HUNTED

Kevin L. Williams

Cover illustration and design by Tomas Ramirez.
Original concept artwork by Malcolm McClinton.

Please feel free to visit my website:

https://kevinlamontwilliams.com

If you would like to find out about my upcoming novels and short stories subscribe to my mailing list!
https://kevinlamontwilliams.com/signup/

This book is dedicated to my family. I love you all! Thank you to my parents and my extended family. Thanks to my kids: Trevor, Jessica, Pablo, Samantha, Elaina, Elijah, EllaGrace, and Gavin. Special thanks to my wonderful editor Leslie Eckard, and Tomas Ramirez, my partner in crime and the fantastic artist who created the cover art, and who is creating artwork for the forthcoming graphic novel!

And, to my Ideal Reader. My love. My guiding light. The first person I ever showed my writing to. The person who has always believed in and supported me...my wonderful wife Susan Elizabeth Williams. I do not deserve your love, but am glad you favor me with it every day. I live to make you proud Susie.

Contents

HUNTED

PART I

NEW MOON

HUNTING GROUNDS

San Antonio, Texas

Several large shapes moved through the shadows of the concrete forest, staying close to the building walls, using patches of darkness between streetlights to hide. To a casual observer this was just a pack of stray dogs roaming the streets. A frequent occurrence this close to the west side. Nothing more. But, these were NOT dogs. The leader of the PACK halted before entering another street, hackles raised. It sniffed the night air, which brought back the lovely aroma of potential prey.

It was an opportunity that could not be passed by.

Joe prepared his makeshift cardboard box home for the night. This was Joe's block. It was his little empire. Joe was a veteran of the streets, but bad luck, life choices, and gambling left him destitute and broke. But, not so broken that he couldn't find a little joy in what he did have. Joe had his home, such as it was, a couple of tins of food, small bottle of whiskey, and his faithful mutt Puddles. The dog was a dirty white and gray poodle mix missing one eye. Old and broken like Joe. Together they made a great pair.

"Come on, Puddles. Time to go night-night."

The dog wagged its tail and walked into the box. Joe was about to slither in after Puddles when a noise from the other side of the alley made him pause.

"What's that, Puddles?"

The dog sensed something too. It leapt to the front of the box and growled. Joe laid a calming hand on the dog's back.

"Don't worry, girl. We've seen bad stuff before. Nothing we can't get past."

Even so, Joe pulled a small blackjack from the pocket of his cargo pants. The blackjack was a staple of inner city police in the sixties and seventies, rubber-coated with a leather strap that hooked around the wrist. Inside was a short length of iron, or lead. Joe couldn't remember which. All he knew was that it felt good in his hand and a knock to the head would make any fool think twice about messing with him and Puddles.

Joe stood up and moved a few paces down the alley. Puddles barked louder and pulled at Joe's pant leg as if begging him not to go.

"Hush now! I want to see who's disturbing the peace down there."

A group of shapes filled the alley.

"Ya'll get now! Go on! Only need one dog over here! Get!"

The shapes moved forward...*toward* him. Joe took another step, then the cold fingers of fear crept up the back of his neck.

His face went slack and his fingers, numb. The blackjack fell to the ground. All sound constricted in Joe's throat. *This can't be,* his mind told him even as he watched one of the shapes *stand up.* Puddles backed into the cardboard box whimpering. The leader closed the gap too fast for Joe to register and leapt. Joe's final thoughts were for Puddles. *Who's going to feed my baby?*

Once the prey was dead the leader called the PACK over to feed. They tore into the meal with a wild frenzy, some of the younger ones fighting each other for the scraps. The leader ignored the inferior canine hiding inside the box. It was satisfied. This was the first of many feasts, and a long time coming.

A half hour later the PACK moved to another side street near an artery of Highway 35 North. Their leader was feeling bold after the night's first successful hunt. They cloaked themselves in darkness and watched stray traffic pass back and forth. No one was out. Minutes later, a taxicab drove up the street. The driver, a sloppy man with food stains on his shirt, lit a cigarette and blew smoke rings at the *No Smoking* sign on the passenger side sun visor. The driver channel-surfed the radio for a bit. As he did, the ash on his cigarette grew longer and longer. It dangled in space, then fell into his lap.

"Damnit!"

He batted at the ash as it slid underneath his butt. The driver was so preoccupied with fighting the burning ember that he looked away from the road just as the PACK began to cross the street. The PACK members sprinted out of the way of the vehicle, but one was a second too slow...

The cab struck the animal and careened into a concrete pillar, slamming the driver into the air bag. The animal was thrown several feet into the air, landing in a patch of grass. The other PACK members loped over to help their comrade. The leader growled when it saw that its subordinate suffered a broken neck. The leader turned to the cab and watched as the driver stumbled from the wrecked vehicle. The driver was so focused on the cab's damaged front end that he didn't notice death moving in his direction.

The leader padded forward. Waited. The street was silent and dark. The accident hadn't alerted anyone yet.

Now, some primitive instinct told the cab driver that he was not alone. He turned and found himself staring into blood-red eyes. The leader loped at the driver who screamed. For a fleeting moment the animal was illuminated under a street lamp before it landed on the cab driver's chest, smashing both of them through the driver's side door and into the front seat. Screams invaded the darkness as the cab driver was eaten alive.

When the leader was done it went over to the fallen one. The PACK descended upon it...eating and consuming every portion until no trace was left.

It was, an act of kindness.

The first police on scene noted the shattered window and smashed panel on the door of the cab. The rookie, Officer Lutz, glanced inside. She ran a trembling hand through her short blond hair and reeled backward, shaken. Her senior partner, Officer L. Barry, a twenty-five-year veteran who stuck around the department like old furniture, shook his head in disgust at her. Officer Barry adjusted his utility belt under his sagging belly and scratched his balls. His yellowed eyes showed the signs of early liver disease. Officer Barry's idea of a good woman was one who served him dinner and beer; while naked.

"Dumb-ass rook," Officer L. Barry growled to himself.

He peered inside with a flashlight. Officer L. Barry dropped it. The flashlight clattered against the pavement, rolling under the cab. He backed away, mouthing a silent prayer he'd learned in Catholic school as a boy. A horrendous howl shattered the night shredding the police officers' nerves. They jumped back in their patrol car and radioed the call in from the relative safety of the cab. Another howl obliterated the night. From the roof of a nearby building, the PACK Leader watched the two humans inside the car.

A low growl of satisfaction escaped its throat.

DANA

The cab was now a crime scene. Police tape was hung, cordoning off the area from gawkers. Crime scene lights illuminated the damaged cab in a swath of bright white light. Network trucks set for up for live feeds. Uniformed officers placed wooden barricades on both ends of the street to block traffic. Across the street, Detective Third-Grade Dana Adams sat in her sedan, shivering from the cold. She turned the defroster up high to fight the icy frost fingers climbing up the windshield. A small photograph of a six-year old girl sat on the dashboard. Dana smiled at the photo then dialed on her mobile. It rang several times before going to voice mail. Dana scowled. Dialed again.

"What?" The voice on the other end of the phone asked.

Dana took a deep breath. Dealing with her daughter wasn't always easy. Well, it had been easy when she was younger, but something happened once Troy turned twelve, and this escalation of tension had continued now that Troy was fifteen.

"Did you do your homework yet?" Dana asked.

"Checking on me, Dana?"

"Well that is my Mom job. No time to slack now."

"You know my grades are good. I'm damn near a genius," Troy said.

"Ok genius, why don't you try to remember to close the lid on the toilet sometime and maybe take the recycle out huh?"

"Under advisement. Anything else?" Troy asked.

"I love…" Click.

Dana stared at her phone. A light rain began to fall from the swollen clouds overhead. It misted the windows, causing everything to look surreal with the intense crime scene lighting set up on the street outside. Dana took another deep breath to clear her mind. The conversation took the wind out of her sails. Dana placed the photo in the pocket of her coat. She stepped from the car and crossed the street, ignoring shouts from the media. The wind was brisk on this January night so she pulled her coat collar up around her neck. Working homicides in winter was brutal, unforgiving work, but she really didn't mind.

As she approached the crime scene tape Officer L. Barry held a hand up to stop her.

"No press."

Dana pulled her overcoat back, showing him the Detective shield clipped to her waist. He frowned but lifted the tape.

"Sorry, Detective. These media rats try all kinds of crap to get access to spread their fake news." Dana wanted to respond to this but ignored him.

Officer L. Barry led her over to the cab. Dana stood back at a distance. She appraised the crime scene with practiced objectivity, taking in clues before she touched anything. Although the crime scene photographers would take tons of photos, Dana liked to take her own to save her first impressions. Dana used her phone to take several pictures of the taxi from multiple angles. It was demolished on the passenger side and it looked like it had been broadsided by a tank. Every window was shattered from the impact. Legs, what was left of the driver, dangled from the destroyed section.

Officer L. Barry shook his head like a wizened sage.

"It ain't pretty, ma'am."

Dana grunted. Not quite a response, but enough to acknowledge him.

"You know what I think? I think them damn gangbangers used a pit bull. See I, remember…"

"Were you first on scene, Officer?" Dana asked cutting him off.

"Yeah. Me and Officer Lutz."

Dana bent down near the driver's side door. She noticed some kind of material wedged into it.

What the hell?

She pulled a small case from her coat, withdrew a pair of tweezers, and tugged at the material. It looked like fur. Dana placed it in a small plastic bag, labeled the bag, sealed the material into the evidence envelope. The sound of a vehicle stopping nearby alerted her to the arrival of either the ME or her partner. Dana glanced back and saw Detective Robin Malcheck making her way through the rubberneckers.

"It might be nice if we show up to a crime scene at the same time for once," Dana grunted at her younger partner.

Robin strolled up munching some kind of sandwich. Robin smiled. "Then where would the mystery be? I like to make an entrance." Robin did a cursory glance toward the cab.

"Ah yeah. Glad I didn't have the pastrami sandwich I was contemplating ordering."

Dana liked Robin, even if her partner was a tad…what was the term? *Rough around the edges.* Robin was in her early thirties. White. A walking CrossFit model, Dana mused.

Robin and Dana were an anomaly in the department. Tough and smart enough to outstrip the men, but savvy enough to get along and be treated with respect.

Dana was the first, and only African American woman to make Homicide. She'd left a pretty good mark during her stint in Narcotics. Been in too many shootouts, run enough warrants to last a lifetime, and sought out Homicide as a way to stabilize her life and raise her daughter *Troy*. Her wild child.

As Homicide units went, San Antonio's was one of the best. It was staffed with several sergeants, over forty detectives, a patrol officer, and civilian support personnel. They were called *The Murder Detail*. As the Lead Investigator, Dana was responsible for the investigative activity on whatever case she worked. In a city of around 1.4 million, it still wasn't enough personnel to cover every homicide that occurred though.

But, the Murder Detail did their absolute best.

Dana was a cop through and through. Raised on the North side of San Antonio in a decent middle-class neighborhood filled with police and military families, Dana had always known her path in life. Service. From a seven-year tour in the Air Force as a fire fighter and on to the academy, all Dana ever wanted to be was a cop. Service and duty. That was the example Dana grew up loving and identifying with. At forty Dana felt she had finally arrived at the place in her life she was supposed to be. A full-fledged adult.

Now, if I could get my personal life in order. Dana pushed the thought away and re-focused on the work.

Robin came from different leanings though. Robin was raised in a prestigious family in Alamo Heights, a wealthy suburban area just west of downtown. Moderate grades, but connected parents allowed Robin to be accepted into the University of Texas in Austin where she majored in Radio, Television and Film. Post grad she decided to become an ESL, or English as a Second Language, tutor so she could travel the world. Robin lived in Japan and South America before the money ran out and she was forced to assess her life options once more.

On a whim Robin took the LSAT for entrance into law school back at UT and was accepted. By the time she graduated, right before taking the bar exam, she decided that she hated lawyers and wanted to become a cop. In true Robin fashion, she tracked down the nearest testing site, aced the test and employment process, and found herself seven years later, fast-tracked to Murder Detail. Robin seemed to operate on instinct. Dana often wondered if Robin ever had a plan.

Yin and Yang, Dana thought. Maybe a good thing.

Dana smiled, "You better not throw up on my crime scene, rookie."

"Come on, Boss. Why you gotta hurt my feelings?" Robin feigned being offended.

Officer L. Barry was intruding into Dana's space. He leaned down, his fat belly almost touching Dan's ear.

"So, what you thinking, Detective? Gang hit?" He said.

Robin frowned. "Do you mind? We need space to work."

Officer L. Barry stood up, trying to use his bulk to intimidate Robin. It didn't work and just pissed her off.

"Hey, sweetie I'm just trying to help."

"By being fat AND stupid?" Robin asked.

Officer L. Barry was not used to a woman talking to him like that except his wife.

"Listen here..."

Robin stood her ground against the man who outweighed her by about one hundred pounds.

"Or what, shit-bag? You know what? I think I need to be downwind because I can smell what you had for lunch," Robin said.

Dana was trying to concentrate. "Robin, cool it. Let's get to work."

"Fat ass," Robin muttered under her breath.

Robin knelt next to Dana. Officer L. Barry wandered and stood a few feet away. He pretended not to be humiliated by cleaning his fingernails with a toothpick.

"See this?" Dana showed Robin the material she pulled from the door.

Dana stood.

"Officer Barry, did you notice anything unusual when you and Officer Lutz arrived?"

He seemed nervous. One of the things that made Dana so good at her job was the empathy she was able to convey. When her colleagues wanted to bust some heads, Dana was almost always able to de-escalate situations. It was a gift she had. Dana pulled Officer L. Barry away from the wrecked taxi so they could talk without anyone hearing them.

"What did you see?" She asked.

"Well…we did our normal canvas right. Then the strangest thing happened…"

Dana waited. She knew that allowing a person to work up to discussing something difficult took time. When he saw that Dana was not going to belittle him, Officer L. Barry continued.

"I felt like something was watching us. Then, we heard it…"

"Heard what?"

"Something…howled."

This is NOT what Dana was expecting.

"Howled?"

"Yes, Detective. That's what I mean."

Officer L. Barry's eyes drifted upward to the adjacent rooftops of the buildings looking down on them. She followed his gaze.

"Officer, what did you mean…?"

Officer L. Barry was already halfway to his car. Dana called over her shoulder.

"Robin, you find any more of that material?"

"Yeah, boss. All over the back seat. It's a freaking mess in there."

"Tell Crime Scene to pay particular attention to that. I want to see the M.E.'s report ASAP." Dana glanced around, irritated. "Where's the M.E.?

Robin strolled over. "Beats the shit out of me. What's with fat boy?"

"I don't know."

Robin could see that Dana was troubled. For the briefest instant, Dana thought she saw twin points of red staring back at her from the roof of a low building near them. They blinked on and off. Dana rubbed her eyes and they were gone the next instant.

"You alright Boss?"

Dana stared at her partner. "I think we're in for a bad one here Robin. My gut tells me this is just beginning."

Robin's phone rang. She listened and jotted notes in a small notebook. She hung up.

"What?" Dana asked.

"You're not going to believe this."

"Another one." Dana answered.

Robin nodded. "Yep. Two blocks from here."

"Swell."

Dana stared up at the rooftops once more, but the night kept its secrets.

Dana was staring at a corpse without a head.

The body lay in a dingy alley just west of downtown, near the local county jail run by the Bexar County Sheriff's Department. A block away many of the city's homeless population had created a shanty town of sorts underneath the Commerce Street bridge. It was a vast collection of pockets of humanity and debris that accumulated with each new human addition. The location of the dead body did not surprise Dana so much as the condition of the body. Unfortunately, as in most metropolitan cities, homelessness and crime strolled hand in hand here. Robberies, muggings, theft, and assaults of all kind were an ever-present risk and way of life for many of these individuals.

These thoughts ran through Dana's head in fast motion.

In all of Dana's eight years on Homicide she'd never seen anything like this though. The corpse was in a sitting position, arms out to the side as if about to push off from the wall. Blood splatter on the alley wall seemed to indicate that the head was cut off while the victim was sitting down. Dana would let the Medical Examiner figure that out. The darkness made it hard to see. A grimy streetlamp cast a dim pale-yellow light down in the alley. She lensed her black flashlight up and down the length of the alley. No head. The uniform who found the body strolled the other end of the alley.

"Anything?" Dana called out.

"No ma'am." The uniform answered back.

"Damn! That is one sweet arterial spray! You find the head?" Robin said.

"Do you see a head?" Dana asked.

Robin scanned around. Even though Robin's humor sometimes burned Dana's fuse, she liked Robin's sharp analytical mind and often reckless abandon.

Dana stood, facing her partner.

"Uniform is searching the rest of the alley."

Robin edged closer to the body.

"You see this?" Robin asked.

"What?"

Dana bent down to see where Robin was pointing. On the edges of the neck wound was a patch of material that looked like….

"Is that fur?" Robin. "That's damn strange. Like the taxicab."

"Detective…?" The voice was strained.

"Sure looks like it. Robin, go check with the uniform and see what's up."

"You got it, Boss."

Dana looked around the corpse more, careful not to disturb it until the M.E. arrived.

"Dana…we found the head."

Robin's use of her first name caused Dana to stand up. It almost sounded like Robin was spooked. Dana jogged to the end of the alley, meeting Robin and the patrol officer. They stared in unison at the head. Well, it wasn't a head anymore, just a half-eaten skull.

The skull had huge indentions and marks on it. The jawbone was torn away and lay underneath a cardboard box like old pizza crust. Bits of flesh still clinging to it. One eye protruding from the skull. Staring in silent accusation at them.

"Yeah, good call on the pastrami," Dana said. A smile played at the edges of her mouth. Robin stared at her partner, then at her sandwich which she'd brought along. Robin pitched it out into the darkness.

"Robin, get the M.E. on the phone NOW. And Crime Scene."

"Yep." Robin moved away to make the call. Dana touched the uniform on the shoulder. He jumped.

"You okay?"

The young man was shaken to his core. Dana could tell that he was a couple of minutes away from popping his cork.

"It's horrible...what…I don't…"

"Why don't you start securing the area. Tape everything off." Dana knew distraction was needed right now.

"Yes, ma'am…uh, Detective…"

The uniform walked back to his car like a drunken man. Robin sidled up to Dana.

"M.E. and Crime Scene on the way." Robin glanced at the uniform grabbing police tape from the trunk of his patrol unit. "Yeah, that guy ain't gonna make it."

"Be nice. We all started somewhere." Dana said.

The uniform made it two steps before he vomited on the side of his unit. Robin suppressed a laugh. Dana glared at her.

"What?" Robin asked. She grinned as Dana walked over to check on the patrol officer.

ALEX

ALEXANDRA STONE felt her mind ripping apart. Pain clawed through her with razor sharp talons...*probing...tearing...consuming* the world around her, leaving nothing but all-encompassing *MADNESS*. The sound of many voices filled Alex's head. She collapsed to the floor into the fetal position, crushing her fists to her temples to stop the sound.

"Alexandra...Alexandra...Alexandra..." The voices spoke her name. Over and over, like a mantra. The voices seemed human but mixed with something feral. Animalistic. *Ancient*.

"LEAVE ME ALONE!"

The voices cut off. The pain lessened. As the minutes inched by the pain became a memory. A fragment. Alex lay on the floor, curled into a ball, afraid to move until she was sure that the voices were gone. Satisfied, she rose to one elbow, glanced around the condo. It looked the same as before. She stood. Shaky, but unharmed.

Alex walked to the great bay windows of her downtown condo and stared into the night sky at the full moon. The celestial body had just appeared from behind the clouds, hanging low like a Christmas ornament, pulsating and throbbing with a silvery energy she'd never noticed before. Alex *felt* the moon's pull through the glass. Strange that it had never affected her in this way before. Now, she wondered if she had dreamed about pain. And yet, it seemed so real a few moments ago.

HOOOOWWWLLL!

The eerie sound enveloped the condo, seeping through the glass, washing over Alex. The wind outside buffeted the condo windows. There was nothing to indicate what made the sound, the only other noises she could hear were the vehicles snarled in traffic stories below, or the occasional plane flying overhead to and from the San Antonio International Airport or neighboring Lackland Air Force Base.

The moon slid behind a bank of clouds as if it was done conducting whatever silent business it was charged with.

Silence descended on the condo.

Her phone rang.

"Answer call." Alex said.

"Call answered." The electronic voice of Alex's digital assistant piped. The voice was pleasant, female, but with a weird, Stepford, robotic quality.

"Ms. Stone?" A man's voice.

"Yes?" Alex said.

"This is David Cupper. Cupper Investigations."

"Hi! I was hoping I'd hear from you. This is sooner than I thought!"

A pause on the other end.

"I'm sorry, Ms. Stone. I wish I had more positive information for you, but the results of your inquiry are inconclusive I'm afraid. We weren't able to find any records for your birth mother, and the foster home you resided in is no longer in existence."

"Anything else?" Alex tried to keep the disappointment out of her voice, but knew she was failing.

"I did try the adoption agency, but unfortunately all the records were destroyed in a fire as well." David Cupper said.

"What do you mean as well?"

"I apologize. The adoption agency and foster home were both destroyed by fire. Curious. Just thought you should know."

"Thank you, Mr. Cupper. I do appreciate it."

"My pleasure. I just wish I could have been more helpful to you. Please don't hesitate to contact us if you need anything else."

"Thank you. Take care." Alex said.

"Call ended." The electronic voice concluded.

Alex felt it again. The loneliness. It crowded in on her. Enveloped her. Cloaked her in a thick blanket that was stifling. She tried to shake it off by touching the delicate necklace she wore. The initials *AS* on it. Alex rubbed it whenever she was stressed.

One step closer...four steps backward.

She wanted to know something about her family. She was certain that she would find the answers this time. But, no. When Cupper told her the bad news it felt like starting at square one. She was alone...Again.

Alex walked from her apartment on the twenty-third floor toward the elevator. She was running late for work. As she passed 23A, her elderly neighbor, Maddie Levitt opened the door.

"Hello, Alexandra!"

"Hi, Maddie!"

The older woman reached out and grabbed Alex's hand. Alex loved this woman like a mother. Maddie had been with her through some rough times and always had a kind word of encouragement for her. She often made little cakes and pastries which she brought to Alex's apartment. The ladies would sit and have tea and pastries. Maddie told Alex stories about when she worked in the Navy on aircraft and her decades-long romance with her late husband. Alex loved to listen to Maddie talk about the powerful love she and her late husband Sammy had for each other. They had loved each other through wars, the loss of a child, changing careers, and other happenings.

Though it all, Maddie and Sammy's love stood the test of time.

"So?" Alex leaned in to Maddie. They walked arm in arm down the hallway like co-conspirators.

"Was he nice?"

Maddie clasped her hands with delight like a girl of fifteen instead of seventy-eight.

"Harold was so wonderful! Oh my! We danced the night away at the Lion's Club. I even remembered how to foxtrot and jitter-bug!"

Alex grinned at her friend as she relived the evening.

"I'm so glad you had a good time. Think you'll see him again?"

Maddie paused. The wetness of a tear in the corner of one eye.

"You don't think my Sammy would be upset do you?" Maddie asked.

Alex hugged Maddie close to her.

"It's been seventeen years, Maddie. I know he'd be happy you found someone nice."

Maddie smiled at Alex.

"You are such a dear, sweet girl." Seriousness swept over her features. "Any news…about your Mother?"

"Nothing yet."

Maddie gave her a reassuring pat on the arm.

"I'm sure you'll find the answers you want. One way or another. Have a good day Alexandra."

"You too, Maddie."

"Oh, Alexandra!"

"Yes?"

"Happy Birthday tomorrow! In case I don't see you dear!"

"Thank you, Maddie!!"

Alex watched Maddie walk back down the hall and disappear into her apartment.

The smile slipped from her face after Maddie closed the door. Alex was happy for her friend. She really was…And yet…would she ever get that same chance? To love someone for a lifetime, and then find love even after that? It didn't seem fair. Alex knew she was a good person. Maybe there was no "fair" in this life. Not for her.

ELI

The East Side of San Antonio. A wasteland of lost and abandoned buildings, derelict neighborhoods, and broken dreams. But, there were signs of revitalization in the neighborhoods here and there. Some new businesses had moved in and the city was making an effort at renovation after forty-plus years of neglect. Things were looking up in small ways.

On one street a red and white church rose from the ashes around the destruction. Each coat of paint was even and had been applied with a loving touch. The grounds were well-maintained. Inside, an elderly African American man moved among the seats. He arranged the rows while picking at small pieces of invisible lint on the carpet. Pastor Abraham Moore was a dignified man of GOD whose faith rose above all else. Every motion he made showed the reverence the man held for this place of worship.

Abraham didn't notice the door open behind him because he was so engrossed. Elijah Moore stood behind his father watching. A smile crossed his face.

"Hey, Pop."

"Did you speak to your mother yet?" Abraham grunted.

This was not the welcome home Eli was expecting. It had been four years since he and Abraham had spoken and Eli thought the past might be behind them for once. Maybe they could act as if all the years and distance were a bridge instead of a chasm.

The smile slipped from Eli's face.

His father didn't even turn around to face him. Eli stared at Abraham, studying him. Over time, as often happens with grown children, Eli felt he'd begun to resemble his father more and more. The lines in his face. The broad, but regal nose. Wide intelligent eyes that hinted at a darkness inside.

Eli was forty-four, in the best shape of his life, and ready to start a new life outside the confines of the United States Navy. He was taller and more muscular than his father, and his skin was a light brown compared to Abraham's dark chocolate. In actuality, Eli was bi-racial. A product of his African American father and German American mother. Of course, the world only saw him as African

American, but he didn't complain. His parents were his parents like everyone else. When Eli moved it was with the supple grace of a panther. A dangerous panther. It was the kind of gait that told other men not to press him.

"No," Eli said.

"Hmm." Abraham continued to busy himself straightening hymnals on the benches.

"I'm out, Pop. My enlistment was officially up as of yesterday. No more Navy."

"Walk with me."

Eli followed his father from the atrium to another room in the back. Abraham's private office. A big mahogany desk dominated the room. The walls were lined with certificates of ministry and prestigious pastoral awards. Photos of Eli's mother and father sat on the desk. No photos of him though, either as a child or grown. There was a photo of his adopted brother Chapa graduating from high school though, Eli noted. On a small shelf, a framed Purple Heart award. Abraham motioned for Eli to sit in the small chair on the other side of the desk. Eli hesitated before sitting. This chair made him feel small. Always had. He sat anyway.

"So, no more glory missions to fight in impoverished nations?"

Eli seethed inside but kept his anger in check.

"I thought the SEALs were your life, Elijah?" Abraham said.

Eli glanced at the Purple Heart. "Used to be yours too Pop."

Abraham opened a drawer and pulled out a pipe. He stuffed some tobacco in it, lit up, and puffed away.

"The SEALs were my job, never my calling. Serving my GOD...your GOD is more important."

"More important than Mom?" Eli stared at his father.

Abraham paused. The sounds of the room were amplified by the silence. Eli half expected to see an angel materialize in the room.

"Yes. She's a strong Christian woman. She understands the meaning of the word sacrifice."

"I'll bet she does." Eli stood and started for the door.

"ELIJAH! Do NOT disrespect me in this house!" Abraham glared at his son.

After a few seconds of staring each other down Abraham's gaze softened.

"Do you have a place to stay, son?"

Eli stood there in the doorway. "You know, Pop, I just wanted to tell you I was out. That's it." Eli walked out.

Abraham opened his mouth to speak, but nothing came out. He spun in his chair and continued puffing on the pipe. He stared out the window into a small garden on the other side.

Going to see his Pops had been a mistake. It always ended in strife, or an argument, or some kind of confrontation. Eli drove from his Father's church and through his old neighborhood. As he maneuvered his Jeep around and between the slow drivers, he thought about how different everything looked. Everything felt *smaller* than he remembered. The last time Eli had come home, which was several years before, things didn't feel this different. Four years ago, the neighborhood seemed to be in better shape. *Or did it?* Maybe that was nostalgia rearing its head, clouding out bad memories the way it often does.

The once proud new houses seemed to have been transformed into derelict structures overnight. When he was growing up everyone in his neighborhood and most of the surrounding neighborhoods kept their yards well-maintained and watered. Now, house after house bore the signs of neglect. Knee-high weeds choked most of the front and backyards with a death stranglehold that might never be shaken. Every other lot was filled with a vacant or abandoned house.

Eli drove by his old middle school. This was a mistake. It suffered from the same absent neglect as the houses. Peeling paint, broken lights, cracked asphalt parking lots, and an ancient multipurpose track and football field that was probably home to losing records. Everywhere he drove it seemed that urban blight and recession greeted him. He skipped driving by his former high school which now boasted one of the highest drop-out rates in the city, record gang activity, and low community involvement.

When Eli was a kid he and his friends could ride their bicycles for miles from their houses without ever having to worry about crime or anything other than finding the next adventure. Summers were once a great time to forget about school and just have fun. As long as you were home by dinner time things were perfect.

Eli swung the Jeep onto the highway and headed downtown. He exited Durango Street (Was it even called that anymore?), past the downtown University of San Antonio campus (When did this go up?), and past Police Department Headquarters which was an ugly, blue-steel low-roofed building on Dolorosa Street downtown. It clashed with the brown and sandalwood Justice building and Bexar County Courthouse located just a few blocks away. This was a place of functionality not aesthetics.

Eli wondered if Dana was inside working. He missed her. It seemed like years since they last spoke, but he could remember every detail about the last time he saw her face. Eli thought about calling her but figured he would get himself settled in first. He drove up Highway 281 and found a hotel. He checked in for one night, planning to stop by and see his Mom tomorrow. That night he dreamed about Dana....

BRICK

Brick's Army/Navy Surplus Store squatted in the middle of a decaying shopping strip that had already died a slow and painful death. Other than the tattoo shop on the opposite end, the surplus was the only store still open. Twenty-five years ago, this section off Bandera Road was a small, vibrant area filled with all manner of shops and businesses. Now, the large, renovated grocery chain across the street sucked all the customers of life and cash like a giant, sprawling parasite, leaving little else for other businesses.

The morning weather increased this sense of misery. Cold rain pelted every surface it could find. Rivers of water flowed through the parking lot painting the curbs a dirty gray. The shabby, white acrylic paint on the surplus store was peeled off in sections, dimpled underneath by sporadic and haphazard fresh coats.

Dan "BRICK" Moore watched the sky outside through one of the grime-coated windows. He fingered the chain around his neck. On that chain hung a key and a crucifix. At six-three, give or take, Brick was two-hundred and eighty pounds of solid black oak. A tree trunk of a man with deep cracks inside.

Like his brother, Brick had served his country. Fighting the good fight for the people of South Vietnam ages ago. He wasn't sure if they'd done any good, but it was his duty so he went. Back then not many options existed for a Black man who wasn't college educated or called to the ministry. Hell, not much had changed in some respects. Brick rubbed his massive hands together and continued to stare at the sky. A huge thunderclap shook the heavens, with the obligatory lighting following a few seconds later.

Lordy, it 'gon come down again.

Brick stepped away from the window and pressed his bulk through the shelves of his store. It was like many other surplus stores that were not franchised. Military uniforms and accessories littered the bulk of the shelves toward the front of the store. Boots from almost every armed conflict the United States had been involved in were stacked along a wall. Further in were display cases that housed knives, old weapons and antique guns. Swords and lances hung on the walls next to shields dating back to the Ottoman Empire.

Younger customers never recognized these finds, but shrewd collectors came from across the country to buy and trade.

The building, prior to Brick purchasing it, used to be a tortilla factory with two levels. Metal stairs curved upward to the second-floor landing where Brick stored lightweight paper items like maps, diagrams, old signs and the like. The room held two comfortable, but battered recliners, a small love seat, and a rickety ceiling fan that shook if the setting was too fast.

Downstairs, behind the main counter, down a short hallway was a tiny office adjoined by a small bathroom. Then a flight of stairs leading down about twenty feet to an underground hallway that resembled a bunker from World War I. This made the building an engineering feat because the majority of buildings in the San Antonio and Hill Country area didn't have basements due to the dense rock located close to the surface. Further down the hallway was a heavy iron door locked with a large padlock. Brick called it *The Vault*. Brick had the one and only key to this padlock around his neck.

All his secrets locked behind this door. *For good reason* he thought. Nobody needed to know what he knew. Well, there was one man who knew. His brother.

The high and mighty Pastor Abraham Moore. Keeper of the Good Book.

Brick stared at his watch. It was a trusty old timepiece from the War. *Which war?* He didn't remember. As he passed his office he heard *it* call out to him. Brick tried to ignore it. He made it to the counter when he heard the call again. Louder and more insistent. The sound was muffled though. Brick crept back to the office and peered inside. He KNEW where the sound was coming from.

The DESK. Always the desk.

Brick sat down in his desk chair. The wood and metal groaning from supporting his bulk.

"Why you calling to me? I been through with you for a minute now. I don't need you."

Brick stared at the desk. There was only one drawer in it. Brick placed his hand on the handle, hesitated, got up.

"No. No sir. Not today," Brick said.

Brick walked out, switching off the light. After a minute he flicked the light back on and stepped in the room. He felt the call again.

Could he really be this weak? This pathetic? A man who prided himself on his strength? Weak like a little old baby fresh off the teat. Pitiful.

Brick sank into the chair again. Opened the drawer, and there it was. He shivered. The anticipation was almost orgasmic. Saliva glands in the back of Brick's throat activated.

There it was. The bottle of SCOTCH. Full. Unopened. Pristine.

You are a weak, foolish man Daniel.

It was his voice but registered as Abraham's voice in his mind. Brick tried to recall the Bible verses about banishing evil.

"Get thee gone…uh…I rebuke you…or…"

Is this how you deal with the problems of the world Daniel? By subjugating yourself to the bottle? Where is your faith? Do you have faith?

"Shut up, Abe. I got faith." Brick whispered to himself as if his brother was in the room with him.

How many years of sobriety have you earned? How many? NONE! You have not earned anything because you have not DONE anything worth doing. You know why? Because you are not WORTHY of sobriety!

Brick slammed the drawer closed. Stood and bolted from the room. For some reason, his eyes were drawn to the staircase leading to the basement. Brick continued to stare as if waiting for some hidden meaning to be revealed. He couldn't shake the feeling that a darkness was about.

And, that darkness came from what he had down THERE.

Sumthin's coming big brother. I can feel it. Yeah…sumthin's coming.

Brick waded back among the shelves, trying to stay busy. He inventoried and sorted and catalogued, but nothing worked. He kept hearing the invisible voice wafting from the back room.

"Shut up now."

Even as he said the words he realized that his feet had taken him back to the room and up to the desk. Brick sat once more and opened the drawer. He took out the bottle of Scotch the way the curator of a museum might handle a precious artifact. He set it on the desk. The bottle stared at him, or at least that's how it seemed to Brick.

Just one drink.

No!

Yes!

NO! don't betray yourself Daniel! Be calm...pray...Let the LORD guide you through this storm.

Just one. It can't hurt. One drink and then you can have the courage to go talk to Abraham.

Brick unscrewed the cap...

Yes! That's what I need...courage.

Brick drank from the bottle. The Scotch washed down his parched throat, coating it in false warmth. Brick smiled.

See...that was easy. So easy.

Brick left the surplus store, climbed into his truck, and drove toward 410, the major highway artery surrounding the city in a giant loop. Twenty-five minutes later Brick eased the truck into the parking lot of Abraham's church. He shut the engine off and stared at the small church. All the lights were on despite the late hour. He sat in the cab feeling warmed by the scotch in his belly...

ABRAHAM

Brick stood outside in the rain staring at the church. He fingered the chain around his thick neck. The door opened. Abraham stood framed in the doorway. Light spilled from behind him casting a halo upon his head.

"You going to stand there soaking little brother? Come inside." Abraham said.

The older Moore walked back into the church without waiting for a response. Brick shivered against the cold rain and followed his brother inside. Brick locked the door behind them and watched his brother fuss with small details near the choir stand.

"He's back huh?" Brick asked.

Abraham gave his younger brother a dismissive snort.

"How do you know? Oh....right...your *sources*."

"C'mon Abe, let's not go there. I do what I gotta' do to get by."

"If you want me to approve of your lifestyle Daniel, I won't. You know right but continue to do wrong." Abraham said.

"We're all sinners Abe," Brick said.

Abraham began to turn away. He stopped. Abraham stared at his younger brother.

"I should have known. You reek of alcohol Daniel. I thought you put that behind you. Seems you still need the Lord after all."

Brick grabbed hold of Abraham's arm. "Yella' needs to know what happened...what IS happening," Brick said. "I know ya'll ain't talked in years Abe, but we gotta tell the boy so we can prepare. You KNOW they comin' after us right? It ain't a coincidence about what we found."

Abraham stared at Brick's hand covering his forearm. His gaze like flint. "Remove your hand..." Brick let go of his brother.

"I will tell him when the time is right," Abraham said.

Brick clapped his hand together like a thunderbolt. The room echoed with the sound. "When? When does the high and mighty Abraham Moore decide the time? Huh? You're such a hypocrite! You talk about showin' compassion, and forgiveness, and all that, but you can't even forgive your own son! So what you and the boy had words

31

before he left? You and I both know you ain't pure as snow, baby!" Brick said.

Abraham didn't want to hear this. He busied himself with cleaning more benches. Brick kept at him.

"The shit we done in 'Nam was about as tainted as you can get." Brick said.

"Do not swear in this house." Abraham said.

"You and me are alot different. And alot the same. We're both killers and none of this churchin', and prayin', and do-goodin' is gonna' change it. Think on that," Brick said.

Abraham stared in the opposite direction. The conversation affected him, but he wasn't about to let Brick KNOW it.

"Good night Daniel. Give my regards to the Bottle," Abraham said.

Abraham walked back to his office. Brick stood in the sanctuary for another minute. He glanced around, shook his huge frame as if shedding a coat, and left. Abraham stared out his office window and watched the brake lights of Brick's SUV fade into the night. He sat back in his desk chair. He opened the desk drawer and pulled out a faded, yellowed photograph of two serious young men.

VIETNAM, 1968

A tiny squad of American soldiers crept through silent woods. Two Navy SEALS, a very young Brick and Abraham leading the way. The soldiers following them were dog-tired, but the brothers moved on like machines.

"Sir...Sir...we're tired Sir. When can we rest?" One of the soldiers asked.

Abraham silenced him. He pointed up the trail with two fingers to his brother. Brick looked ahead. Abraham signaled the squad to halt. A small village. The soldiers fanned out at Abraham's signal. They waited in the brush while Abraham and Brick moved forward.

The village looked deserted. Empty hutches, fires burning, food cooking...and then...a dead dog. Gutted open.

Brick whispered, "Abe...NVA."

On the ground were several dead and mauled North Vietnamese army regulars. Torsos ripped open. Arms and legs missing. Some without faces. Skulls chewed off.

"What happened here?" Brick spit out. He fingered the cross around his neck.

"Don't know brother, but we need to leave now!" Abraham whispered.

ROOOAAR!

The sound galvanized the men. They turned and glimpsed one of their soldiers yanked backward into the dark jungle. Screams erupted. Then...silence.

"Abe! On your right!"

A massive canine shape with burning eyes leapt at Abraham. The brothers FIRED....

Abraham put the photograph back in the drawer and slammed it shut, clasping hands in front of his face and prayed. The words silent but spoken nonetheless. Tears streamed down his dark face, finding every crevice and line. He opened up the bottom drawer and took out a leather-bound book. He took his favorite pen from a coffee cup on his desk and began to write in the book.

Close to nine o'clock, Abraham locked up the church, climbed into his battered late-90s Ford pickup truck, and drove home. As he drove Abraham's thoughts drifted back to his conversations with both Elijah and Daniel.

Am I too judgmental? Why?

Abraham had long quested for these answers but the Lord deemed fit to keep them a mystery to him. He knew the Lord had his own reasons for this. Abraham's truck bounced into the driveway. He got out and hobbled up the back-porch stairs. Every step a battle with arthritis.

His wife was upstairs doing something, so Abraham poured some milk into a glass, shambled into the den and turned on the TV. Abraham watched the basketball game from his favorite plush leather chair without really watching it. Ellen Moore floated into the room.

Even late in life she was graceful, and beautiful. She captured his soul every day. He was blessed to be married to Ellen. She kind of resembled one of the ladies on that old prime time soap about the Texas oil family. The one with blonde hair, Abraham thought.

She sat next to him. Laid her head on his chest.

"Why so quiet? Normally you are shouting like a banshee for your team." Ellen said.

Abraham muted the TV.

"Elijah's back. He's out of the SEALS."

Silence. Abraham turned to his wife. She was NOT surprised.

"You already knew, didn't you?"

"Eli's been writing me since he's been in. We video-conference whenever we can." Ellen said.

"Why didn't you tell me?" Abraham asked.

"So you could lecture him? Didn't seem like a good idea Abraham." Abraham stood. He paced the room like he was in the pulpit.

"You and that boy always kept things from me! I don't know why he can't just talk to me. Heck, Damien is more open than Elijah! I always knew when Damien was in trouble because he would come TELL us! But, not Elijah..."

"Abraham, you know why. Because he is too much like you. Both of my men are so bull-headed."

"Bull-headed? Really?"

Ellen made bull's horns with her index fingers on the sides of her temples, breaking the tension. He hugged his wife.

"I just don't know how to talk to him. Elijah's so guarded." Abraham said.

"You were too, when you came back from the war. It took you many years to open up. Maybe he needs the time too."

"I know. I know."

"The last few months something was different in his letters, but he didn't...or couldn't tell me what was wrong." Ellen mused. She noticed her husband wasn't answering. Abraham was lost in his own thoughts. Ellen touched Abraham's arm.

"Promise me you'll talk to him."

"I will, Momma."

"Not *lecture*, just talk," Ellen said.

"I just need to figure out where to start," Abraham said.

"Tell him you love him. I think that's a good place."

Abraham smiled at his wife of fifty-plus years. "Wisdom, thy name is woman."

Ellen smiled. She nestled her head in Abraham's shoulder as they continued to watch the game.

Abraham sat up.

"I was so distracted tonight I think I left the back door unlocked. I should go back and check."

"It's late. Just wait till morning love."

Abraham stood.

"As much as I still love where we live, the neighborhood has gone downhill. I wish it was not so, but that is the truth of it."

He kissed Ellen.

"Back in a few."

Ellen stared at Abraham.

"Be safe."

He smiled on his way out.

Night shrouded Abraham's church and the small parking lot in darkness. Inside, the elder Moore checked the lock on the back door and placed the last of the offering buckets on a table near the podium. He looked back over the darkened seats of his church and smiled.

A low animal growl emanated from the back of the building. Another from his left. Then from his right. Abraham realized he was surrounded. His face remained calm.

The LORD is my SHIELD.

The growls were closer now...

Abraham faced his unseen enemy with a straight back. Dark shapes moved just outside the small ring of light near the podium. The shapes paced back and forth. Abraham's eyes were like flint, and for this brief moment, a glimpse of the fighting man he once was came blazing through. A ferocious howl shattered the silence of the small church.

Abraham stood still and quiet. Bible held out in front of him.

"Your time has come, Shepard..."

The voice was savage and oozing with malice. Abraham tried to adjust his eyes to the darkness beyond the podium. A woman of brutal beauty with a slash of silver cut through her dark mane of hair stepped from the shadows. Her head and shoulders the only parts visible to him. The rest of her form seemed to blend with the darkness of the room.

"Do what you will, demon. In the end the Lord will prevail." Abraham said.

Even as he said the words Abraham knew it was his time. Here was one of the devil's minions come to test his faith. She had come once before, but only to taunt. Now, she demanded payment...in flesh.

FOUR YEARS AGO

Abraham closed up the doors of his church as he had done every day for over forty years. He stepped back and admired the small building, proud of what he and his deacons had accomplished with so little. This life had not provided monetary wealth, but he was rich in the love of his flock and his dear Ellen. Even though he wasn't speaking to Elijah much Abraham knew that Elijah was doing well out in the world and for him that was enough. Abraham was also glad that Chapa's wild ways were behind him and that his adopted son had found his calling in life.

He turned from the building, trudged to the parking lot, climbed into his truck and started the engine. He flicked the headlights on and was surprised to find a woman standing in front of the truck. She appeared to be in her early forties, but Abraham had the strange sensation that she was much older. The woman had dark hair with a white streak in the middle, but her eyes are what stood out to Abraham. The woman's eyes were red, like some kind of demon.

Just a trick of the light he thought.

Abraham stepped from the truck.

"May I help you miss?" He asked.

"Not in the way you think Shepard." She said.

Some instinct made Abraham stay near the truck.

"Well miss, unless there is something I can help you with, I will say goodnight."

The woman displayed her teeth in imitation of a smile. Abraham looked away for an instant to climb back in the truck. When he looked again she landed in front of him as if she had leapt the distance of the twenty feet which separated them. She grabbed him by the throat and lifted him off the pavement. Abraham clawed at her wrist as he felt his throat constricting, shutting off his air flow.

"How does it feel Shepard? Is it terrible to feel this suffering? To feel your life slipping away? To feel the FEAR? Tell me...are you afraid?" She asked. Her white teeth seemed sharper than he remembered. Her red eyes burned like amber coals as she glared at Abraham. He tried to struggle but she was too strong. Stronger than any person should be.

"Curse...curse you demon...in the...name...of the Lord.." Talking was difficult with her vice-like grip on his neck. Abraham knew he was going to pass out soon.

"Remember this fear Shepard! The same fear you brought to my kin! Know that I shall erase your seed from Mother Earth and they too shall know the pain you have inflicted."

The woman stopped squeezing and dropped Abraham onto the pavement. And, in an instant, she ran off faster than his eyes could follow. Abraham crawled over to the front tire of his truck and sat back against it. His throat felt like it was on fire and his entire body hurt. But, more than this, he was terrified because he KNEW what she was...

Abraham's mind careened back into the present, and he watched as the woman stepped backward into the shadows. The sound of flesh reforming and bones extending crawled from the back of the sanctuary toward Abraham. Then, from that darkness her red eyes glowed in the black space. Abraham began to recite the *LORD'S PRAYER.*

Our FATHER, who art in HEAVEN, hallow be THY name...

Now he saw the animal that stepped from the shadows and wished he had more time. Just a bit more. To spend with Ellen...with Chapa...with Elijah...

It growled at him.

THY Kingdom come, THY will be done...

The animal lunged at the old man, knocking him into the darkness. Abraham never made a sound. The rest of the PACK converged on the same spot.

Take me Lord...

And the LORD took his son Abraham home.

HUNTED

AFTERMATH

Alex got up early, dressed, and went for a quick jog at Gevaudan Park. It was an old park with hundreds of ancient trees and ground cover, peppered and crisscrossed with running trails. Some paved, others not. Morning mist hung in the air, saturating the ground. Small drops of dew fell from the overhanging branches and leaves, just catching glints of sunlight spearing through the treetops. Alex ignored all this beauty as she jogged along. She breathed hard, each step bringing with it stabbing pain.

Out of breath, Alex stopped, hands braced on her knees. Chirping birds sounded throughout the forest canopy. Alex walked farther up the trail, a slight limp in her step. The birds stopped chirping and the woods became *too* quiet...

From deep inside the forest, several canine shapes watched her. Alex stopped. She thought there was a hint of movement out among the trees. The woods were silent so Alex continued walking. The mysterious shapes paced her, staying just out of sight. Alex stopped. Did she hear voices? Was someone calling her? Alex stood still to listen. All she heard was the sound of the forest around her and the birds chirping. From this deep in the running trail she couldn't even hear the sounds of vehicles on the freeway nearby.

Must be my nerves. I've been working too much. I need to slow down and maybe take some time off.

On the way back to the parking lot, Alex could not shake the feeling of being watched.

Mena Zulachi, Alex's administrative assistant, smiled when Alex arrived at the office. She rose from her desk and met Alex in the doorway.

"Good morning!" Mena beamed. Alex smiled at the younger woman. Mena handed Alex a sheet of paper and coffee mug.

"Hi, Mena."

"Here's your morning agenda."

"Thanks. Is the conference room set up?"

"Yes, ma'am. Everything's ready. So..." Mena fidgeted with nervous energy. She balled her fists up and tried to tamp down the smile that threatened to eclipse everything in the room. Alex put her briefcase and purse down. She waited for Mena to spill.

"So...?"

"He asked me! We're getting married!" Mena said.

Alex smiled.

"Oh, Mena! That's wonderful!"

Mena held out the ring for Alex's inspection.

"Very nice." Alex reached out and hugged Mena.

"Do you mind if I take a few days off? Roger and I want to go back to Wisconsin to tell our parents."

"Oh yeah! Of course! The guys can pick up the slack when you're gone."

"Okay. I'll get them up to speed asap!"

Mena closed the door behind her, but opened it back up a few seconds later.

"Thank you, ma'am. I really appreciate how supportive you've been since hiring me."

Alex smiled again.

"Girl power...Besides you deserve some happiness, Mena. Go have fun." Alex said.

Mena shut the door.

Alex took a sip of her coffee, then settled into the day's business. At thirty, Alex was one of the youngest Executive Vice Presidents of Comet Holdings, a new player in the finance game. She brought in big clients and took home a queen-sized salary. Alex was at the top of her game. She looked the part too. Alex always wore pants suits and skirts that cost north of several grand. And her shoes? Fuhgeddaboudit. Alex had a massive shoe closet the size of some department store sections.

After her promotion to VP she did a stint in Chicago, then Los Angeles. But, San Antonio's downtown reminded her of the childhood Baltimore she'd grown up in. For some reason she'd been drawn to San Antonio, now over three hundred years old, with its rich history, textured and shaded by the many people who fought and struggled over the land. First, the Native Americans, Payayas, who encountered Spanish Catholic explorers, then the Mexicans, who were for a time displaced by white settlers who ended up referring to themselves as Texans. The town was built on the banks of the San

Antonio River and housed five Spanish Missions, the most famous of course being the Alamo. Like many other states, Texas was founded on conflict over land.

Alex was a student of history and liked feeling connected to a city. Here in San Antonio, she connected with the deep well of pride exhibited and exemplified by the Mexican-American culture. She tried to attend as many cultural events as she could. Fiesta, Night in Old San Antonio, the King Williams Fair, and even transplant events like the Taste of New Orleans made Alex feel like she belonged.

And, that is what she wanted…to belong. To something. Here at least Alex could see a path laid out for her life, regardless of her past. For Alex, belonging meant not being lonely ever again.

A LIFE ENDED

POLICE swarmed in a flurry of activity inside the church. Blood, body parts, and entrails saturated the length of the sanctuary floor. Every chair, table, and pew had been demolished. Dana and Robin surveyed the damage. The body of Abraham Moore, or what was left of it, lay beyond the podium.

"No matter how many we see, it's still a life ended," Dana said.

"It's a stiff, Boss. Get over it." Robin answered.

Robin was already jaded even though she had less time on the force and Murder Detail than Dana did. Still, Dana felt like she should be more horrified about this awful violence. But, as a cop you became hardened to the violence you saw…detached. It had to be this way otherwise more police officers would kill themselves or go insane. There was just no other way to process dealing with death and misery on a daily basis year after year.

"Whoever did this had alot of rage." Dana said.

A Uniformed Officer came from the back room holding something.

"Detectives, you may want these."

Abraham's Navy dog tags.

"Thanks," Dana said.

"Yes, ma'am." The Uniform walked off. Dana rubbed the dog tags between her gloved fingers.

"A soldier deserves better than this." Shock registered on her face. *Oh, GOD.*

"I knew this man."

"How?" Robin asked.

"Abraham Moore. He was Eli's father." Dana said.

Robin made the connection. "The Navy guy?"

Dana heard Robin, but her gaze and thoughts were miles, no, *years* away.

I was so preoccupied…I didn't even notice.

Dana collected herself, allowing the professional demeanor to surface again.

"I'll call his wife."

Robin nodded acknowledgment to her partner. "I'll get started in the back."

Robin made her way back toward the office as Dana stood near the podium. Crime Scene techs placed a special black tarp over the remains.

"Detective! There's some guy outside...Says his father works here!" Dana spotted the young officer pointing outside the sanctuary doors at someone she couldn't see.

"Says his name's Elijah Moore."

Time seemed to freeze for Dana. All the air left her body.

What am I going to tell him?

She tried to regain her composure, walked to the front, and exited the building. Dana spotted Eli several feet away on the grass, staring up at the church steeple. His black Jeep parked on the curb. Dana motioned to the officer. "I got it. Thanks."

Eli faced her. They made eye contact.

In that single instant they shared a connection. Years ripped away like gossamer, leaving the remembrance of the last time they were together. Years ago. *How many? Ten? Eight?* Eli attempted a smile, but he knew the presence of the police was not a good sign.

"Hey, Dana," Eli said.

"Hi, Elijah."

The silence. Like they used to share in intimate moments. *How does he feel about us? Stop it Dana. Focus.* Then, the connection was gone like smoke as Eli's eyes took in the police activity around them.

"What happened? Some kind of break-in? Where's Pop?"

"Elijah..." Dana began. But she couldn't bring herself to say the words. To tell him his father was dead...murdered. And not just murdered but *torn apart...*

She wanted to shield him from the pain she knew was coming. Protect him by saying nothing. And yet...this was her job. To deliver horrible news to good people.

Elijah didn't give her the chance though. His eyes turned into slits. Rage bubbling to the surface. He moved toward the doors. Dana stepped into his path. This is the part of him she didn't know Dana thought. *The warrior. The killer. The hunter of men.*

"What's going on?" Eli asked. His voice was icy and removed. So unlike their last meeting.

"We found him this morning." Dana said.

"NO!"

Eli refused to believe what she was implying. Images of his father flashed through his mind. Each a memory of pain and frustration. Of disappointing Abraham. Eli couldn't stop the tears from streaking down his face as he thought back to the last conversation he'd had with his father.

"I'm so sorry." Dana said.

Eli pushed past Dana. She laid a palm on his chest, stopping him.

"Elijah...I know you're hurting but let me do my job. When I'm done I'll give you all the information you need."

"How...did he die?"

"I don't know. But, when I do I'll find you."

"I'm not leaving, Dana." Eli said.

Dana dug in her coat pocket. Took out a business card. Eli shoved the card into a pocket in his jeans.

"You need to tell Ellen. She needs to know as soon as possible." Dana said.

Eli pulled his eyes from the silhouette of the church back to hers. She was right. He had to tell his mother. Eli spun around without another word and stalked back to his Jeep. Dana stood outside the church as his Jeep pulled away and cleared her vision. She wished there was a way to take his pain away.

Dana walked back into the church.

Brick sat inside his favorite bar, a place called *Full Metal Jacket*, nursing a shot of scotch. The old place was a haven for old veterans who like to trade war stories and talk shit to each other. The building was nestled inside a dreary, plain brick shell on Vance Jackson street. It sat near another super grocery store like the one across from the surplus. That was a bad omen Brick thought to himself as he drank.

The patrons were men between fifty and eighty who remembered the old conflicts that most civilians had forgotten. Sometimes younger vets of the campaigns in Iraq and Afghanistan came through and these men and women were welcomed with open arms as younger siblings who knew the cost of defending one's country.

Brick signaled to the bartender to bring him one more. He'd already had four and it was starting to affect him. His eyes were glazed over and sweat covered his brow. The bartender frowned and sliced a hand across his throat, signaling the water was cut off for Brick.

Brick smiled and stood. He dropped some money on the table and staggered to the door.

"Hey brother. Let me give you a ride. You don't need to be driving." One of the vets said.

"Yeah...guess you right." Brick fished his keys from a pocket and tossed them to the vet.

"Gonna take a leak. Out in three...maybe four."

"Gotcha Big Man! I'll be outside."

Brick gave him a thumbs-up and wandered into the restroom.

Brick stood outside, inhaling the crisp night air. He walked over to his truck, patted the hood like the vehicle was a trusty horse, and looked around for the vet who offered him the ride. The parking lot was empty except for cars and trucks. Brick was confused. He looked at his truck again. The driver's side door was open and the truck was on as if the vet had started the engine to warm it up.

"Maybe he had to pee too." Brick giggled to himself.

He decided to walk to the side of the building to check to see if the gentleman might be relieving himself on the side of the bar. Brick came around the corner and saw the man laying on the pavement. It looked like he was sleeping.

"Hey! Thought you were gonna give me a ride? Looks like you might need a ride too! HAHAHA!" Brick ripped out a good loud snort and walked over. He kneeled down to shake the man.

"Come on. I think I can at least get you back inside. Maybe I'll call one of them...ride songs. No...ride shares? Whatever those damn things are! Gonna call one for both of us."

Brick gripped the man's shoulder and rolled him over. He froze.

The man's neck was an open wound. Blood pumped from his severed carotid artery. Brick could see all the way to the bone inside the man's ruined neck.

Brick staggered backward, falling against the wall.

"Oh no...LORD'Y...No!"

Then he was aware of a presence near him. He looked to his right and saw an animal shape squatting under a burned-out lamp post. He glanced the other way and saw another blocking the way he'd walked out from the parking lot. The animals sat there. Unmoving. Watching him.

The woman with dark hair and the white streak came from the shadows in front of him. He hadn't noticed anything before, but here she was. She smiled at him and squatted a foot away. She stared into his eyes with those glowing red eyes of hers.

"Your brother, the Shepard, is dead soldier."

Brick couldn't move or speak. He was petrified with fear.

"You might like to know he died as a soldier. No fear. No begging. Just silence. I hope you can die with such dignity, but alas, I fear you will meet death trembling. Begging for your life. Or you will drink yourself to death in shame, knowing that you did NOTHING to help him. Yes. This is how I think you will go. Or, perhaps you will take your own life. Use one of those fancy pistols of yours from the curio shop to blow your brains out...hmmm? How will you meet your end?"

"Wha...what...do you want?" Brick croaked out.

"Why, to see you ended." She said.

The woman grabbed Brick's skull with tremendous force and slammed it back against the building wall. The blow so powerful it almost knocked him unconscious. She gripped the sides of Brick's bald head in both hands and pulled him inches away from her wild face.

"Be ready soldier! I am coming for you! Not tonight! Perhaps not even tomorrow, but I am coming nonetheless. Prepare yourself! Prepare to meet your death!"

She released Brick and signaled to the waiting animals. They ran off into the darkness. She smiled and strolled away, laughing.

Brick slid down the wall sideways. Tears flowed down his dark face. This was HIS fault and now DEATH was coming home to roost.

COLD CASES

Seven-thirty the next morning, Dana and Robin sat at their desks in the Murder Detail squad sifting through the autopsy report on the headless John Doe victim. Dana snapped her fingers to get Robin's attention. "Listen to this."

Robin rounded the desk and perched on it while Dana read.

"Wound lacerations consistent with animal attack bite patterns. Saliva compound on wound typed as Canis Lupus."

"Well, that's some bullshit…So, what now?" Robin sighed.

Reports and paperwork were not high on Robin's list of adrenaline-inducing activities. Dana leaned back. She tossed a pencil into the ceiling, making it stick there next to the other twenty or so pencils hanging in the ceiling already.

"First, let's send the samples from the headless John Doe, the homeless man, and the taxicab attack to the lab. Maybe they can match them to the sample from the Moore killing. Second, we interview..."

Dana shuffled through the case folder. Scanned a page.

"...Dan Moore. Abraham's brother. Nickname is "Brick." Might have some answers."

Robin glanced at the report in Dana's hands. "Is he the big guy ATF tried to stick a gun charge on couple years ago?"

"The same."

Dana leaned back so far in her chair it threatened to tip over. She aimed and tossed another pencil into the ceiling tile. Robin stared at her partner. She started to climb onto Dana's desk.

"What're you doing?" Dana asked.

Robin gestured at the ceiling. "You have pencils as decorations."

"Leave them. Helps me think."

Robin hopped off the desk.

"Whateves." Robin said.

Robin stretched her lithe frame.

"I'm going home. Maybe I can have sex with my girlfriend before she goes to work. I'll drop the samples by the lab."

"See you later." Dana said.

Robin started to walk away. She turned back.

"Wow. Not even phased by my comment. I like it. Hey..."

Dana glanced up from the folder.

"Don't waste all your energy on this one. Probably just a dog attack. We've got real criminals to catch." Robin said.

"Get some sleep, Rookie."

"Peace."

Robin disappeared down the hall. Dana examined the autopsy report again.

"What killed you, Mr. Moore?"

She walked over to a filing cabinet next to Robin's desk. Pulled out several folders from a section marked UNSOLVED COLD CASES. Stacked them on her desk. Opened the top folder. Her finger trailed down the page, stopping at a small section.

"That's weird." The section listed the causes of death according to the Medical Examiner's Office: ANIMAL BITES; ORIGIN UNKNOWN. Dana snatched another file. The SAME result.

Animal bites; Origin unknown...

She scanned to the bottom. *John Doe.* Urgency set in. Dana blew through the stack. Each time reading the cause of death and victim's names.

John Doe, John Doe, John Doe...Animal Bites; Origin Unknown.

The list continued...She closed the file in her hands just as the phone rang. It startled Dana.

"Yeah, Doc. I've been waiting on the reports."

Dana listened to the person on the other end of the line. "Uh huh. Right. Got it. Oh...next time we give you a call from a crime scene, how about maybe get your folks to show up on time?"

A heated voice on the other end made Dana smile. She hung up while the person was in mid-sentence. The phone rang again.

"Detective Adams." Dana paused.

"Elijah...Hi! It's okay. Tonight? Sure. You remember how to get there? Ok. See you tonight."

Dana hung up and stared at the phone. *He's coming over.* Dana's mind raced. A deep, terrible fear crept up from her belly, settling in her heart. *He won't, can't understand.* Dana chewed and chewed at the thought. She had to commit to doing the right thing even if it tarnished any friendship she had with Elijah. But, thinking this brought back the sadness she had suppressed for so many years. It also suppressed the hope that Dana kept locked away in a tiny place inside her heart.

Soldier on, Dana.

Her Father's voice. Tony Adams had been a big-hearted policeman who died in the line of duty. The world's best single parent and Dana's hero. Gone in an instant of violence. An act which had propelled her into Homicide. Always chasing the ghost of her Father while trying to catch his killer. Or killers like his.

Do what needs to be done and move on, Dana. Don't leave anything behind baby girl. Leave it all on the line.

God, she missed him! Big Tony was the only parent she had ever known.

When Dana was around ten, Big Tony took her on ride-alongs in his patrol car. It wasn't department policy, but he indulged his only child, and she loved it. Loved HIM because of it. Big Tony always made Dana feel like the only one on the planet. He doted on her, taking her to back yard barbeques with his cop friends. Baseball games and trips to the amusement park. Life outside the force with Big Tony felt like one giant party to Dana.

All that was ripped away when Dana graduated from high school. Big Tony was serving a warrant with a special unit on a drug house. Shots were fired, and in the chaos Big Tony was dead. They found him on the second-floor landing. Smoke pouring from the barrel of his 357 Magnum. No sign of his killer. Just like that. Dana's hero was *gone*. She hated that the police never found out who killed him.

Oh man. Troy.

She needed to make sure her juvenile delinquent-in-training had gone to school this morning. She dialed, praying that Troy would not pick up the phone this time. Voicemail.

"Breathe, Dana. Breathe. Troy is at school. She's not running around the streets. Right? Right!"

Dana pulled the school number up in her phone directory. Her finger poised above the call button.

"Nope. I trust her." Dana hung up and reviewed the rest of the stack of folders.

BROTHERS

The Moore house was modest as to be expected for a pastor. It was one story with a high, old fashioned porch and shutters that could be opened and shut lining the windows. A high, pitched roof, steeper than most in the neighborhood seemed to resemble a church steeple. Eli did not think this was an accident. The house was painted yellow and white because his mother Ellen loved the colors and this was the one indulgence Abraham gave in to. Abraham preferred to keep a low-key modest profile.

Eli had to admit though that Abraham had loved Ellen with a fierceness of passion that Eli never saw with his friend's parents. Abraham doted on his wife as if she was the sun, and he a moon in her orbit.

Eli wandered through the house of his childhood in a daze. Photos and other mementos showed the life of Abraham Moore as it used to be. Eli entered the living room. Sat down on a couch. Like Abraham's office, this house made Eli feel small. The ghosts of Eli's childhood drifted around him in a swirl. Most good memories, some not so much. He loved Abraham, but his Father had been a hard man to please.

Eli noticed a collection of photographs hung on the west wall of the room. Of *him*. From his first birthday all the way to a photograph taken last year by Chapa of Eli in full tactical kit as a SEAL. He walked over and stared at the photos. The collection was very organized, almost like a shrine. He glanced behind the SEAL photo. An older one sat there. Eli was thirteen. The second summer after Chapa came to live with them. Eli smiled.

This one held a special place in his heart. It had been a good summer to be a kid. He and Chapa rode their bikes miles from the house without any kind of questions from his parents. They often stopped at a small pond, dropped their bikes, and went for a dip, knowing the ride home would dry them off before Ellen noticed. Of course, Mom being Mom, Ellen always noticed. But, she never scolded them. Her statement, after mandating they take off their filthy sneakers was: *Boys will be boys. Clean up before your father comes home.* She said it with a twinkle in her eye and a smile on her lips.

That was the summer Chapa and I became REAL brothers...
Ellen walked in. He could see the grief on her face. Ellen was worn down. Exhausted. Eli hated it. This was the first time she looked *old*. All the vibrancy that his mother owned seemed drained out of her. Her skin was so pale Eli thought she was almost translucent. It seemed to sag off her like an old shawl. The powerful, beautiful, courageous women was still inside he thought, just muted. He didn't know how to help her. How to fix her.

Maybe he couldn't. *That* thought bored a hole in Eli's soul.

"Mom..."

"I know baby. I know."

Ellen hugged her son as only a mother could. She placed her hands on his face, kissing his forehead.

"Your father made peace with death a long time ago -- just like you, I think." She said.

Tears filled her eyes.

"Can you stay here awhile? This house feels bigger than it used to." Ellen asked.

"Of course Mom...When did you put those pictures up?"

"The ones of you? I didn't. Your Father did. About a year ago."

"I thought he was angry?"

"Eli...he loved you. Always did."

They sat on the couch holding each other. Eli could almost feel Abraham's presence with them. It was a strange, but somehow comforting feeling. He glanced at his mother's profile. Such a strong woman. She had to be. Raising two badass young boys on her own while her husband sailed the world for the Navy.

"Coffee, son?"

"Sure."

Eli and Ellen moved to the kitchen. It was a lovely room, bright with green and pastel colors that enhanced the light coming in through the kitchen windows. The kitchen was Ellen's refuge. The place where she showed her family love. Everyone was welcome in her kitchen. His mother treated friends that he and Chapa brought over like family. There was always an extra space at the table and enough food to eat. Ellen Moore was known on the block as Momma Moore, which made Abraham laugh since Ellen was white. He always joked with her, saying:

You know what won my momma and grand-momma over on you not being Black? Ellen asked what? Abraham said "those beans that you cooked for them when they first met you! They said that girl put her foot in it! They said if any white girl can cook like this I guess she's a keeper!"

Ellen's phone vibrated. She read the text. Smiled.

"Can you wait a few more minutes? Someone just came by I want you to see."

"As long as you need, Mom."

Ellen walked from the room. A few minutes later, Eli heard a man's voice in the other room. She walked back into the kitchen.

"Look who's here." She said.

His brother Chapa walked in.

He sported a beard now, but still had the same boyish charm from the last time Eli and he were in the teams together. Chapa was Latino of Mexican descent. *Damien Jesus Antonio Chaparia.* His father, who had been the center of Chapa's life until Cartel crossfire took his life during a trip to Juarez, was from Mexico City and his mother from El Paso. When Chapa's father died his mother never saw the world the same. She moved them to San Antonio, and by the time Chapa turned eight, she went from anti-depressants to heroin. By the time Child Protective Services took Chapa from his home she was so far gone that she didn't even remember she had a son.

His mother overdosed soon after.

"Chapa! Man! It's great to see you!"

"Eli. Whew! I missed you, bro'!" Chapa said.

The men hugged each other as brothers and men who had been through bad times and back. Their love had been tested through blood and tears. The men stared at each other without any words. Chapa walked over to Ellen and folded her in an embrace. Tears filled Chapa's eyes.

"I don't know what..." Chapa started.

"He loved you too, Damian. SO much" Ellen said.

Ellen stared at her sons...her boys. She knew they were about as broken right now as she had ever seen them, which scared her considering the profession of violence they had both been in. She did what mothers all over do and thought about them before herself.

"Why don't you guys go out and do something?"

"I'm not leaving you, Mom." Eli said.

She glanced around the kitchen.

"It's okay. The service starts this afternoon. I need to go through some old things and I need to do it by myself." Ellen said.

"We can help." Chapa said.

She reached out, cupping both their faces with her hands.

"Oh, my boys. I love you both. You make me proud to be your Mom."

The men smiled at their mother.

"Don't worry. I'll be alright. Eli, why don't you stay with your brother? I know he missed you."

"You sure, Mom? I can stay." Eli said.

"Eli...go." Ellen said.

"Ok Mom."

Each of her boys kissed Ellen on the cheek before leaving the kitchen.

They drove across town back to the North side, near the highway junctions of Loop 1604 and Interstate 10, or I-10 as locals called it. Not "the 10" as Los Angeles-based folks did. Chapa lived in an upscale apartment complex off the frontage road near the La Cantera Shopping Center. It was not Eli's style, but it suited his brother. The complex was just gaudy enough to be the center of attention, and that described Chapa to a tee. Chapa's apartment was lavish. Decorated in what Eli had once heard was "modern chic" or some nonsense. It was all bachelor pad.

"Damn, Chap! You a drug dealer now?"

Chapa laughed at his older brother.

"Where can I drop these bags?" Eli asked.

"Toss those anywhere, bro," Chapa said.

Chapa made his way into the kitchen. Dug into his fridge. Held out two beers.

"Beer?"

"Water."

"Since when did you ever pass up a good ale? What gives?" Chapa asked.

"Just want to keep a clear head," Eli said.

Chapa tossed Eli a bottled water. Eli settled on the couch.

"I can't believe he's gone, Chapa."

Chapa sat in one of the chairs near Eli.

"Me neither...I hope you weren't mad...about what she said." Chapa said.

"About Pops loving you? Please. You were always a member of this family. He loved you. Hell, probably more than he loved me. You're my brother. Always will be."

"Pops didn't ever have to bail YOU out of jail for shoplifting or fighting, or drinking, or whatever." Chapa said.

"Well, it's not like you could go home, as screwed up as your family was. Someone had to get you out of trouble." Eli mused.

"For real. It's funny, Eli. Who would have thought a crack baby with two criminal parents would make it all the way to the United States Navy SEALS? I sure didn't." Chapa mused.

Eli lifted his water in toast to him.

"Well, you did...WE did."

"Damn, Skippy," Chapa said.

They clinked water bottle to beer bottle.

Abraham and Ellen took Chapa in when he was a rowdy ten-year-old living in his fifth foster home. Ellen worked for Child Protective Services at the time. She told Chapa years later that she fell in love with him the moment she saw his face. Ellen spoke with Abraham and they decided that it was GOD's plan for them to adopt the troubled boy and give him all the love and support he had never been exposed to. It turned out to be a win-win for everyone in the Moore family. Ellen and Abraham got another son. Eli, the brother he always wanted. And Chapa, the family he deserved. As a sign of respect for his new-found family Chapa dropped his first name and used part of his last name to honor his Father. He took the Moore last name as his own.

Chapa stared at his brother for a while. He smiled, "What's up with the cop?"

"What do you mean?"

"Don't play dumb. I know you're gonna see her."

"Actually..."

"Here it comes." Chapa said with a smile.

"Actually, dumb ass, what I was GOING to say was that she is THE investigating detective on the case." Eli said.

"No shit?"

"Really."

"Is she still hot?" Chapa asked.

54

Eli gave him a stare. It became a grin.

"Yeah...she is. But, that's not the point. The cops, including her, don't have a clue."

"That's a shocker."

"She's good, though, Chapa. I mean real good. Like on those cop shows." Eli said.

Chapa snorted. "Maybe she'll catch the bastard who did this."

"I hope," Eli said.

They sipped their drinks more.

"How are the ribs? Still hurt?"

"Shit! Nothing can stop the Chapmeister! I've broken more bones playing football with you and those sissies around the corner from the house. Remember that?"

"Yeah. The McAlister brothers. What a bunch of knuckleheads." The memory made Eli smile.

"Their sister wasn't," Chapa said.

"No, she was not."

"Man. Those were good times Eli. Good times."

"The best...."

Eli swallowed.

Why can't I just say what I mean instead of over-thinking?

He looked at his brother.

"Sorry I've been out of touch for a while. I just needed to be alone. Know what I mean?" Eli said.

Eli walked to the window. Watched traffic pass by on the highway.

"What happened?" Chapa asked.

"To what?"

"You and Pops? Once you joined up, everything seemed tense between you guys. I was waiting to hear from you, then after Panama, nothing." Chapa said.

He was concerned about Eli. The last months before their discharges from the Navy, Eli had been more and more remote. Then he cut off all contact. Chapa wanted to help him but wasn't sure how. Eli was a pretty sociable person under the right circumstances, but also a loner. Chapa never pushed Eli when he needed space.

"How about we go see Uncle Dan?" Eli said.

This made Chapa sit up straight. "Now, THAT is what I'm talking about! When?"

"Later tonight. I need to see Dana before that."

Chapa laughed. "Man! She's already got the leash on tight brother!"

Eli smirked at his brother. "Whatever. Where am I bunking?"

"First one on the left."

Eli got up, grabbed his bags. Started down the short hallway.

"Hey Eli…"

Eli faced his brother.

"Glad we're both here. I missed you man."

Eli smiled at Chapa.

"Me too."

Chapa flicked the TV on as Eli disappeared into the spare bedroom.

Abraham Moore's funeral was held at Fort Sam Houston National Cemetery. It was the official cemetery for all military personnel, managed by the United States Department of Veteran's Affairs. It sat adjacent to Joint Base Fort Sam Houston on the city's east side. The cemetery, established in 1926, covered more than one-hundred and fifty-four acres of land with over one-hundred and forty-four internments. Like most military cemeteries, the space felt tranquil and ordered. Row upon row of white markers were sectioned off with military precision. Most of Abraham's parishioners showed up to give their condolences to Ellen, Eli, and Chapa. Old war buddies, ministers from various churches of faith around the city, as well as several council members came by, one after another.

Eli was touched and moved that his father had such an impact on so many others. At one point Chapa leaned over and whispered, "Man, I didn't know Pops knew so many folks!"

"Neither did I." Eli whispered back.

Dana walked over and hugged Ellen. "I'm so sorry Ellen. If I can do anything for you, please let me know." Ellen smiled at Dana. The older woman pulled her close and whispered in her ear. "Tell him."

Dana tried to smile. They hugged again. She moved over to Eli.

"I…uh…I'm sorry Elijah." Dana said.

"I know. Thanks." Eli said. He smiled at her. This made her less uncomfortable. She moved over and shook Chapa's hand.

"Hey Dana." Chapa said. "Appreciate you working on the case and all."

Dana nodded. "We're trying."

The choir from Abraham's church began singing one of his favorite hymns. Everyone stood, joining along with the singing. Eli tried to feel something, but found his attention wandering. He stared out at the sea of markers and focused on the soft breeze that caressed his face. He moved his eyes back the other way and spotted Brick standing near a tree, almost hidden, but watching the funeral. Brick met his eyes. The big man nodded and Eli nodded back. Eli was glad Brick showed up. He knew why his uncle held back. His mother did not like Brick and never had. His uncle was always respectful of Ellen's opinion and kept his distance, which she appreciated in turn. Not one big happy family.

Whose family was perfect anyway?

Eli kept waiting for rain to begin pouring down like in the movies, but the sun was high in the sky, shining down as if to herald Abraham's return. Eli smiled. It sucked that he couldn't tell his father what he thought now, but at least he was at peace.

And that mattered more.

CHANGES

Alex hung up from the hourlong conference call and stretched. She wanted to go home, but the oppression of her remaining workload hung over Alex like a dark cloud. She left her office, noticed that everyone including Mena was gone, then strolled to the restroom. Alex peed and went to the sink to wash her hands.

Alex splashed water on her face. She opened her eyes.

A hideous *wolf-like* beast was staring back at her from the mirror…

Alex screamed.

She fell backward, scrabbling away from the sink and into a stall. Alex covered her mouth and glanced at the floor under the stall walls. The restroom was quiet. The only sound Alex's breathing.

She was alone.

Alex crawled to her feet and walked toward the mirror, looking at the floor. When her thighs bumped the sink, Alex worked up enough courage to look. The only thing staring back at Alex was her own reflection. Same as it ever was.

"Get it together, Alex."

Just as she started to laugh at herself for being silly, pain surged through Alex's body. She spasmed and collapsed to the tiled floor. The pain crashed on her in wave after wave. A never-ending blanket of agony.

"Alexandra…" The voice seemed to issue from her mind, yet reflected off all the surfaces in the restroom.

"Join us…"

Many voices. A chorus. Just like that night in her apartment. Closer though. Very close.

"Please…help me…somebody…"

Alex flopped from her back to her stomach. She crawled toward the door. Inches seemed like miles as the pain hammered into and through her. She tried to focus on getting to the door and back to her office to call for help. Alex managed to shift to her knees and make it to the door. She plodded, animal-like, into the hallway. Tongue hanging from her open mouth, trailing a pool of saliva behind her. Several feet down the hallway she fell face-first, spent.

An eternity later, Alex opened her eyes.

She was staring at the ceiling, still laying in the hallway. The pain was gone, replaced by a dim memory and aching back. She stood up, looked around. The hallway was still empty. She checked her watch. An hour had elapsed, but Alex had no memory of it. Back in her office, She grabbed her laptop and purse, shut the lights off and left. The sensation of being watched heightened.

Alex checked and rechecked the hallway before leaving.

Alex pulled up outside the gate to her apartment building in her Jaguar. Keyed the remote. The gate opened. As she started to drive in, something ran past her car. Alex hit the brakes, causing the back end to bounce up and down. She flicked her high beams on.

The driveway was empty...

Get it together Alex. Don't lose it now.

Alex parked the car in her spot. She climbed out, purse and briefcase slung on one arm. A file full of documents in her hand.

Then...she heard it...

A sound from outside.

Alex dropped the file. The papers scattering on the ground. A long howling was carried to her ears by the wind.

"Hello?"

Why did I say that?

A low growl from somewhere in the garage drifted back. Alex stared, but couldn't see anything in the dark. The growl was not menacing.

It was almost *inviting.*

She took a tentative step *toward* the sound. The full moon hung low over the Earth, casting a bright glow into the parking garage. Alex walked back to the car, bent over to retrieve the file and papers. Bright red drops of blood hit the folder, staining it. More drops rained down on the ground.

Alex grabbed the folder and noticed her hand was bleeding.

"Damnit!"

Blood covered her index and middle fingers.

She moved to the elevator, careful not to drip blood on her suit. Alex hit the button for the 23rd floor. She stepped inside while inspecting her injured finger. A small incision ran from the nail to the first knuckle on her index finger.

"What's this...?"

She shrieked and fell to the floor, just like at the office. Her body convulsed. The pain intensified a thousand-fold. The world fell sideways and a gray cloud settled over Alex's eyes and mind.

4th Floor...

Alex was jerked into consciousness. She was laying on her side. She lifted her head enough to stare at her hands.

OH GOD, OH GOD, OH GOD! OH MY GOD!!!

Her hands were bloody. As she watched, the flesh ripped backward and long sharp claws extended from her fingers.

"AAAAAAAAAAH!"

6th Floor...

Alex's eyes rolled back in her head. She screamed again. Then passed out.

9th Floor...

...A tearing noise brought her back from unconsciousness. Her expensive French boots were shredded. Claws protruded from what was left of them.

"No this can't be happening! Wake up Alex! WAKE UP!"

The elevator continued to climb...

11th Floor...

...Every muscle in her body contracted, and just as suddenly relaxed. Alex thought the worst was over. She breathed deep.

"AAAAAAAAAAAAH!"

The sound of Alex yelling turned into a yelping noise she did not recognize as her own...

12th Floor...

...Then a growl mixed with a gnashing of teeth...

13th Floor...

...Then a howl. Alex's body morphed and doubled in size. Her clothes were ripped to pieces.

14th Floor...

...The elevator filled with the noise of bones breaking and reforming.

As her tendons and muscles grew, the sound of snapping ricocheted and bounced off the walls. The sound, like rubber bands snapping.

16th Floor...

...Alex stood on all fours now. Hands and feet changed into paws with five digits. She howled in pain.

17th Floor...

...Her spine lurched up underneath the skin like someone snapping a bedspread. The ripple traveling from her neck all the way down her spine.

20th Floor...

...Alex struggled to turn her head. She glanced back at her hips. A long, pink, hairless tail extended from just above her anus.

Her body was drenched in a gooey combination of sweat and gelatinous skin.

21st Floor...

...Alex tried to speak, but a growl issued from her throat. Fur sprouted from every pore in her body.

It wriggled and crawled across her skin like worms. The fur moving with terrible purpose, covering the rest of her exposed flesh.

22nd Floor...

...Alex's ears disappeared into her head. Large pointed canine ears erupted from her cranium, pushing through the flesh. Alex howled one last time. As she did, her face elongated and contorted. Her jaw snapped in several places, the face transforming into a snout. Her teeth became long, razor sharp canines. Saliva dripped from her mouth onto the floor.

DING!!

23rd floor...
...The door opened.

Alex stood there staring into the mirrored wall across from the doors. The same savage, wolf-like animal with grey fur and ice-blue eyes that stared at her from the mirror in the office restroom.

Alex padded onto the floor, forgetting the pain of the experience and her torn clothes inside the bloody elevator. She stretched out to the mirror to get a better look at herself. Outside the windows, the full moon was at its peak. Alex rushed to the window and stood up, bumping her head on the ceiling. She pawed at the glass.

Maddie Levitt from 23A opened her apartment door. Alex didn't recognize her at all. She smelled *prey* and rushed forward. Hurtling with all her might. Ready to lunge and rip the flesh off the stinking carcass.

Alex roared and jumped...

Maddie screamed. Slamming the door just as Alex slid into it. Alex's body crashed against the door, splintering it. Maddie screamed again as Alex forced her way past the splintered wood. Saliva dripping from Alex's massive jaws. Maddie tried to run further into her apartment when Alex lunged at her...

Minutes later, Alex headbutted the exit door and raced down the stairs. Metal and concrete flying past her at frightening speed. Alex burst from the door into the parking garage. She stopped, looking left and right. A chorus of howls pierced the night. Alex sniffed the air. She smelled *THEM.* Alex moved on instinct now. She loped past parked cars and out of the garage.

Alex ran to the security wall that ringed the apartment building. The wall was fifteen feet high. Alex increased her speed, jumping up and out, and clearing the wall. Alex sprinted in the direction of the howling....

...to the PACK.

SECRETS AND LIES

5:00 pm

Dana tried to concentrate on cooking dinner, but her mind kept drifting back to thoughts of Elijah. As her spaghetti turned into mush on the stove, Dana thought back to when she and Elijah had spent a weekend in Austin. Just the two of them. Dancing, eating, making love most of the time. Dana almost felt his breath on her skin, Elijah's hands on her thighs. He entering her.

BUZZ!

The doorbell ripped Dana from the memory. She glanced down at the boiling mess in front of her.

"Shit! Troy! Can you get the door?"

No answer.

"TROY! Answer the door!"

Still nothing. Dana turned everything off and stalked into the front room. She stared upstairs to see if Troy was coming down.

"Damn it."

BUZZ!

Dana tried to fix her hair, but it was a lost cause.

Oh well. Alright. Don't be nervous.

She opened the door. Eli stood there smiling.

"Hi. I brought wine."

He held up a cheap bottle of wine from the grocery store. Dana smiled back.

"My favorite. Come in please."

Eli stepped inside and stood in the middle of her small living room. Dana tried not to stare as he moved past her. *He smells good.*

Dana had a small, two-story, three-bedroom house not too far from Chapa's place, just down 1604 near Culebra Road. Dana picked the area because she wanted Troy to go to a good high school with high-level academics. She really tried to make sure Troy had as stable a life as possible despite living with a single Mom/Cop.

"I like the new colors. They're pretty." Eli said.

Dana shrugged. "Thanks. I got tired of gun-metal grey. Went a little more girlie I guess."

"Troy here?"

Dana smiled. "Yeah. She doesn't know you're here! Big secret! I'll be right back."

"Sure."

Dana jogged upstairs and knocked on Troy's door. Silence. Dana slammed the door open.

"I was calling you."

"And?" Troy answered without even looking at Dana. Troy had a pair of headphones on. Dana could hear the music blasting away. Dana crossed the room and snatched the headphones off Troy's head.

"What the hell, Dana?"

Dana glared at her.

"We have company."

Troy adjusted her headphones.

"You know...your cop friends really need to get a life," Troy said.

Dana grabbed Troy's mobile device.

"Enough with the attitude. Who I spend my time with is my business."

"I have friends too, Dana."

Dana snorted, "Your friends are delinquents and into shit, you shouldn't be into. You know...I don't want to have this conversation right now...Elijah's downstairs."

Troy dropped all the attitude. Her face changed into that of a very happy young lady.

"Really?" Troy jumped up and ran downstairs. Eli saw her as she turned the corner into the living room.

"TROY!"

Troy jumped into his arms and hugged his neck like a life preserver. They held on as if they were the only two people in the world. Dana walked in and watched them. She smiled and wiped away the wetness of a tear before either one saw her. Troy nestled her head in Eli's chest.

"You ok, kiddo?" Eli asked.

Troy smiled and pushed her face deeper into him.

"I am now."

Dana ordered Chinese take-out for them since she destroyed the spaghetti. They ate and laughed through the night. Troy lingered near Elijah the entire time. They laughed at the dumbest jokes and kidded around with each other.

So, this is what a real family feels like? Dana thought.

"Time for bed Troy. School night." Dana said.

Troy hugged Eli's neck. He smiled.

"Will you be here long? In town I mean?" Troy asked.

"Yeah. I'm done with the Navy."

Troy beamed. Tears in her eyes.

"You mean…"

"I'm here for good." He said.

Troy couldn't believe her ears. She kissed him on the cheek and bounded up the stairs, turning around long enough to wave. He waved back and she disappeared out of view.

"Can you stay a few more minutes Elijah?"

"I wish. I gotta get up early and help Mom."

"Yeah. I'm working night shift anyway. Well, maybe we can all do this again sometime?" Dana said.

Eli stood.

"You bet."

Dana walked Eli to the door. He grabbed his jacket.

Tell him.

"Elijah…"

"Yeah?"

Dana stared into his eyes. The need to say something right there, but fear crashed in on her.

"Can you meet me for coffee tomorrow? Dell's?" Dana asked.

"Yeah. Text me when you get a sec." He said.

Eli and Dana looked at each other. Things unsaid on their lips. She leaned in and gave him a hug. Eli felt her sincerity deep in his chest. He wanted to crush her in his arms and hold her, but now wasn't the time.

"Thanks for coming. I've haven't seen Troy this happy in a long time. It means a lot to her." Dana said.

"And you?" Eli asked.

Dana smiled at him. "Me too."

"Good. See you tomorrow Dana."

Eli walked out the door. Dana closed the door and gazed through the front window and watched him all the way to his Jeep. She drew back from the window and leaned against the door.

Coward.

Her phone sprang to life. Dana walked over to the end table it was on.

"Hey Robin, what's up?" Dana frowned as she listened to Robin talk. She felt the pull of death calling her name.

"Yeah, I know it. Give me thirty minutes."

Dana locked the door, shut the downstairs lights off and walked upstairs to change.

8:00 pm

Dana stepped off the adjacent elevator on the 23rd floor. She noticed the trail of blood running from the elevator to the wall. Bloody paw prints were everywhere. They extended all the way to Mrs. Levitt's door. Crime Scene Techs swarmed over the crime scene. Robin waved at her from inside the other elevator. It was open and locked so only the police could access it. Dana walked inside. Blood was splashed on the walls and floor. Shredded clothes lay in a pile in the corner of the elevator.

"Hey, Tony. What's up, Robin?"

Tony Samuels, a Crime Scene Tech, nodded at her and continued to work. He was a slim man so pale that he seemed to fade into the harsh work lights set up just outside the elevator doors. At almost seven feet tall Tony was always mistaken for a professional basketball player who played for the San Antonio Spurs, Robin's favorite team. This amused Tony since he preferred volleyball and had played in college. He also had a tendency to hunch over which made him look a bit like Quasimodo from *The Hunchback of Notre Damme.*

Robin grinned, loaded up with more sarcasm than usual.

"Pretty gross huh?" Robin was smirking.

Dana stared at the elevator. Clumps of material were stuck on the floor. She pulled a pair of gloves on. Squatted down.

"Tony, if you got what you need, why don't you give us a minute." Dana said.

"Sure thing, Detective." Tony said.

"Hey Tony!" Robin said.

"Yes?"

"Think you're gonna get traded this summer or are you gonna exercise your player option?" Robin asked with a grin.

Tony smiled. "Ha, ha."

Tony left the elevator.

"Where's the body?" Dana asked.

"Boss, we got blood galore, ripped up clothes, a dead old lady down the hall. But, nobody. It's all *Fubar*. You know, fuc...."

"Got it."

Robin screwed her face up, trying to figure out what this meant. "This...it's just weird."

Dana noticed the torn boots and purse in the corner. She walked over. Picked them up.

"Saint Laurent...nice. Who's the vic?"

Dana started to rifle through the purse, but Robin stopped her. Robin had dialed on her cell and was holding it to her ear. She covered the mouthpiece.

"On hold. Already did it. Name is Alexandra Stone, hot-shit investment banker. Works for a company called Comet Holdings."

"And the other one?

"Maddie Elizabeth Levitt. Eighty-three. Found in her apartment down the hall. Her body got mangled pretty bad. Looks like parts were torn off, like from an animal or something."

"Anyone hear from Ms. Stone? Check hospitals yet?" Dana asked.

Robin nodded.

"Checking right now. I'm on hold. So far, nada. No other signs of assault. Beaucoup paw prints from the old lady's door to the exit stairwell."

Dana knelt by the clump of material she'd noticed earlier.

"I'll check those. Prints?" Dana pulled tweezers from her pocket.

"Just the vic's. And these paw prints." Robin said.

Dana looked at the clump.

"More fur. Same as the cab."

Dana stood up in order to let Robin inspect the clump of hair.

"Do the usual. Canvas the neighbors, her job, the whole nine. We need to figure out if this blood is Ms. Stone's or someone else's." Dana said.

Robin was preoccupied with the call. Dana tugged at Robin's sleeve. Robin hung up in frustration.

"I hate being on hold!" Robin said.

"You know what I'm thinking?"

Robin groaned. "Don't say it."

"The Moore case..." Dana said.

Robin groaned again.

"I told you not to say it. Boss, you know, once you get that big brain of yours working, we get into trouble." Robin said.

"Hey..."

"Yeah?"

"Have you checked the cold cases lately?" Dana asked.

"Nothing but ghosts in there." Robin said.

"I found quite a few old cases with animal attacks. All the vics were listed as John Doe. All of them homeless." Dana said.

"And?"

"You were the detective on some of them. Did you follow up?"

"Boss, you know Cold Case Detail does that. Why the hassle?"

"I'm not implying anything, Robin. I just think that with the strange stuff we've got going on we should explore every angle; that's all. Even the cold cases. Maybe there's a pattern we're missing." Dana said.

"Damn, this and now more shit..."

"Just get on it, Robin!"

Robin got quiet. Dana didn't often raise her voice, so it surprised her. Dana could see that Robin was distressed about disappointing her. She softened her tone.

"Let's not miss anything. Alright?"

Robin nodded at her partner. "Okay."

"Check with them and see if anything turns up."

"Hey...Sorry for...."

Dana smiled. "We're all tired. Forget about it."

Dana walked from the elevator. Headed down the hallway to Mrs. Levitt's apartment. Another Crime Scene Tech was taking pictures inside. The door was demolished. Dana looked inside. Glimpsed a bloody torso covered by what used to be a nightgown.

Oh, Jesus.

Dana crossed into the apartment.

Later, Dana headed to the exit stairs. She tracked the bloody paw prints down to the parking garage level. More prints stretched out toward the perimeter. Dana glanced around and noticed a small blood trail near Alex's car. She walked over. Several dried brownish-red spots on the ground caught her eye. Dana flicked open her personal knife. She scraped a dried blood sample into a small plastic bag. Dana stood up. Her mind processing the various scraps of evidence and possible connections. Since this blood was dried it meant that someone had bled before the attacks on the way to the elevator.

Things made sense. And yet, they didn't.

Why would an animal attack the person in the apartment upstairs?

She remembered a case from the nineties in San Francisco when a young woman was attacked and killed by two savage dogs inside her apartment building. Maybe they were dealing with something similar? Perhaps she thought. But what about the taxicab and Abraham Moore at his church? Who would take the time to transport attack dogs to each crime scene unless it was something personal? *Vendetta?* It frustrated Dana that she couldn't make it all fit into a nice neat picture. In all her years on the Murder Detail she had never experienced this sensation of not knowing where to start. There was always something that gave you a clue about why the crime was committed. But this…?

I don't know what we're dealing with here…and it's getting worse. It's time to start thinking outside the box Dana.

Dana pulled her phone from her pocket and dialed Robin's number.

"What's up Boss?"

"Robin, I need to get at this thing with fresh eyes. I'm going to see an old contact."

"Who?" Robin asked.

"Left-Foot Tony. Used to run gambling and dog fights over off Flores Street. Some of his clients had some savage animals. He might know something."

Robin snorted or spit on the other end of the phone, Dana couldn't tell which and didn't want to know.

"I'm in." Robin said.

"Meet me outside. We'll take my car." Dana said.

"Be right down."

10:15 pm

Dana and Robin drove through the abandoned warehouse district on Flores. It was one of the last few areas within a mile or so of downtown that was just starting to see some renovation happening. But, the area they drove through had not yet undergone any changes. It was a five block stretch of empty or half-empty buildings peppered with graffiti and decorated with refuse and trash. The buildings that did house businesses had parking lots surrounded by fences to keep nefarious individuals out, or at least less interested in stealing.

Dana maneuvered the car into a large parking lot near the middle of the stretch. A sign read *Pete's Autos*, but Dana knew it was a front for illegal gambling, dice, cards, and fighting of all kinds; human, canine, and foul. Dana hated this place with every ounce of her being. A dark corner of her mind always thought about firebombing it whenever she drove by. *Ah it sucked to be a cop sometimes!*

About fifteen cars lined the parking lot as Dana parked. She climbed out and stared around. Robin sat in the car.

"Uh, this place is a shithole. You sure?" Robin asked.

"Yep. See that corner over there by the dumpster? There's a service door behind it. Only folks in the know can get in." Dana said.

Robin climbed out, still looking dubious. "They're gonna make us as soon as we walk in Dana. We look, dress, and smell like cops you know?"

Dana smiled. "My Dad used to roust half these guys…and I plan on carrying on the family legacy."

Robin smiled back. This was why she loved working with Dana. When Dana was on the hunt she did not quit…EVER. She would follow the scent or lead wherever it took her, no matter the cost or effort. And, truth be told, Robin needed someone to provide that example. Someone to push her to another level of effort and discipline. Dana was that person and Robin would follow her into hell if need be.

Dana and Robin walked to the corner of the building. The sound of voices and music filled their ears. Robin saw the door Dana talked about. It was dark grey, painted to match the side of the building and almost invisible from the street at night. The side of the building was dark. The only illumination came from a single light bulb several feet away from the door. There were no markings, numbers, or anything on the door to indicate it was functional.

Dana rapped on the door once and stood back.

The door opened. A giant Latino man stepped out. Bald, tatted, and hairy. He frowned at Dana and Robin. He made them as cops in an instant.

"What?" The big man said. The sound of his voice made it clear they were not welcome.

Dana stared up at him. "I'm here to see Left-Foot Tony. We go back."

Big Man stared at both women.

"Step bitches."

He started to close the door when Dana kneed him in the groin. Big Man doubled over and Dana stuck her finger into his right ear and dug in. Big Man grunted. Dana leaned down and whispered.

"I really don't like that word...now open the door and lead us to Left-Foot before I call SWAT. Those guys don't play. Now get your ass up."

Big Man stumbled to his feet. He frowned but led them inside the building. Robin grinned from ear to ear.

Big Man led them through a small maze of corridors which terminated into a much larger space, similar to an auto mechanic's bay. It was sectioned off into four distinct areas with low walls made up of wire mesh about four to six feet high. Very bright work lights hung overhead so all the spectators could have an excellent view of each ring. Groups of men and women clustered around the circular mesh fight arenas betting money and drinking. The motorcycle chop-shop crowd.

The first two rings held cock fights. The next two, were set up like MMA sparring rings. Inside muscular men attacked each other with abandon. Since this was what was known as a "smoker" there were no rules. The referees stood near the fighters and made sure no one died. Other than that, the fighters could do what they wanted. The animals fared worse of course. The roosters clawed and scratched one another until they were a bloody mess.

Dana shook her head in disgust as they walked by. Robin grinned at the MMA fights.

"These guys are taking an ass-whooping! Damn! Makes me want to go a few rounds!"

"You fight?" Dana asked Robin over her shoulder.

"Not now, but back in law school to earn some extra cash. My record over three years is 15-0, with one draw. Not bad huh?" Robin said.

Dana wanted to smile but kept her game face on. She growled at Big Man.

"You're starting to piss me off. Where's Left-Foot?"

Big Man stopped at thick dark curtains hanging from the ceiling. They split the other fighting rings off from this area. He jerked his thumb inside.

"He ain't gonna be happy to see no Cop bitches I can tell you that."

He smiled at Dana as if challenging her. Dana stared hard at Big Man. Before she could do anything...ZAPP!

Robin tased Big Man in the side of his thick neck with her hand-held, police-issue taser. Big Man flopped backward to the floor, convulsing like a fish pulled from a lake. The women watched him with a kind of morbid fascination. Big Man was alive but unconscious. Drool sloshed out of his open mouth and pooled onto the concrete floor.

Robin smiled. "Damn! I musta' had the voltage on this thing too high...For the record, I don't like that word either." Dana nodded and smiled at her partner. Robin glanced down at Big Man as she holstered her taser.

"I almost feel sorry for him...Nah!"

They parted the curtains and stepped through.

This was the "elite" section.

The crowd was filled with semi-high rollers. Pop/Hard-core Hip-Hop blasted from unseen speakers. People sported fake expensive watches, nice haircuts, and fashionable wardrobes. Stacks of money were laid out on long metal tables. One guy was in charge of taking and placing bets. The people lining the ring sat in nice comfortable chairs instead of standing around like their lower caste cousins in the other room. A man and woman in white shirts, dark slacks, and dark vests served drinks.

Even the walls were pained in lush colors and adorned with high-end paintings that matched the décor. The lights were dimmed and accentuated with low-intensity neon lights that gave the entire room the appearance of a posh nightclub. The only areas lit with harsh lighting like the other side of the curtains were the dog fight areas. These were identical to the ones outside, covered in wire mesh and blood.

Dana scanned the faces searching for Left-Foot.

Then she spotted him.

Left-Foot Tony was a large, greasy fat man in a tailored suit who resembled a Latino rapper she'd seen on television before. He was whispering in the ear of girl in a skin-tight dress. She giggled back at him like she was enjoying his dirty talk. They both sipped some kind of exotic drinks.

Disgusting, Dana thought.

Dana caught his eye from across the room. Left-Foot Tony almost choked on his drink. Dana walked past one of the dog rings and glanced inside. Two pit bulls tore into each other with a frenzy. Blood sprayed the floor of the ring, coating the dogs' fur. Dana looked away.

Robin trailed her. She looked inside the pit bull ring too.

"Sonafabitch!"

Left-Foot Tony started to stand up but Dana held a hand out. She stared at the girl in the skin-tight dress.

"Who the hell do you think...?" The girl started to say when Robin displayed her gun and badge to the girl.

"Fuck off," Robin said.

The girl turned white as a sheet and ran off. Dana plopped down in the chair next to Left-Foot, intruding into his space. Robin kept standing with her back to the wall so she could watch the crowd in case something went down.

"Hey, Tony! I'm going to give you a choice about how this goes down. If you're straight with me I might go easy on you. If not, my young friend here goes bananas on this room and I call Vice. Got it?

"Yeah...yeah. I thought we were cool and all? You know I knew your Pops right? Me and him had an understanding. I gave him shit from time to time about stuff going down, and he left my joint alone. Them same rules apply right?" Left-Foot Tony said.

"What I remember about your arrangement with my Dad was that he said you were a lying piece of shit snitch who'd sell out his own mother if it would benefit him." Dana glanced at the patrons of Left-Foot's establishment.

"Hmmm. I wonder how many of these fine, upstanding individuals would like the fact that you snitch to the PoPo? Hmmm? Not many I'd guess." Dana said.

Robin looked over at Left-Foot and frowned.

"I think we should bust his ass and destroy all this shit. Fucking disgusting." Robin said.

His eyes got wide. Sweat poured down his thick face.

"What you want? Just tell me!"

"Last few weeks...homeless folks getting attacked by savage dogs. Ring any bells?" Dana asked.

"I ain't heard nothin' about that. Swear on my Moms life!"

Dana didn't buy it.

"You ALWAYS know what's up downtown. So, don't give me any of that "I don't know anything" crap!"

A few guys walked near the table, trying to figure out what was happening. Robin glared at them as she displayed her badge.

"Keep steppin'." Robin said to them.

"*Puta`*" One of them breathed as they kept walking.

Robin shook her head. "Again, with *that* word. Boss...I am gonna go buck wild on these fools I tell you!"

Dana glanced at Robin, then back to Left-Foot.

"You see...she's already getting twitchy. Tell me what you know." Dana said.

Left-Foot was trying to perform mental jiujitsu about how to get out of this situation. Dana watched his wheels turning and became impatient. She looked up at Robin.

"Here we go!" Robin began striding toward the dog ring.

"WAIT! I got you!" Left-Foot Tony was on the verge of panic. He could sense his clients, business, and *profits* floating away.

"Just keep that crazy bi...I mean detective away from my customers!" Left-Foot said.

Robin heard and veered back toward them. She took up position on the wall again.

Left-Foot continued. "I been hearing rumblings about strange shit. Like packs of wild dogs roaming the streets. I didn' think much about it until this cat named Joe told me he'd seen some ranging down near Commerce Street Bridge. Then another cat said he was almost attacked by a big-ass dog but the train scared it off."

"Where was this?" Dana asked.

"You know those tracks that run through downtown, past the jail, splitting Colorado Street? Right there."

"I know it." Dana said.

"Dude said he was walking by the tracks when this big ass dog came up snarling and shit. It was just on the other side of the tracks and looked like it was going to run at him when the train whistle went off. Guess it got scared. Stood its ground for a few, then when the train rolled past it ran off like a shot he said. That's all I got. For real."

"Bullshit! You don't know anything and just want us gone! Boss, let me put a cap in his ass! Just one!" Robin said.

Again, Dana kept her game face on. She waved Robin off and stared Left-Foot Tony in the eyes.

"Nothing else?" Dana asked.

"Honest! So...we good? I don't need beef with you guys. I'm just tryin' to get my hustle on you know?"

Dana nodded. "We're good...for now." She stood, then leaned over him. She patted his fat cheek. "Don't make me come back."

"No...no! You won't hear a peep outta' me! Promise Detective!" Left-Foot Tony said.

Dana motioned to Robin. They left him sweating.

"Detective! One more thing!" The sound in his voice stopped Dana. She turned back and walked up to the table so she could hear him over the music.

"My boy said the strangest thing. Right before the train came. When the dog was on the other side of the tracks. He said...it STOOD UP."

Dana didn't think she'd heard him at first. "What's that?"

"He said the dog stood up...like a MAN. Yeah, I thought that was weird as shit too."

"Thanks Left-Foot," Dana said.

After Dana and Robin disappeared from view through the curtain Left-Foot Tony gained a bit of his manhood back. He glanced around for his servers.

"I need a damn drink up in this bitch!" Left-Foot Tony said as he wiped sweat off his forehead.

Dana and Robin sat back in her car.

"Bust a cap? Really?"

"It's all I had at the moment. But I have a question. You just going to let that shit go? Those dog fights and all that?" Robin asked.

"Nope," Dana said. She dialed on her mobile. Waited for SAPD Dispatch to pick up. "Yes. This is Detective Adams, Badge number four, seven, nine, four…Give me Vice. I have a tip for them. Yeah…we're sitting on the place right now."

"I think I'm in love with you Dana," Robin said with a smile.

THE TRUTH

7:50 pm

Brick peered through the front window. Squinted. A dark-colored, hard-top Jeep was parked in the lot outside his surplus store. Brick reached behind the counter and grabbed his sawed-off shotgun. He placed it behind the door. The sawed-off was good for "close encounters." Brick opened the door. Eli and Chapa were outside. Before Eli could react, Brick picked him up in a bear hug.

"Damn boy, it's good to see you!" Brick grinned a huge gap-toothed smile.

Eli gasped for air.

"Uncle Dan…you're choking me."

Brick, still smiling, put him down.

"Sorry."

Chapa was grinning in the background.

"Hey, Tio'!"

"My favorite knuckle-head! Come here boy!"

Brick snatched Chapa up, too. The men laughed before going inside. Brick led them through the surplus store and upstairs to the recliners. While Chapa and Eli settled themselves, Brick pulled a huge Cuban cigar from a small silver box and lit it. He leaned back in his favorite lounger and blew smoke rings at the rickety ceiling fan swaying back and forth. Brick offered one to Eli. Eli declined. Chapa frowned.

"Those things will kill you, Tio'."

Brick laughed. A big, hearty sound that threatened to shake the timbers of the building.

"Boy, I danced with death too many times to let one of THESE kill me!"

Brick leaned back. Took another deep breath and blew a huge smoke ring up into the air. It was dissipated by the movement of air around the ceiling fan. Eli stared at his uncle. He loved this man with a fierceness that was only rivaled by the love he had for Chapa. Brick had always been there for him and Chapa. Always. He had so many great memories of times with Brick. Maybe more than with his

77

father. Brick had been the surrogate father Eli and Chapa went to for advice about girls and other matters Abraham did not want to be bothered with.

Brick, like Chapa, had street smarts that he passed on to Eli. Things that were hard to quantify, but that helped guide him in a dangerous world. It didn't matter if they needed their bikes fixed after crashing them for the thirtieth time when they were young, or if it was doling out advice about the most vulnerable spot in the body to hit someone, or how to talk to girls. Brick was the man who shared the pain and humor over life's circumstances. Eli wanted it to be Abraham, but for whatever reason, Abraham had never been available to Eli and Chapa on an emotional level.

When they went to Abraham Moore for advice it was about practical matters like money, grades, how to treat your neighbor, or their personal prayer life. Abraham dispensed the intellectual and the practical, while Brick dispensed street wisdom and heart. Even though it troubled Eli sometimes, like life, it just was.

The humor slipped away from the men. They were left with grief and the inability to say what they were feeling. Like so many veterans of war.

"I'm sorry about yo Daddy, Yella. Abe was a great man."

Older African-Americans like Brick sometimes referred to light-skinned or biracial folks as "high yellow." Brick used it as an affectionate term for his nephew. When Brick used it Eli almost felt like a boy again.

"Thanks for showing up today. Mom said she was going to call you."

Brick shifted in his recliner.

"Yo' Momma never did have much use for me, but she's a wonderful woman. Guess can't say as I blame her much. You been to church lately?"

"NO." Eli answered harsher than he meant to. He stared at his feet.

"Yella', as long as you been breathin', you been in the church. Yo Daddy, GOD rest his soul, havin' been a preacher and all. You slippin'?" Brick asked.

Eli picked up a cigar. Rolled it between his fingers.

"Slipped I guess. I don't know, Uncle Dan. After all the stuff Chapa and I've seen, places we've been to. Faith seems like a lost art." Eli said.

Brick smacked the recliner arm with his meaty fist. It startled Eli and Chapa.

"Yella', me an' yo Daddy been through mo' shit than a lil' bit! What we did is enough for a whole lifetime full of nightmares."

He leaned closer to Eli.

"Know what I'm tellin' you boy? If yo Daddy didn't never lose his faith in the LORD ALMIGHTY after two tours in Nam...Killing NVA...seeing children burn and..."

Brick stopped, choked up. Tears formed in his eyes. He wiped them on his sleeve. His thoughts went back to his last conversation with his older brother.

"Matter of fact, he started his church as soon as we got stateside." Brick said. "That's all he talked about when we were over there. It's all he wanted. To raise up a flock of good Christians."

Eli sat back, pondering this. Brick's tone softened a bit. He took hold of Eli's hand. Squeezed it.

Eli stared at the floor, "I miss him."

"Me too Yella'. Me too" Brick whispered.

"Uncle Dan? Do you know what happened to him? Dana...the cops aren't talking, but Homicide Detail was there. If you know something please tell me."

Brick shifted in his seat. He rubbed the tender spot on the back of his head where the werewolf woman tried to marry it and the wall together. Eli waited. He watched his uncle with a frightening intensity.

"Yo' Daddy was murdered."

The words were out there. Brick let them sink in. Eli sat back in his chair. He and Chapa were stunned. Above their heads, the rickety ceiling fan creaked away, making noise with every pitiful turn. Water dripped somewhere in the apartment.

"Sumthin' killed yo Daddy."

"Who?" Chapa asked.

Brick chomped down on his stogie, "Not who, but WHAT."

Both men were confused. Brick hauled his huge frame out of the recliner and motioned downstairs.

"Come on. I need to show you boys sumthin'. It's time you found out the *truth*."

Brick, Eli, and Chapa walked into the back room, past the small desk, and down the ancient staircase. Brick led them up to the metal door. He pulled the key from the chain on his neck. Used it to unlock the huge padlock securing the door. Brick lifted the heavy bar off the door and placed it on the ground.

Brick opened the door. It groaned as he tugged at it. A rush of warm dusty air hit them. He moved backward from the door and grabbed Eli by the shoulders.

"Yella', if you and Knuckle-head go through this door, yo lives is gonna' change. I mean it. NOTHING will ever be the same. If you wanna' know what killed yo Daddy, go inside...I'll be waitin' right here."

Brick hugged Eli and Chapa, stepped to the outer door, re-lit his cigar. Eli stared at the door for a long time. He stared at his brother.

Chapa shrugged. Eli started to walk inside the Vault when the smell hit. He gagged, covering his mouth with one hand, and stepped over the threshold. Chapa gagged too.

"Hey Tio', you got a collection of dead cats in here? It's fuckin' rank!" Chapa said.

"Just go inside, knucklehead."

Chapa followed him inside. The room was dark. The only light shone from the doorway. Just as Eli turned around to call out to Brick, light flooded the room. Eli waited for his eyes to adjust. He rubbed them, blinking to get his vision back. Eli jumped back from what was displayed on a small wooden platform.

A stuffed animal.

Some kind of hybrid between human and wolf.

Eli stared at the hideous face. It seemed to scowl at him. Long fangs bared in a ferocious death grimace.

The face old...*ANCIENT*. Wrinkles creased the snout and eyelids. Dangerous claws tipped its fingers. Claws that both Chapa and Eli knew could rend a man's insides and expose them to the world. So strange that it had hands instead of paws.

The animal was *BIG* too. Standing at least seven feet tall. Eli could not comprehend how such a monster could exist in the real world. But, the truth of it was standing right before him. This animal, this creature...this thing of legend was *REAL*.

Eli spoke, his words a whisper.

"I've seen one before...in Panama..."

Chapa stared at his brother. Both men shared the same horrible memory of Panama. One they saw unfolding again here, in their city. A memory Eli never expected to confront again....

FIREFIGHT

PANAMA: *0300 HOURS. U.S. NAVY SEAL TEAM TWO MISSION:*
COVERT EXTRACTION. CLASSIFIED TOP SECRET.

EIGHTEEN MONTHS AGO

Steam rose from the green canopy and enveloped the trees above. The denseness of the vegetation gave the impression of a solid wall of forest. Near a small clearing, a patch of shadow moved. Then another. United States Navy SEALS. The men moved from position to position with precision and exactness. Weapons trained at the ready to engage any hostile target. The Eli signaled a halt with one gloved fist. The Team froze.

Eli, squatted down and pulled a small plastic-enclosed map from his thigh pocket. He checked coordinates on the map with a compass. Eli was on the short side of retirement and one of a few active African American SEAL officers. This was his last operation with SEAL Team Two as a Captain.

For Eli it had never been easy being a SEAL, but it had been fulfilling. The life had been good to him. On the other hand, easy was for other men. In Eli's world there were only two kinds of folks...operators and non-operators.

Eli's impressive physique and sharp mind had been honed by twenty years of constant training and enduring rigors that most people could never understand, much less survive. Confidence, discipline, and physical skill radiated from him. Everything about Eli screamed leader. Twenty meters behind him, on the right, was Kronkowski, who had a lightweight M-60 machine gun perched in front of him on a tripod. Beck, the Radio Telephone Operator, or the RTO, was about ten meters behind Eli carrying the Satellite Radio.

Eli replaced the compass and adjusted his night-vision goggles. Through the goggles, the jungle turned bright green. Night turned into day. Tonight, the mission was to extract General Mendez from his fortified compound. The General had filled the vacuum left from multiple years of parliamentary in-fighting by seizing control of the civilian government and declaring himself "The People's Leader". The Team had performed this kind of rendition numerous times, but even as trained as the SEALS were, caution kept them alive.

Something darted past his field of vision.

Eli swiveled his head to track it and saw a shape in the middle of a small clearing. He low crawled toward the moving shape to a get better look. Eli stopped about seventy meters from it. From his point of view the animal appeared to be canine. Like a wolf – but MUCH larger. It was feeding on something. As Eli mused on this the shape turned its big shaggy head and stared at him. Its features still indistinct in the darkness. It dropped the object that was in its mouth...a small human leg...a CHILD'S leg.

Eli grimaced.

The beast stalked toward him on all fours, covering the ground at a rapid pace. Eli trained the sights of his weapon on the animal's head.

Sixty meters...

Fifty meters...

Forty meters...

Twenty...

"What the...?"

Eli glanced to his right. Chapa, then Chief Petty Officer First Class, stared at the fast-approaching animal. Chapa was slack-jawed.

Ten meters...ROOOOAAARRR!!!!

The sound pierced the night sky. It was ferocious and full of rage.

Five meters...

Now the rest of the team stood next to him.

"That thing just stood up." One of the Team said.

The beast charged.

Shit...decision time...

Eli shouted, "Open up!"

Howling and shouts joined with automatic gunfire. Team Two opened fire as it raced toward them. Red tracers from the team's weapons lit up the jungle, mingling with shouts and terrific roars.

The beast jumped at Eli. He tucked and rolled, landing just clear of the slashing claws. PFC Johnson sighted in with his MP-4, firing five shots into the hairy hide. Before he could fire again the thing leapt on his chest, crushing him to the ground.

Johnson opened his mouth to scream, but it tore his throat out with its large fangs.

Kronkowski and Chapa pumped multiple rounds into its back. The thing snapped its head up, green eye blazing. It slashed out at Kronkowski. Four-inch long, razor sharp claws puncturing his body armor, ripping the right side of his chest open.

The beast flung Kronkowski's body forty feet away into the darkness.

"You sonafabitch!!" Chapa shouted.

Chapa ran over and fired into one of its eye sockets. Blood spurted in a great fountain all over him. It howled and used its big bony head as a battering ram, slamming into Chapa, propelling him backward into the underbrush. By this time Stiefel, Davis and Davenport came over firing shot after shot into the animal. The beast reacted to the hits.

The team surrounded it.

Blood oozed from dozens of wounds that should have been mortal. How is this thing still standing up? Eli thought.

It was weak.

With the moon obscured behind the clouds the exact features of the animal were still unclear. Eli crept closer, pulling his father's age-old silver knife from a sheath on his thigh. The animal snarled and bared its canines.

"Hold your fire," Eli said.

The beast stood in a clearing. The team surrounding it. It breathed in and out in great ragged gasps, as if each breath was agony. The animal tilted its shaggy head toward Eli as he neared it. Eli stopped about a meter away. There seemed to be a keen intelligence in those feral eyes. Eli was surprised. Then the beast roared.

The animal raised up on two legs like a human and charged. Eli ducked under the slashing claws, plunging the silver knife to the hilt into the animal's breastbone. It had an immediate effect. The beast staggered backward, howled up at the starry sky, then crashed to the ground. Twisting and convulsing until it died.

The team walked over and stared at it. Chapa limped over. Eli grabbed him to support his weight.

A dead quiet hung over the clearing. Each man tried to grapple with what they had seen. The cracking and splintering of bones surprised them. A few flinched until they realized it was the body at *their feet creating the sound. These men of war were shaken by the experience in a way they had never been shaken before.*

"Oh, sweet Jesus…that can't be…" One of Eli's team said.

"Listen up! We go to extraction point Bravo right now! Davenport…" Eli said.

"Yes sir." Davenport said.

"You and Stiefel pick up Johnson and Kronkowski. NOBODY gets left behind."

"Roger that, Cap." Davenport answered.

"Let's move out." Eli led the way with Chapa on his shoulder.

CONTACT

Brick stood in the doorway with folded arms. Stogy clamped between his teeth.

"I'm not certain, but when it died, it started changing..." Eli said.

"Into what?" Brick asked. An uncomfortable silence passed between them.

"It looked almost...human." Eli answered.

"Yella, the same thing happened to yo' Daddy and me in Cambodia. 1968. Damnedest thing I ever seen."

Brick stubbed the cigar into an ashtray shaped like a crucifix.

"This here one we found dead in the woods near Gevaudan Park. Old Ranger buddy of mine stuffed it fo' me."

"Why?" Chapa asked.

"Don't know. Maybe to remind myself of what's out there."

Eli backed away from the animal on the podium. Eli, Chapa, and Brick stared at it with a mixture of loathing, fear, and grudging respect.

"Brick, what are they?"

"Werewolves." Their uncle answered.

The former soldiers shared a silence. The natural sounds of the building seemed louder than normal for a few seconds. Chapa and Eli waited for their uncle to smile or crack a joke, showing that gap-toothed smile, but no. Brick did not smile or grin. He was serious. More serious than they had ever seen him. This unnerved the fighting men who had seen their fair share of trouble.

"Not those Hollywood Lon-Chaney-types, or American Werewolf in whatever country things! I mean honest-to-GOD, rip your-throat-out monsters." Brick said.

He stared at the men to let it sink in.

"Werewolves that live in this city right NOW."

Werewolves...Eli thought the word might evaporate if he said it out loud.

"It's Panama all over again." Chapa said.

"I don't care what they are. I'm going to hunt them and kill every last one." Eli said. Brick nodded his head.

"You just tell me what you need, Yella."

"Weapons, ammo, you know the drill." Eli said.

"Got it covered Yella'. Got it covered."

"What the hell are we going to do Eli?" Chapa asked. "I mean, if they're here too there might be hundreds of them. There's only three of us."

"I doubt there are that many. They would've been discovered already. No, I think there is a small pack of them running around this city somewhere."

The men stood there...transfixed by what they understood as the most dangerous threat the three of them had ever faced. It was almost overwhelming. However, the three professional military men accepted this news with a taciturn mindset which would not make sense to a civilian. A civilian would pour over the news. Agonize about it. And in the end do nothing. It was left to men like this to take stock of the threat, prepare, then go out to meet it headlong. In civilized society it had always been this way.

These men were Spartans. A lone few who did what many could not.

Brick started to open his mouth to say more but closed it just as fast. He'd told his nephews what needed to be told and there was nothing more to say. His encounter with the deadly woman just upped the ante.

Chapa wanted to act. Right now. He wanted to go out and hunt these animals like they had hunted insurgents for many years. No mercy. No quarter. But, he would follow Eli's lead. His brother would know what to do. Eli made the missions and Chapa prosecuted them. Simple.

Chapa watched his brother. He knew to wait until Eli came up with a tactical solution.

"I've got to think. Come on. I'll drop you off." Eli said.

Eli and Chapa headed to the door.

"See you, Brick."

"Bye Tio'."

Brick hugged his nephews.

"There's one mo' thing." Brick said. This stopped the brothers.

Eli turned. "What?"

"When Abe and I found this one something was moving in the woods near us. It came out from the trees into a patch of moonlight. Big, black one with red eyes. Had a streak of white in its mane. We aimed at it, but it growled at us then ran off in a flash. I think it was the leader. And…I saw her again the other night"

Eli smiled, but it was not pleasant.

"Good. Then I know which one to kill first."

9:23 pm

Eli dropped Chapa back at his apartment. Chapa again asked if Eli was alright. When his brother didn't answer Chapa dropped it and walked inside. Eli pulled onto the highway. Everything was a blur. The cars, the city. Eli stared into the rear-view mirror. Dark circles ringed his eyes. Eli hadn't slept much since his father died. His dreams were infiltrated by dark, shadowy animals, hunting him. As a practical man, Eli knew what the dreams were about, but they disturbed him anyway.

As these restless thoughts pushed at his mind Eli decided to drive to his father's church. He pulled in the driveway and noticed the yellow police tape covering the door handles. Eli climbed from the Jeep, walked to the doors and stared down at the tape. He ripped it apart and kicked the doors in. The wood buckled and splintered.

Eli sighed and stepped inside.

The devastation caught him by surprise. The violence that had been inflicted caused Eli to cry out. He shouted at the rooftop, his cries echoing off the walls, filling every space and corner. Eli fell to his knees and let all his frustration, anger, pain, and sadness overwhelm him. He cried and cried until there was nothing left except an emptiness that carved a path in his soul. Once the emotions began to fade he stood up and gathered himself, trudged to his father's office, opened the door and sat in Abraham's chair.

The arms of the chair were cold to his touch. He caressed the leather as if rubbing it would make his father appear like rubbing a bottle hoping for a genie to rise.

SAN ANTONIO, TEXAS: TWENTY YEARS AGO

Eli's bags sat on the floor, next to the front door. Ellen stared at the bags, then at her son. She hugged him, squeezing his neck, afraid to let go. Eli had finished BUD/S training for the SEALS and was being sent on his first mission. Of course, he couldn't say where he was going. Ellen knew (and worried) that when Chapa graduated from BUD/S in a few weeks he would be deployed right out of the gate like Eli.

Two Brothers...Two Sons...Two SEALS.

BUD/S stood for Basic Underwater Demolition/SEAL. It was a six-month training course held at the Naval Special Warfare Training Center in Coronado, California, designed to find and develop men of the strongest character and place them in grueling tests that were the most physically and mentally demanding in the world. This was followed by two more years of continuous training in different environments and terrain, which required the new SEALS to utilize all their training, intellect, and independent thought to complete whatever mission they were tasked with.

Once a candidate survived BUD/S and subsequent training he was changed, forever. He was a man who was willing to lay it all on the line for the men on his team.

"How long will you be deployed, Eli?"

"Don't know Mom...And..."

"I understand. Abraham?"

Abraham had entered the room. He stood near Ellen. A frown covering his face like a storm.

Ellen took their hands. "Let's pray over our son."

They bowed their heads.

"Father GOD...Bless Elijah and his men as they march forth into battle. Give him the wisdom and courage to do what is right. Protect him and hold him close so that he may come back to this family whole. In Heaven's name we pray. Amen."

"Amen." Ellen whispered.

"Amen. Thanks Pop."

"Be safe but know that if you go out that door you're not welcome back here."

Ellen was stunned. She squeezed her husband's hand.

"Abraham...please."

"No. You disobeyed me, Elijah. Not only that, but you swayed your brother to follow you as well. Now, I face a future where both my sons take the path of violence. And I shall not have it! Your

Mother and I have provided for you, sheltered you, clothed you. And how do you repay this love? Rebellion. Utter disregard for your Mother's feelings. And for mine."

Eli didn't know what to say. He felt trapped. He wanted to please Abraham. That was all he'd ever wanted. But, there was no pleasing him.

"Pop...you can't make me choose. Not right now...I...I have to go. Don't you understand? I have to go."

Eli reached out for his Father. Abraham turned his back on his son.

"Then go.... Your war awaits you."

It was always conflict with Abraham. Always. He wasn't sure why. Eli had followed the rules. He got excellent grades, excelled in athletics, performed community service. Eli had been the poster for great kid. In college he graduated Magna Cum Laude, with Distinguished Honors in Philosophy, Sociology, and Communications from the University of Texas at San Antonio, then received a Master's in Arts from Our Lady of the Lake University, a Catholic university on the west side of San Antonio. Eli did all this while serving in the Navy reserves. Once he graduated with his Master's, he went active duty and applied for BUD/S.

But, for some reason, Abraham either ignored his accomplishments, or minimized them. This was part of the reason Eli decided to join the NAVY and become a SEAL. Because both his father and Uncle Dan were SEALS. Eli wanted to be part of the Moore legacy. To earn the SEAL Trident, and the name. Now, it was too late to earn praise from Abraham. Too late to earn anything.

Eli pushed the past into the recesses of his mind.

Eli opened the desk drawers. He wasn't sure what he was looking for. The desk held three drawers. The first was empty except for the old photograph of Abraham and Brick in Vietnam as young men. Eli smiled the way most people do when they see true evidence that their parents were young at some point in their life. It was hard for Eli to reconcile this image of his father with the young man in the photograph.

Eli opened the second drawer. It was empty. When he opened the third drawer he found a leather-bound book. On the front was a cross. Eli opened it. The first page read:

ABRAHAM MOORE – *Journal of a Pastor*

Eli thumbed through the journal. It began in 1960, before Abraham and Brick went to Vietnam, and continued up to the present. His father had catalogued his thoughts and feelings over a lifetime in this book. Eli flipped more pages until an entry caught his eye.

ELIJAH:

FEAR is what I feel.
Fear for you my son. I feel the naked trembling fear of a man who must release his child into a world of hatred, anger, violence, poverty, sadness, and bigotry. I fear that as I release you (and your brother Damien) I and your mother will no longer be able to protect you from it. Protecting your child is one of the most solemn duties of a parent as we raise our children. Protecting them from physical dangers when they are younger, but also protecting them from spiritual dangers as they grow and mature. And there are many spiritual dangers you will face, my son.
Which brings me back to the fear...
I fear that I have not done enough to harbor you from the world. I fear ultimately, that I have not done enough to comfort you. This is MY fault alone. We are commanded to love by our Lord and Savior, and I have done this for my flock, and your dear Mother. But, I know now that I have NOT done enough to show YOU that love. I have not been able to express my love.
Why?
I could blame my own Father who gave me nothing but the firm hand of discipline. I could blame my Mother who tried in her own self-absorbed way to be there for me, only to stay mired in her own failing health. I could blame the War for crippling my emotional impulses to the point that I shut down and ran from intimacy. I could blame a great many things. But, none of this would be the truth of it.
The TRUTH is that I was always afraid of disappointing you and not being the Father you needed. Ironic that this very fear led to self-actualization, and now I have indeed become just that.

For this my beloved son...ELIJAH...GOD's chosen...I am SORRY.

I love you more than even these words can express and I am sorry for every hateful thing I have said to you, or the times I did not listen to or support you. I am sorry for not taking the time to listen to you as a Father should. I am sorry for not swooping you up into my arms when you were little and kissing your tears away. My life, while satisfactory, has been empty without you and I want you to know that I am PROUD of the man you have become.

A man of honor, courage and sacrifice, willing to lay down his life for country and family. As you read these words I know that we have not spoken to each other in love, so if you find this, please know that I LOVE YOU son. And I always have.

Your Father,

ABRAHAM MOORE

This entry was written the day Abraham was killed. The very day Eli came back to San Antonio and visited his Father.

Eli was stunned. The words flowing from the page were the words that Eli longed to hear all his life. It never occurred to him that his father loved him so much or could express that love in such a vivid way.

Eli stood and placed the journal back in the drawer. He made a mental note to tell his Mother about it at some point. He left the office and walked back to the front doors. He stared at the ruined wood. Eli frowned and went into the back storeroom to look for some way to lock the sanctuary. He found a large padlock and key. His kick had splintered the door jam, but Eli was able to secure the padlock through the metal handles. It would have to do for now. When he locked the padlock Eli picked up the torn tape and tied it together through the ruined handles of the door. He strode back to the Jeep and drove from the parking lot, certain this was the last time he would ever see his Father's church again.

11:00 pm

Eli pulled the Jeep in the emergency lane on IH-10, stopping near the guardrail so he could get his mind right. He needed a plan of attack, just like when he planned operations for the SEALS. Eli happened to stare out the window toward Gevaudan Park on his right. He could see the tall trees from the overpass he was parked on.

Something was running along the edges of the tree line in the park.

No! This isn't possible!

Eli reached underneath his seat and pulled out a loaded semi-automatic Glock handgun and extra ammunition clip. He checked both clips, chambered a round, set the hazard signal for the Jeep. He slid over to the passenger side door and got out. He glanced around for traffic. No cars either way. Eli leaned against the guardrail to get a better look.

Then, he spotted them.

Six large *WEREWOLVES*. Loping through the woods.

Eli lifted his Glock and fired. The bullets hit the ground near the PACK, causing them to scatter. One of them stopped to figure out where the shots came from. Eli locked eyes with the animal. It had RED eyes!

"You're dead! Do you hear me? DEAD!"

Eli fired several more shots, just missing the werewolf. It used a tree for cover and growled at him. Eli glanced around for a way down from the overpass. There was a large tree just left of him. Sturdy-looking branches a few feet underneath the overpass. Eli put the Glock in his waistband and spare clip in his pocket. He jumped out into space, dropping onto the tree. He almost lost his grip, found his balance and shimmied down the trunk, landing with a spring at the bottom. Eli drew the Glock. He crossed the gap between the highway and the tree line, scanning for movement as he did.

The werewolf crept out from behind the tree. Bold. It stared at him. Eli shot it center mass. The werewolf flopped backward, howling in pain. It kicked its hind legs along the ground like some kind of crab as it tried to escape. Eli pulled the trigger again and again. Pumping five more rounds into it. The animal lay still.

Eli covered it with his weapon, advancing forward inch by inch. Eli was about a foot away when the werewolf roared. It jerked up, slashing at him with sharp claws. It had hands instead of paws. Eli fell backward, jerking a shot up into the air. The werewolf squatted on its hind legs and stood up.

Oh shit.

Eli ejected the magazine, pulled another from his pocket. Rammed it home and fired. The shots hit the werewolf center mass again. One connected to the head, throwing the beast backward. It was in great pain, but not dead. Eli couldn't believe it.

A crashing sound on Eli's right made him swivel.

Another werewolf came into view. It was big and grey, with ice-blue eyes. It seemed different. Not aggressive. More curious. The werewolf stopped. It seemed surprised by the human and werewolf squaring off against each other. The black one howled once more and took off running. Eli covered the grey one. He started to pull the trigger but stopped. It's eyes finally found the barrel of the Glock. They widened and it darted into the woods faster than Eli could see.

Eli heard a vehicle approaching. He didn't turn. He kept staring into the woods where the werewolves vanished, hoping to catch another glimpse. He considered chasing them into the woods, but that would have been a bad tactical move. Eli heard doors opening. A voice blared from a loudspeaker.

"Don't move! Drop the gun and put your hands up! Now!"

Eli complied. He dropped the Glock and interlaced his fingers on top of his head.

"Get on your knees! Cross your feet!"

Eli followed the instructions. A few seconds later a pair of rough hands grabbed and handcuffed him. Another pair of hands grabbed him on the arm. He was yanked over to a patrol car and thrown onto the hood. One officer rifled through his pockets, pulling out his wallet.

"What were you shooting at Mr. Moore?" The senior officer asked.

Eli didn't answer.

"Check this out. Military ID." The junior officer said to his partner.

The senior officer tapped Eli on the shoulder with his own wallet.

"I asked you a question. Seems pretty strange for a Navy officer to be shooting up the park at night."

Eli still didn't answer. *What am I going to say? Hey officers, I was shooting werewolves! Yeah right.*

With his face turned, Eli could see the patrol car had driven into the park by a service road. Another vehicle approached. A plain sedan. As it got closer it maneuvered behind the patrol car, so Eli couldn't see who was driving. He heard the door open and close. Low voices. One officer kept Eli secured. The other talked to the mystery cop. The officer holding Eli stood him up and unlocked the handcuffs.

"Thanks guys. I owe you." Eli knew the voice.

"No problem Detective. Thanks for helping my guy out last week." The senior officer said.

"Anytime."

The patrol unit drove off. Eli turned around and stared at Dana's annoyed face.

"Hi." Eli tried to smile. Dana was not amused.

"You want to tell me what the hell you were doing?" Dana asked.

"Letting off steam."

Dana frowned.

"Just…go home, Elijah. I know you've been overloaded. I get it. I'll cover this, but I am a cop…don't push it."

Dana handed Eli the Glock and empty clip.

"You could've killed somebody." She said.

Eli put the Glock in his waistband. Slid the clip in his pocket.

"I only kill what I mean to kill." Eli said.

"I won't even ask about a permit."

Eli smiled again. "In the Jeep."

Dana gave him a dismissive wave.

"Go home."

"Yes, ma'am."

Eli glanced at the woods once more. He jogged away up the service road. Dana watched him go. A minute later she could see Eli on the overpass climbing into the Jeep. He drove off.

Dana walked the edge of the tree line, picking up the shell casings from Eli's Glock and putting them in her coat pocket. A brownish substance on the ground caught her eye. It was blood. Near the blood, was fur. Similar to the crime scenes she and Robin had been investigating. She pulled out a small baggie and a pair of gloves from her pocket. Dana scrapped the fur and some of the blood into the baggie using her knife just as she had done in Alex's garage.

CRACK!

A branch snapped somewhere in the woods. Dana drew her service weapon fast as lightening. She aimed at the trees, looking for a threat. The woods were so dark they seemed impenetrable. Dana was alone. She holstered her weapon and left the area but her cop instincts tingled all the way back up the service road.

Eli was filled with adrenaline from his encounter with the werewolf. As he drove back to Chapa's his hands shook so hard it was difficult to grip the steering wheel of the Jeep. Now he understood what they were dealing with. These animals were savage, strong, and fast. He'd never seen an animal move that fast before with the exception of a cheetah, and he didn't think trying to fight them in open ground was a good idea after tonight.

No, this mission required stealth.

He, Chapa, and Brick would need to hunt these things SEAL-style. Under cover of darkness, using the elements to their advantage. Thinking about it more, Eli was convinced that even CQB, close quarters battle, was possible since the werewolves wouldn't have the advantage of speed. If the former SEALS could force the predators into a small space they could inflict some real damage. By cutting off the werewolves' ability to surprise their prey they would be vulnerable. And THAT was what Eli wanted. To take the fight to *them*. And WIN.

THE PACK

11:38 pm

Alex sprinted through the woods, her powerful body moving like a machine. She increased her speed. Ran faster and faster. When Alex reached a small rock-face half-covered with moss and ivy she stopped. A dark *opening* beckoned to her. It seemed to be a cave of some sort. Alex took a few tentative steps forward using all her senses to figure out what this might be. She smelled something familiar. A scent or scents not unlike her own. As she began to walk inside a rustling of leaves and tree limbs startled her. An alarm bell sounded inside her animal brain and she jumped back just as Red Eyes landed in front of her.

Alex stood her ground. The werewolves paced around each other. Red Eyes was much larger, but Alex was still formidable.

They exchanged growls then Red Eyes spun around and squeezed through the entrance. From inside, a bark issued. Alex paused as her suppressed human mind wondered if it was wise to enter. This moment was fleeting though and Alex padded forward on silent paws, crossing the threshold.

Each step she took was tentative. Deeper inside the cavern she heard what sounded like a voice.

"Alexxxxxandraaaaa..."

A *human* voice.

Alex stopped to sniff the air for a few seconds before moving further inward.

"Alexxxxxandraaaa..."

The voice floated to her from deep inside the drainage pipe. The tunnel lead into a large space that split off into different directions. In the middle was a space the size of three large rooms. A large drainage junction. Refuse, old boxes, pieces of plywood, and newspaper littered the ground.

But...the setting is not what shocked Alex...it was the Twenty PACK members sitting in a circle. All the animals looked just like her. The beasts were all different ages. Some had dark brown fur. Others, black. A few of them had gray tufts of fur on their ears, throats, or backs. From a distance, the PACK members looked like timber wolves. With one exception, they were much bigger.

The size of full grown tigers.

A dark-haired woman stood in the middle of the PACK. She was stark naked and her eyes seemed to glow with a primordial light. The woman had a shock of white in her hair that stood out like a strip of sunlight in the cavern. Alex noted this woman was the most beautiful person she had ever seen.

Alex glanced around and saw that all the PACK members had green eyes. Alex wandered down into the center. The woman walked over while the PACK closed ranks around Alex and waited.

Alex howled in pain. Her eyes rolled back in her head and she fell to the hard ground. She began to change, but this time in reverse. Alex's limbs shriveled and shrank, withdrawing into her body as if pulled by magic. Her canine teeth fell out of her bloody mouth, replaced by her original human teeth. Clumps of fur and excess flesh fell from her body, mixing together and striking the concrete with a wet slapping noise like meat dropped onto a butcher's block. As Alex's jawbone transformed her canine ears shrank into her skull even as human ears burst from inside with a loud popping noise.

As the change took hold, the PACK members exulted in Alex's full transformation with a mixture of joyous yelps, whines and barks. When the PACK moved back, the human Alex lay curled on the floor of the cavern in the fetal position.

Alex wondered how they could do this. It was the most horrible thing she'd ever undergone. How did they stand the pain of changing? Alex felt *violated*. Like her body had betrayed her.

It was sickening.

Worse, how could she go through this again?

Alex tried to stand, but she was weak. Weaker than she had ever been in her life. She stared at the chunks of dead flesh and wolf body parts strewn in front of her. Bile surged in her throat and Alex vomited.

The dark-haired woman bent down toward her. A compassionate look on her savage face.

"The pain will subside Young One. It is always worse the first time." She said.

"What...am I?" Alex asked.

"You are one of the PACK now." She said.

"I don't understand...who are you?"

"I am called Wenona. I once had more names, but I shed them as I did my human skin long ago."

"What is the PACK?" Alex asked.

Wenona helped Alex to her feet, supporting her as if she weighed nothing. Alex could feel enormous strength flowing through Wenona's lithe frame. Wenona was curvy but well-muscled with strong child-bearing hips. When Wenona moved it was with a fluid grace and unabashed sexuality that Alex had never known. Wenona was a creature confident in her abilities and place in the world.

"The humans have called us by many names over the centuries. Shapeshifter, Loup-Garou, Wolfen, Ukumar, Thags Yang, Taw, Kung-Lu, Bisclaveret, and Werewolf. Our kind has roamed the Earth from Tibet to Russia; Turkey to Japan; France to Germany. Now, we are here in the New World." Wenona said.

"How?" Alex asked.

"Every generation, all over the globe, there are a hundred human babies born of a PACK member and human male. The PACK member mates in human form then waits until the child undergoes the CHANGE from human to PUP. This normally occurs after two and ten score years, or twelve human years as you understand it."

Puberty Alex thought.

"The PACK will watch the child until this time. Once the pup has gone through the CHANGE, the PACK will call to it and lead the pup to a place of sanctuary. The pup is welcomed into the PACK, given the opportunity to hunt with the lead hunter, and then able to live as PACK member." Wenona said.

"This is impossible. I'm human. I mean I have parents. A father...a mother." *But, do I really?*

Wenona placed a hand on her shoulder.

"Search your feelings, young one. You have known the truth your entire life." Wenona said.

The crushing weight of something hidden from view for a lifetime rushed at Alex. She staggered from the physical shock as much as the emotional. Alex dropped to one knee, gasping for air. Wenona pointed at Alex.

"See? You no longer feel the need to cover your flesh as before. Shame and embarrassment do not matter for the PACK."

Alex realized she was naked but didn't move to hide it.

"Why didn't I change when I was younger?" Alex asked as she stood. The moment of weakness had passed and Alex felt better.

Wenona paused.

"It is recorded that on special occasion a human will not go through the CHANGE until they are at least three score years." Wenona said.

The women walked through the darkness of the cavern. As they did Alex realized that her eyes were far more attuned to the darkness than ever before. She could also hear and smell things with a clarity that gave her a headache. The night sounds made by small animals scuttling through the woods. The shifting and swaying of the trees as they sang the ancient song of their line. The wind howling and swirling overhead. Cars and trucks speeding by on the highway at least a mile away trailing noise and noxious exhaust.

It was as if her brain and all her senses were absorbing millions of bits of raw data and streaming it to her body at a high rate of speed. The feeling was exhilarating and overwhelming. Every nerve ending in Alex's body was on fire.

"You are a werewolf now. Your fate is linked to the fate of the PACK. If the PACK is in danger YOU are in danger. Just like tonight."

"Danger? What kind of danger? From that man? He had a gun but didn't even shoot at me. Why can't you just live in peace? Hunt in the forest? Why do you have to hunt humans?" Alex asked.

Wenona roared. A sound so terrifying that the werewolves in the cavern backed away and huddled together in submission. Alex could see a great swell of rage in Wenona. It seemed to boil off her in waves.

"Because THEY will not let us! We fight for our very survival every day! Our entire existence depends on our secrecy. Look!" Wenona pointed at her torso. Alex could see several small holes. Bullet wounds. Wenona parted her hair and showed Alex a small gash.

"Oh my God! You got shot! Does it hurt? Are you okay?"

Wenona grimaced. She dug a fingernail into one of the wounds and plucked a flattened lead slug out. She tossed it on the ground.

"Pain is a way of life for us. These weapons hurt us, but most of these lead bullets cannot end our lives." Wenona said as she struggled to control herself. Alex waited.

"Alexandra, you must do something."

"What?" Alex asked.

"Go back and destroy all traces of your life. If the humans become too suspicious they might discover the PACK and try to hunt us. They have developed more powerful weapons over the ages. Weapons that could annihilate us and wipe out all our kind. But, if we are careful, our numbers will grow until we are the most powerful race on Mother Earth again." Wenona said.

"Let go of your old life and start anew. Now, go. Eat. Rest yourself, Alexandra. I will reach out to you soon."

Alex nodded, unsure of what to say to everything Wenona told her. Wenona motioned to a box in a corner. Alex opened it. Inside was clothing for women of different sizes. A large assortment of winter coats, hats, and boots were stuffed down toward the bottom. Alex checked a few sizes and changed into the clothes. She walked to the entrance of the cavern.

"One last item," Wenona said.

Alex wheeled around to listen.

"If you choose to keep your old life, know this…The animal part will keep growing until it drives you mad, or you submit. If you do not submit the PACK will kill you. It is the way."

Alex stared at Wenona a long time before answering.

"How do you know my name?" Alex asked her.

Wenona smiled at Alex.

"I know many things, Young One. Au` revoir." Wenona said to Alex as she left the cavern.

TROY

Dell's Coffee House was a dinosaur. A remnant from an era when small business owners could open a neighborhood venture and thrive in the community. It sat in a gentrified area a few blocks east of downtown near the historic King William area, which was a small but regal section of houses modeled after the huge Victorian estates and mansions on the East Coast. The same family had owned it for fifty years and had passed the love and care from generation to generation.

Dana drank coffee while she waited for Eli to show. She loved Dell's coffee. It reminded Dana of Big Tony. He and Dana frequented Dell's every Sunday because they ran a police officer's special. Sally, Dell's granddaughter, ran the place now. She smiled at Dana. The best thing about coming to a place like Dell's was that they treated you like family.

Eli wandered in, spotted Dana in her favorite booth. He walked over and sat across from her.

"Hey," Eli said as he picked up the menu.

"Sleep much last night?" Dana smiled at Eli.

"Yeah...about that..."

"Forget it," Dana said. *Do it now, Dana. Don't chicken out. He'll understand.*

"Any leads on the case?" He asked.

"It's complicated. That's all I can tell you right now. I'm sorry."

They were quiet.

Dana opened her mouth to say something. Stopped short. Stared down into her coffee. In her mind all Dana could see was the two of them in that hotel room overlooking downtown Austin. Their bodies slick with sweat. Moving in time to a rhythm that connected them on a sexual and spiritual level.

"Where're you staying?"

"With Chapa until I get myself squared away."

Dana grinned. Happy to change the subject.

"Is he still crazy? Couldn't tell at the funeral." Dana said.

Eli smiled. Thinking about his brother always made him smile.

"Got that right. Still out there...You know...doing his thing."

103

Dana's eyebrows went up.

"And you? Become a ladies' man?"

"Nah, I like to keep my feet on the ground," Eli said. Dana tried not to show the excitement she felt inside.

Dana sipped her coffee and turned her head to look out the window. Eli stared at Dana's profile. He loved the way a single lock of hair drifted across her eyebrow. He stared at her hands. They were lovely. Strong, but feminine. Eli had almost forgotten how beautiful Dana was. Every single time he was deployed on a mission he thought about her. Every time he figured he wouldn't make it, Eli thought about Dana. Her hair…her face…the way her body felt. The way she made *him* feel.

Thoughts of coming back to her at some point is what got Eli through. It made him press on even when he didn't want to. Eli needed to tell Dana that he had not come back to San Antonio to see his family. He came back for HER. Eli pondered why he never told Dana the way he really felt. Perhaps because the life of a Navy SEAL wasn't the kind you just dragged somebody into. When he was being honest with himself, Eli guessed it was his hyper-masculine way of trying to protect Dana from that. And Troy.

Maybe he was just trying to protect his own feelings.

"How's everything with you and Troy? I thought I sensed some tension between you two." Eli asked.

"She's a teenager. I don't know if it's me or all parents, but we just don't seem to connect anymore. She's so distant. I gotta tell you, it's sucked more than it's been fun. Pretty shitty huh?" Dana said.

"No. I can't imagine how hard it's been for you, raising her alone."

"Troy's a good kid. She is SUPER smart. She's a junior and about to graduate with honors ahead of everyone else. Crazy."

"Does she want to go to college?" Eli asked.

"Well, when I can get her to talk, she talks about Georgetown University. If I can keep her from getting arrested we might make it happen. Although sending her off to college, unprepared and so young scares me."

"What protecting herself?" Eli asked.

"No…it scares me that she won't ever come back."

"Dana…you are a great Mom. She knows it even if she doesn't want to say it."

Dana shifted in her seat. She pulled the photo of Troy from her purse. Passed it to Eli. He smiled.

"Man. That seems like so long ago. Look how small she is. What was she? Seven? Eight?"

"Seven. Well, a few weeks before her birthday." Dana said.

"They grow up fast, huh?"

"Yeah."

Eli started to flag the server down, but she appeared with a pot of coffee and a cup as if by magic. She poured a cup for Eli and left them alone.

"I was surprised she remembered me. It's been so long since we saw each other."

Dana reached across the table and took hold of Eli's hand. He smiled. Surprised.

The moment of truth.

"She would never forget...her *Father*..."

The words were out. Never to be taken back.

Dana held her breath. She could almost see the words. Swirling around in the air above Elijah's head like fairy dust, then settling down over him in a blanket. Eli blinked several times as his mind tried to process what Dana just said.

"What? She's what?" Eli asked.

Dana stared into his eyes.

"She's your daughter Elijah...OUR daughter."

Eli glared at Dana. Pulled his hand from her grasp.

"Why didn't you tell me?"

"I...I knew you didn't want...it just seemed easier for both of us."

"Easier? I just found out I have a daughter I hardly know. Does she know?"

Dana didn't answer.

"She doesn't know." Eli said.

"But, she loves you."

Eli stared out the coffee shop window. He watched people walk by...families.

I've lost so much time. Time I didn't even know I was losing.

Eli stood and placed some money for the bill on the table. Dana stood also.

"I'm sorry, Elijah. I'm sorry I didn't tell you. We were both so young then. I figured...you know...most men would be relieved."

Eli stared at Dana.

"I'm not most men."

He left without a backward glance.

Eli drove back to Chapa's apartment complex. He sat in his Jeep, opened his wallet and pulled out the photo of Troy. In the picture she was smiling at the camera like she had a secret. Eli smiled.

Wow. Troy's my daughter.

It was incredible and heartbreaking. Yet, on some level, he had always known. He and Troy shared a connection that seemed so right. Truth be told, Eli had wanted Troy to be his daughter, but never knew how that could happen. But, the question stayed with him...

WHY?

Why didn't Dana tell me before now?

Eli wondered if she was going to tell Troy and when. How would Troy react? Would she accept him or hate him for not being around all these years? The thought of Troy hating him terrified Eli. Now that he thought about it he could see so much of himself, and Dana, in Troy.

What an idiot! It was staring me in the face all the time and I never even knew it!

Eli let himself into Chapa's place. The apartment was empty. Chapa was gone. Eli went to the spare bedroom where he was staying, threw his boots on the floor, and collapsed onto the bed. His mind drifted back to Abraham. Eli wished that they could have said more to each other. Now that his father was gone, Eli wanted to tell him all the things he couldn't say in life. Tell Abraham about his granddaughter.

That seemed to be the way it worked though. You never tell the ones you love how much they are loved until it's too late. A mistake that haunted most folks their entire lives.

It was a mistake he would *not* make with Troy.

Minutes later Eli was asleep. Dreams of shadowy monsters circling a little girl dotting the nightscape of his mind.

REGRET

Alex stood outside her condo, staring up toward the top of the building, wondering how she got there. It seemed alien in some way to her now, when just last night it had been home. She noticed a police cruiser parked outside across the street, but it didn't set off any alarm bells. Alex entered the building and took the only working elevator to her floor. Inside the elevator she felt a strong sense of de' ja' vu. The feeling was disorienting, and for a moment Alex felt dizzy.

The higher the elevator climbed, the more claustrophobic she felt.

As the elevator climbed Alex realized she wasn't wearing her own clothes. She was wearing a suit when she left work, and now for some reason, she was wearing baggy winter pants, high fur-lined boots, a long sleeve t-shirt, and an overcoat.

Why am I wearing someone else's clothes?

Alex reached for the thought but her mind was blank. Not blank really. More like shrouded. Inside was a grey curtain through which she could see shapes dancing back and forth. When Alex attempted to peek behind the curtain what was there became dense and solid.

She had no memory of anything that happened last night other than meeting a strange woman with jet black hair shot through with a streak of white. This was punctuated with fragments of running through the woods and entering some underground cave-like structure.

What a strange dream that was.

The door opened.

Alex almost fell from the elevator. She staggered away from the doors and held herself up against the window in the hallway across from the elevators. It was then she noticed the crime scene tape pasted to the adjoining elevator. Alex walked toward her apartment. When she noticed Maddie's smashed door that's when it all came rushing back...

Her   transformation...the   Blood
Lust...Maddie...SCREAMING...running   from   the
building...following Wenona to the PACK.

Alex remembered EVERYTHING. And she hated herself for it.

She stood outside Maddie's door. Unable to move or breath. A hand touched her shoulder. Thick fingered. A scream. It was Alex's own. It was a police officer.

"Whoa! Don't be scared ma'am!"

"It's…it's okay. I'm sorry. You just startled me." Alex managed to point at the ruined door in front of her.

"What happened?"

I already know. I did this.

"One of your neighbors was killed last night I'm afraid. It was bad."

Alex tried to speak, but the sound just clicked in her dry throat.

"Do you live on this floor?"

"Yes…Yes…the end of the hall. 23D."

The officer checked his notepad. He glanced up.

"Alexandra Stone?"

"That's right? What's going on?"

"Uh…you were reported missing last night also. Do you mind waiting at your apartment? I need to call the detective in charge of the investigation."

Alex frowned. "Sure."

The officer seemed apologetic. "Sorry. Procedure. They'll probably have some questions for you."

Alex entered her apartment.

She walked to the windows as she had many times before. Now, she knew what it all meant. The strange, hypnotic pull of the moon…the feeling of someone watching her…the voices in her mind, an invitation from the PACK.

The gears clicked into place and for the first time in her life Alex felt like maybe she belonged to something…to a *family*. Wenona's words came back to her: *Let go of your old life and start anew.*

How?

The brand-new condo Alex lived in was expensive. One of the perks of the high corporate package she earned. This place had all the bells and whistles. It resembled a large cavern, with high, sloping walls, and a skylight in the ceiling. The colors, while trendy, were stark and cold though. Architects and art students might want to study Alex's condo, but it was doubtful they would want to live there. Even though others thought her place was severe it was comforting to Alex. The view was the selling point though. It gave her a one-hundred and eighty-degree angle on the Alamo City. Plus, she lived across from the Majestic Theatre where all the Broadway shows played. But, the view gave Alex something else. Whenever the moon was out it streamed through the tall windows of her condo, bathing the entire room in a preternatural glow.

Alex thought about Maddie.

Oh Sweet Maddie. I'm so sorry...so sorry! Noooo! I can't believe I did that to you!

Alex fell onto the couch. She felt trapped. She couldn't stay here. Too many memories. Panic hit her. What was she going to tell the police about what happened? Would they believe her? The questions pummeled Alex.

What am I going to do? Think! Think!

Without thinking she changed clothes, grabbed her purse and headed to the door. She cracked it open. The police officer was not in the hallway, although she could hear a voice somewhere. Alex guessed he was standing next to the elevators.

She crept out and left through the exit stairwell next to her apartment. The same stairs she had bolted down on paws, dripping blood, the night before. Alex jumped in her car and drove to a bar at the Pearl north of downtown that featured hotels, apartments, retail, dining, and cultural outlets. Alex picked a trendy sports bar with darkened lighting. It fit her mood.

Early Happy Hour. Men and women of the after-work crowd sat in small groups. Light dance music pumped from hidden speakers. The music quiet enough that people were able to carry on conversations at normal speaking levels. Alex sat at the bar by herself. She glanced around while nursing a whiskey sour.

Maybe she could pick a random person for sex. Make her forget everything for a few hours. She didn't care if it was a man or a woman. At that point, any red-blooded human would do.

Human. Sounds so strange to me. I don't even know what the word means anymore. Am I human? Was I ever?

"TGIF?"

Alex heard the voice but didn't answer. She thought it might be in her own head.

"Yeah? TGIF am I right? You know…Friday night. Let go of your stress-filled work week."

"Excuse me?" Alex turned to see the source of the voice. A middle-aged man of about forty-five. White. Kind of a Wallstreet-wanna-be type. Nice suit, but not expensive enough to indicate he was in the game. Just on the periphery. Fake Rolex watch. Dress shoes from Target. This was a guy used to trolling in shallow waters.

"No offense, but I just want to enjoy my drink and leave." Alex said.

The man slid into the seat next to Alex without being invited of course.

"I don't think I can let you do that." His voice dripped with faux-charm.

Alex was amused for the moment. "And, why is that?"

"Because beautiful women…"

"…should never drink alone. Right?" Alex said.

The man was flustered. His game whittled down a few points.

"What's your name?" Alex asked him.

Now he was on the defensive. Advantage, Alex.

"Uh…Brian."

Alex cast a glance down at Brian's hand.

"Brian the married man I take it by the ring on your finger."

"Look, I was just…"

Alex smiled. "Fuck off Brian."

Alex turned her back on him. He climbed off the bar stool and skulked back over to his laughing buddies. As they gave him shit about getting shot down Brian glared at Alex.

Alex was among the last to leave the bar. She strolled toward her car. It was parked along a narrow street on the side of an upscale apartment complex. Alex reached the car. She unlocked it. Instead of getting in Alex stretched her arms up. She sniffed the night air, catching different kinds of scents floating along. Her mood had lifted. She still wasn't sure what she was going to do, but at least the thoughts weren't as prevalent for now.

The alcohol had helped with that.

A pair of rough hands grabbed Alex by the shoulders. Brian spun Alex around and stared at her.

"No slut does that to me!"

He was expecting fear, but Alex smiled at him. The smile, feral, wild.

"Boy…did you pick the wrong woman."

Alex clamped a hand on Brian's throat. Her grip like iron. Brian tried to move it but couldn't.

There was *fear* in *his* eyes now.

Alex tossed Brian over her head, over the car, and into an alleyway behind them. His body collided with the side of a dumpster, falling into a near-senseless heap next to it. Alex stalked into the alleyway. Her features hidden in the near darkness. Her eyes seemed to glow with some primordial, savage light.

The animal inside her was taking over and Alex couldn't stop it…

"You're a naughty, naughty boy Brian."

"Please! Don't hurt me! I'm sorry!" Tears, spit and blood saturated the front of his fake expensive suit.

Alex growled. "You're sorry? You're sorry? Brian, you are a pathetic piece of SHIT!"

Brian staggered backward into the alley. He moved on instinct. Terror pushing him to escape. Brian could hear the sound of something leaping or climbing behind him. He turned. Alex was gone. He stepped backward, his back meeting the building. Nowhere else to run.

Alex dropped from the fire escape behind him…

"You shouldn't hurt women Brian. You could get hurt too."

Brian spun around to face her. Alex's eyes had changed. They were more WOLF than human. The irises were filled with yellow and the normal ice-blue color of Alex's eyes seemed more penetrating. These were not the eyes of a human anymore.

"Noooooo…..!"

A series of savage growls erupted from the alley…then…*silence*…

MEETING

Robin bent over the corpse that used to be Brian. Dana flashed her light around the scene looking for anything unusual while Robin chatted away.

"Ok. So, we have a serial dog-killer? I mean serial killer-dog? Oh whatever! It's all FUBAR anyway! Yeah…and that smell. Fantastic. Designed to bring up the ole' lunch know what I mean? What more could a girl want on a Friday night? The sweet aroma of dead bodies and garbage. Just lovely. I could be throwing down on my girl, but No! I gotta be here with you…No offense…"

Dana smiled. "None taken."

"…Like I said…Here with you, cataloguing and sifting through some guy's guts." Robin checked dead-Brian's wallet. "Hey. I remember this dickhead from a few years ago. Brian Delaware. Busted on a sexual assault charge but the victim didn't follow through. I seem to remember some stuff about domestic abuse against his wife too. What a fuckwad."

"Guess it caught up with him," Dana said.

Robin turned to Dana. "Remind me why I picked Homicide again?"

"Because, secretly you WANT to be here with me on Friday night, instead of with your girlfriend, looking through all this mess. That's what I think."

"Oh yeah." Robin smiled. "Guess I do love this shit. Besides, I gotta learn everything so I can take your job. Hahahaha!"

As the detectives examined the scene Dana thought back to her conversation with Elijah. It came out all wrong. She meant to tell him that she loved him and that she was sorry about keeping the secret from him for so long. But, no. She just blurted it out. Threw up all that history all over him and then expected him not to get angry. It wasn't fair to him. She should have told him before now.

A flash of metal caught Dana's eye. She knelt down and picked up something off the ground. Alex's necklace.

"I know one thing," Dana said.

"What?"

Dana held the necklace up for Robin's inspection. "We're looking for something besides an animal."

Her phone rang.

"Adams…Really? How long ago? Ok. Thank you. Bye."

Robin looked over. She knew the look on Dana's face. This was a break in the case.

"Seems our vic showed up."

"Who?"

"Alexandra Stone."

"No shit?" Robin asked.

"Yep. Finish here. Have patrol do a canvas. I'll go talk to Stone." Dana pulled her gloves off. Robin frowned.

"Thanks a lot."

Dana smiled at her junior partner as she walked away.

"Hey! You said you wanted to learn everything. Gotta work your way up the food chain!"

Robin stared down at the mess in front of her.

"Damn. I should'a stayed in law school."

Alex returned to her apartment because she didn't know where else to go. She wasn't ready to go back to the PACK. She was scared and disgusted with herself. She parked in the garage, stepped from the Jag and stared down at the ground. She could still see the blood stains on the ground. Alex shuddered. For an instant, she remembered loping on all fours through this parking lot and jumping over the concrete wall. Then the memory was gone. It all seemed like a dream, until she stared at her hands. They were smeared with blood…BRIAN'S blood.

Oh no…No…NO!!!!!!

Alex searched her mind for the encounter with Brian but came up short. All she could remember was them talking outside her car. Her black outs were becoming more pronounced as the animal pushed it's way into her soul. As a result, her human mind was beginning to shut down.

Alex reached inside her glove compartment. She found some napkins and wiped off as blood as she could. She shoved the soiled napkins into her pocket and trotted to the exit doors that led up to her floor. She used her security access code to open up the door and began the long climb up to the 23rd floor.

Dana knocked on the door to Alex's apartment after checking with the embarrassed uniformed officer. He stared at the ground as Dana asked him several questions. The main question: Why he didn't keep an eye on Alex? Dana didn't beat him up too bad though because she was certain he wouldn't make that mistake again. Mistakes can be their own lessons she mused.

She knocked once more just as the door creaked open. A blonde woman with ice-blue eyes stared back at her through the links of the security chain across the door. Dana held up her Detective shield for inspection.

"Yes?"

"Detective Dana Adams, Homicide. Can we talk? I have a few questions for you Ms. Stone."

Alex scanned the badge.

Dana fished in her coat pocket and pulled out a business card with her name, grade, and the *San Antonio Police Department* logo. Underneath this: *Homicide.* She handed it to Alex through the tiny gap. Alex closed the door.

Okay, guess she doesn't want to talk.

The door opened. Alex stood back to let Dana walk in.

"Come in Detective."

Dana was struck by how expensive the furnishings were in Alex's place compared to her tiny house. *Man, I need an upgrade.*

Alex motioned her over to a huge leather couch that seemed so plush it could swallow a person whole. Dana opted to sit in a chair near it instead. She balanced her butt on the edge and stared at Alex. Dana noticed several empty moving boxes stacked in a hallway. She noticed something else...Alex had been crying. Dana could see smears of mascara under Alex's eyes where she had tried to wipe it off.

"Nice place. Moving?"

Alex glanced over at the boxes. *Does that seem suspicious? I should have left them in my bedroom.*

"Never really unpacked. Would you like some tea Detective?"

"Thanks."

Dana watched as Alex poured tea from an antique kettle into very small, fine porcelain cups. Alex walked them back over and placed a cup on the end table near Dana. Alex sat on the human-swallowing leather couch. She sipped her tea. Dana ignored hers. She pulled a notebook and pen from her jacket. Waited.

Why isn't she asking me anything? Alex thought. She could feel anxiety rising inside her like a tide. She wanted to be anywhere but here right now.

"What happened to you last night Ms. Stone?"

Dana watched Alex for a reaction. She got one.

Alex's hands started shaking.

"I don't remember. At least not all of it."

The first lie. I can see it. Dan thought.

Dana was always very sensitive to victims of violent crime. They sometimes had trouble processing events that had happened, or trauma they had been through. She never ever prejudged anyone. But, something about Alex just felt OFF. Dana couldn't put her finger on it. Something instinctual told her that Alex was more than she seemed. Dana wanted to be wrong because Alex seemed like a nice person. Then, again, Dana had seen lots of sociopaths who were nice, polite people. Right before or after they murdered someone.

Alex stared out the window. This was the second night of the full moon. Dana didn't look at the moon though. She was more interested in Alex.

"What DO you remember Ms. Stone?"

Alex's throat felt dry. It seemed to constrict tighter and tighter each time she swallowed or took a breath. *Detective Adams KNOWS. She knows I killed somebody!*

"Well…I came home from work…dropped my folders. I uh, noticed I was bleeding. Then I got on the elevator and…and…"

Can I trust her?

Maybe I should tell her…explain what's happening to me.

Alex stared at her hands as these thoughts swirled around in her head.

Dana was patient. She could wait as long as it took to allow the person whatever amount of time it took them to work up the courage to speak. Whether it be a confession, a witness statement, or just spilling their guts. People needed to talk eventually. Dana was trying to determine if the pause was because of fear or something else.

"I woke up this morning on the other side of the city. That's all I remember."

"So, you don't know how your clothes were torn off you?" Dana asked.

"I'm sorry Detective Adams. I don't remember anything."

Dana was all business. She jotted some quick notes on her pad. Alex watched Dana as she wrote. Alex knew she couldn't say anything. No one would believe such an insane story. At best they would commit her...at worst arrest her, THEN commit or execute her. She could see the headlines now:

Former VP goes insane and murders innocent woman and man! The vicious killer known as the WEREWOLF LADY is the most insidious murderer since Charles Manson's clan!

On and on and on this spun around in Alex's mind.

No. She would keep her secret until she figured out a way to deal with it. Maybe she could find a cure. There had to be some kind of cure...Unless she WAS insane of course.

"Are you hurt?"

"Excuse me?" The question snapped Alex back to the present.

"I asked if you were hurt. Perhaps you vomited blood. Are you injured in any way?" Dana asked.

"No." Alex answered. *Not the way you would understand.*

Dana leaned forward, keeping her face neutral, but still conveying the compassion she really felt when dealing with crime victims.

"Ms. Stone. I understand if you don't want to talk about it. But, it's important that we find out as much information as possible so we can catch the person who did this. We don't want it to happen to anyone else."

Alex stood. She walked to the window.

"Believe me Detective Adams...*This* could not happen to someone else."

"I'm not following."

"Sorry. I'm babbling. I guess I should let you know that I experience blackouts from time to time. This has happened to me all my life. I think, maybe I had one of my episodes."

Dana scribbled more notes.

"I understand that, but we found YOUR clothes, torn and bloody, in that elevator."

Alex rubbed her eyes. Her head was pounding.

"I'm sorry. I don't have an explanation for you."

"One of your neighbors was hurt as well."

Alex walked back to the couch. She braced herself even though she knew it was coming.

"Who?"

Dana consulted her notebook.

"Maddie Levitt, 23A."

Images of Maddie screaming as she tried to close the door rushed at Alex. She made a choking noise and had to work hard to close off the bile that rose in her throat. Her eyes watered.

"Is she...dead?"

"I'm afraid so Ms. Stone."

Alex began to cry. Tears cascaded down her cheeks, spilling onto the plush leather couch. She covered her face and sobbed.

Dana watched her with the detached empathy needed for the job. After so many senseless murders and grieving families, she was used to shutting off a part of herself in order to focus. The only way she could help these injured souls was to solve the murders of their loved ones. To bring some sense of justice to the living and the dead.

To help people the way she couldn't help Big Tony.

"I'm sorry. It's just that she was a beautiful person...and she was...my friend."

"My condolences."

Alex tried to regain her composure.

"I'm really tired Detective. Can we finish another time?"

Dana tucked her pen and notebook away. She stood.

"Sure. I may have some more questions for you down the line. Thanks for your time."

Dana headed for the door. Turned the knob.

"Do you have children Detective Adams?"

The question threw Dana.

"Yes...I do. A daughter."

Alex was facing away from Dana. Staring up at the full moon. Talking more to herself than Dana.

"Mothers and daughters share a special bond. Let her know you love her. You never know what tomorrow may bring."

Dana didn't know how to respond, so she backed out and closed the door. Alex continued to stare at the full moon.

PART II

FIRST QUARTER

THE STRAPP LEGACY

Alex walked over to the door and locked it. Her mind was racing. *I'm not going to kill anyone else. I'm not a monster. What am I supposed to do? Maybe someone can help me? But, who?*

She opened her laptop and Googled werewolf, curses, mythology, shapeshifters. Too much information. She needed to narrow the focus. A few listings caught her attention. One was from a university professor in Minnesota. *Siodmak University.* Professor Val Rubin taught several exotic-sounding courses like *Werewolves Among Us: Shapeshifters, Myths, and Legends*, and *Lycanthropy: To Howl, or Not to Howl*. A week ago, Alex would have found these ridiculous. Not now.

Alex found the department number and called. She asked the assistant if she could speak to Professor Rubin. A few minutes later, the assistant informed her that Professor Rubin was out of town for several days. Alex hung up.

Strike one.

Alex pushed away from the table and walked over to one of the boxes on the floor. Inside, on top, was a large manila envelope. The words **MY PAST** written in black permanent marker on the front. Alex opened the folder. It was a detailed, but thin, report from Cupper Investigations about the search for her adoption records. She stared at the one-page sheet for what seemed like hours, willing her past into the present.

"Call Cupper Investigations."

The electronic valet spoke in her robotic, but pleasant tone. "Calling Cupper Investigations."

Alex walked back over to the table, taking the sheet of paper and a pen with her.

"David Cupper speaking."

"Hi Mr. Cupper, it's Alex Stone."

"Ms. Stone! This is a pleasure!"

"Sorry for calling so late. I wanted to ask you a few questions if you don't mind."

"Not at all. How can help you?

Alex tapped the pen on the counter to work out her nervous energy.

"When you were investigating the information from my background you said something about a fire destroying the foster home and adoption agency records. Is that right?"

"That's correct."

"I remember the foster home, but you said fires destroyed the agency records too?"

"Yes."

"Can you tell me where it was located?"

"Of course, Baltimore, Maryland."

"Thank you very much Mr. Cupper."

"My pleasure Ms. Stone. Don't hesitate to call me if you need anything else!"

"Thanks."

"Call ended."

Alex wrote the words: BALTIMORE, MD on the paper.

All she remembered from her childhood were a couple of fosters homes she had lived in. and these memories, like most as people age, were hazy. Bits of information. Images here and there of playing in front of a brownstone building with some little girls. Sitting in public school trying not to get beat up because she was the only white girl. Alex's strongest memories though were of her first African-American friend, Paula Voss. They met at school, as new friends often do. Alex was sitting by herself and Paula came over, and introduced herself. Paula treated Alex like a little sister from the very beginning and invited Alex into her circle of friends.

Those were the good times.

Paula came from an upper-middle-class family. Her parents were educators, both PhDs at Johns Hopkins University. They wanted Paula to experience the public school system for a time even though they could afford private school for her. Once Paula became her friend the other neighborhood kids accepted Alex. Paula was smart and tough. Together they made a good team. It was also good that Alex was graceful and athletic.

Some of the kids called her the *White Wolf.* Even back then she was fast. This earned the other kids respect. Paula and Alex were double trouble on the track team. The fastest two sprinters in the school system. People called them *Salt & Pepper.*

Alex remembered saving Paula from five girls from a different neighborhood who jumped her. Alex's ferocity shocked them all, even Alex. Paula dismissed it, thanked her friend, and that sealed their sisterly bond forever.

I guess the signs were there of what I would become, but I ignored them.

She missed Paula in the way siblings miss each other since Paula was the closest she ever had to a sister. Time and Alex's corporate moves had gotten between them. Paula reached out more often than Alex did. They had not seen each other since they were children but talked as often as life let them. Which was not often enough.

Alex made a mental note to look Paula up if she went back.

She scrolled through the Google searches again. Another interesting listing jumped out at her. Not because of the name, but because of the location…Baltimore, MD. The title: *A Curious History of Baltimore Urban Legends*, written and collected by DR. ARTEMIS STRAPP. Forward by WYSTAN STRAPP.

"Interesting."

Alex clicked the link, but it came back with a *URL Not Found* error report. She tried again. Same response. Alex made a list of all the libraries in San Antonio that had a Special Collections section. She called and asked each one if they carried the book. No one did.

Strike two.

She did another search for specialty bookstores in the local area. This turned up two near the San Antonio Zoo off Broadway. It was a short drive from her apartment.

The Second-Hand Bookstore, despite its boring name, contained a large collection of antique and vintage texts. A relic from a time when people wanted to read paper-bound books instead of turning on the latest device of choice. The bookstore was a yellow and white four-bedroom house converted into a maze of small alcoves and crevices with interesting nooks and places to sit and read. It sat facing the street allowing the morning sunlight to stream through the large-paned windows next to the front door. Inside it smelled like musty books, mixed with the slight pang of old furniture. For book-lovers, this place offered a treasure-trove of riches if one was willing to search.

The owner, Katherine the Great (Alex couldn't figure this one out), seemed to have stepped out of the pages of one of the tomes on the shelves. Katherine the Great was a short woman of about fifty, with wispy blonde hair cut short, who dressed like a hippie not long from Woodstock. She wore long flowery pants, sandals, a loose strapless blouse which threatened to expose her small chest, and a long silk shawl that rode down to her slim ankles. The clothes and her attitude fused together almost made her seem to glow with an inner light that Alex didn't understand...and yet, Alex felt that Katherine the Great was the kind of woman she could trust.

"What's the name of the book again dear?"

"*A Curious History of Baltimore Urban Legends*, written and collected by Dr. Artemis Strapp. Forward by Wystan Strapp. I checked the Special Collections section of every library in this city. Couldn't find it at the chain bookstore or online either."

Katherine the Great screwed up her nose at the mention of online.

"Heavens dear! How far we have fallen as a society when we read books that aren't bound in physical materials! You may not remember this dear, but there was once a time when books were ONLY found in libraries and bookstores! Quaint I know!"

Katherine the Great laughed. A huge belly laugh that seemed to emanate from her soul and more suited to a large man than a petite woman.

"I am very fond of Artemis Strapp's writings. He was a surgeon and one of the foremost authorities on Baltimore."

"Perfect. How can I reach him?"

"Only by means of the great beyond I'm afraid!" She laughed again. "Dear, Artemis Strapp passed away almost a hundred years ago!"

All the energy left Alex's body. For some reason she felt that this book would lead her to some kind of answers. That it would clear the mist surrounding her life.

"Oh! Wait here dear!"

She waded back into the stacks while Alex pondered what the hell she was going to do next. Katherine the Great returned holding a large book, bound in some material the animal part of Alex's brain seemed to recognize.

Leather maybe...or human skin? Hard to tell which.

"Aaah yes! THIS is a treasure. Took me a long time to find it! Almost got killed looking for it." She said.

Alex paged through the huge manuscript. The writing was elegant, punctuated by broad strokes that spoke of an intelligent mind and affinity for the quality of the letters on the page. Inside were all manner of notes, illustrations and official documents.

Alex stopped on one passage:

Journal Entry:

Winter...More killings have occurred. Each more savage than the next. The victims' throats were ravaged and mangled as if by some fierce animal. I have examined the bodies of the victims attacked and killed by the "wolf". I dare not say this aloud, lest my colleagues and the authorities think I am mad, but it is NOT a wolf....

Dr. Artemis Strapp (October 16th, 1861)

"What is this?" Alex asked.

"Selected readings from Artemis' works. A few journal entries. Illustrations, etc. This is not by any means a definitive edition but should get you started in the right direction!"

Katherine the Great stared at her. "Let me see your hands child."

Alex thought it was an odd request but held out her hands anyway. Katherine the Great took hold of them. Alex felt a chill run through her body. Katherine the Great was staring at Alex. Somehow, she *understood* what was inside Alex. Somehow.

"It's been said that the Shapeshifter has a different energy about it. The energy

and spirit of the BEAST... ...Pain, pleasure, anger, desire...they all seem to merge together in the thrill of the hunt."

As Katherine spoke Alex felt herself swaying...the room fading away. She glanced around and found herself in the WOODS, beyond the walls of the store. In the distance, Alex could see herself, standing in a clearing, surround by dark canine shapes. Alex walked over to this vision of herself...she reached out and...

Katherine the Great stared at her.

"Strange huh?" Katherine asked.

"Yes...I'm not sure...what happened."

"All the women in my family have Second Sight in some variation or another. My cousins in the North, up Minnesota way, are gypsies. Feel things stronger than I can. See visions too." She said.

"And you?" Alex asked.

Katherine the Great ripped out that belly laugh again.

"Dear, the only visions I see are after a pint of vodka...I just help to "push" a person to see their own if they are willing...and YOU my dear...seem more than willing...Anyway Fifty dollars..."

"Excuse me?"

"The book. It costs fifty dollars. That going to be cash or charge? Gotta pay the light bill you know."

Alex Googled *Wystan Strapp*. Her search returned only one hit. A professor of Archeology working out of Johns Hopkins University. When she called Johns Hopkins Archeology department they told her Professor Strapp no longer worked at Johns Hopkins. They suggested Alex contact several community colleges in the county where he taught as an adjunct. Alex called a few schools. She schmoozed one assistant into giving her Wystan's number by posing as a former colleague. Alex felt bad about lying, but desperate times called for something else.

She called the number.

"Hello?"

A pleasant voice. Rich tones.

"Professor Strapp...Wystan Strapp?"

"This is he. Who am I speaking too?"

"My name is Alexandra Stone...I'm not sure how...or where to start, but...I need your help sir. Can we meet?"

"Uh...why do you want to meet me? I'm a very busy person you know."

"Please. It has something to do with your book."

"I've written many books. Which one are you referring too?"

"The one by Artemis Strapp. *A Curious History of Baltimore Urban Legends*. You wrote a forward for it."

Silence. For a minute, Alex thought Wystan hung up.

"Hello?"

"Yes...I'm still here. Where did you find this book Miss?"

"Alex...Stone. It doesn't matter. Can we meet? It really is urgent."

The silence again...

"I really am busy. I'm not sure if I have the time right now."

"Please Dr. Strapp. It might be life or death...please."

Alex's heightened senses picked up the vibration of Wystan's heart rate speeding up. He was either scared or excited.

"Do you live in Baltimore?" He asked.

"No, but I can be there tomorrow."

"I've got your number from this call. Text me when you land. Go to the National Aquarium."

"I'll find it. Thank you."

"I look forward to speaking with you then Ms. Stone."

Alex hung up. Maybe she could hold off strike three for a bit.

CHARM CITY

BALTIMORE, MARYLAND

Alex's plane touched down at Baltimore-Washington International Thurgood Marshall Airport around noon. The airport serviced flights to Washington, D.C. and Baltimore, and all points between. It was located about 20 minutes southeast of downtown Baltimore, situated in the middle of a circular maze of service roads amid tall trees on either side. Alex got a rental and drove up Interstate 195, merged with 295, and on up to the city. The minute she drove past Camden Yards baseball stadium she had the feeling she was arriving at her second home.

The city had always intrigued her with its blend of urban facade and old East architecture. It seemed like the perfect mix of old and new. The bustle of city life and pull of nostalgia.

Alex rented a room on the 22nd floor of the Radisson Hotel in the Inner Harbor which overlooked Baltimore Harbor. She could see large and small ships moving back and forth like great sea creatures. Alex scanned the horizon and could make out the National Aquarium rising just over the tops of the other buildings. She texted Wystan. He said he could meet her in an hour. Alex decided to pass time by walking to Fell's Point.

Fell's Point, an historic area of Baltimore, had been established on the north shore of Baltimore Harbor and the northwest branch of the Patapsco River. Some of the first Navy vessels were built in Fell's Point shipyards. Frederick Douglas once worked as a slave on the docks in 1835 where he learned to read and write. The doomed poet Edgar Allen Poe died a lonely death in an alley near here.

Now Fell's Point was home to restaurants, coffee bars, music stores, shops, and hundreds of pubs. A tourist hub for twenty and thirty-somethings who most likely had no idea of the city's great history. Still, when Alex walked along the cobble stone streets she could feel the maritime past of the former seafaring town.

Alex walked past all the bars and shops. Just as she was turning to head back toward the Inner Harbor a sign on a door caught her eye. It read: *STRAPP CURIOS*. The store was closed. She stared through the murky front glass. She could make out knick-knacks, books, but not much else. Curious digs for a Professor of History. Alex glanced at her watch and hustled back.

She made it to the National Aquarium in time to see a tall man standing near the doorway glancing at tourists as they walked inside. Alex figured this was Wystan. He was about six feet one, lean, with a rakish mop of brown hair that threatened to cover his eyes each time he sneezed. Which was a lot. Alex wondered if it was a nervous habit. He seemed like a rocker inside a professor's body. Alex waved at him. Wystan smiled and walked over.

"Ms. Stone I presume?"

"Hi! Wystan right?"

"Aaa-choo! Oh! So sorry! Terrible allergies. Yes, I'm Professor Wystan Strapp."

That smile again. It warmed Alex for some reason.

"I'm sorry for my appearance, but I was pursuing a rare book and the seller would only meet me at a specific time and location. All very clandestine. Not sure why. But, in the end I procured it and am very happy about this particular find. It is a rare text about ancient Armenian legends detailing the Wendigo myths that few have heard of. In fact…"

"Wystan, can we go talk somewhere?"

"Oh yes! Apologies! I tend to blather on sometimes when I'm in a time crunch. Not that I don't have time for you, but that my time is limited. I mean I DO have time for you…just that most of the time, time is limited. My time I mean. And I do like to be on time when time permits."

Alex thought he was so cute. Trying so hard to be impressive but failing on an epic level.

"Well, why don't we go to my shop? It's not far. Just up in Fell's Point. Did you know that Fell's Point has an interesting history?"

"I was just there. Outside your place."

He smiled.

"Delightful. Then if you don't mind, I can regale you with tales of yore about Fells' Point and other interesting facts about Baltimore that many do not know."

"Please do," Alex said.

After a short walk and history tour of Fell's Point Wystan unlocked the door to his shop and let Alex inside. He locked it behind her.

"No customers today?"

"No. To be honest Ms. Stone, I don't really sell much of anything. I am just complying with legal restrictions so I can continue to live here. My apartment is upstairs. This is my collection."

"Call me Alex."

"Is that short for Alexandra? What a lovely name. Quite a rich historical context applies to the name…but lovely indeed."

Alex smiled. "Thank you Wystan."

The first thing that struck Alex were all the books on the shelves, the floor, and almost every available surface. The place reminded Alex of Katherine the Great's bookshop in San Antonio except this felt more like a small museum. Quality art pieces and paintings were arranged so that light fell on them in just the right way to highlight a certain element or accentuate a feature.

"I thought you were a teacher Wystan?"

Wystan sneezed. He seemed nervous. His heart rate increased.

"I…I was released from academia. An unfortunate set of circumstances I really do not want to discuss."

"Ok. Sorry. Is this your place?"

"It was my Grandfather's, and his fathers before him, etc. A Strapp has owned this building for many generations. Now, it is my legacy. My great-grandfather Artemis was a physician. He used the downstairs for his practice. Right behind you there was once a table where he performed emergency procedures."

"Are you going to pass it to your children?"

"I am the last Strapp unfortunately. I never married. No siblings to fight for control over this place. Once I leave this Earth the Strapp's will have vanished forever."

Alex stared at Wystan as he talked. She could almost feel the shadow of his family passing into oblivion. He seemed so lost. So alone. A feeling Alex knew something about. Wystan stared back at her. Alex blushed. He motioned her to a chair. She sat.

"Now I am fully entrenched in the Internet. I blog about the unknown…well…not the unknown, but a more clarifying word might be the "undiscovered". It seems that in this end I am in line with my family's line of thinking."

"How's that?"

"Since you asked about my great-grandfather's book I'd like to show you something."

Alex followed him upstairs to a small sitting room. Inside was a small oak desk covered with drawings and more books. Next to the desk, was a giant stuffed leather chair that seemed to double as a bed. Wystan cleared space on the chair and offered it to her. He knelt down under the desk and dragged a rugged metal box from underneath. He pulled a key from a chain around his neck. Wystan unlocked the box. Inside was a manuscript similar to one Alex purchased. Alex glanced around and noticed a portrait of man who very much resembled Wystan. He saw her staring at it.

"My great-grandfather Dr. Artemis Strapp. Uncanny resemblance yes?"

Artemis was tall, handsome, and had a shock of dark hair very much like Wystan. Alex wondered if Wystan tried to emulate his great-grandfather. Artemis wore an eyepatch over his left eye.

"I look more like him than my own father. Quite interesting. My father and grandfather were both short and fat. Remember when I asked you where you procured the manuscript from? It's because I was under obligation to donate the manuscript to a library. I'm not sure how it ended up somewhere else but a couple of years ago I discovered another manuscript. And this one is far more detailed. It is almost entirely composed of journal writings with some detailed maps, whereas the one you have I'm sure most likely contains illustrations, news clippings, some journal entries, and other oddities correct?"

"That's right."

"Make yourself comfortable. I would like to read some of this if you don't mind."

"That's why I'm here Wystan."

Wystan opened the manuscript and started reading…

A Curious History of Baltimore Urban Legends

Journal of Dr. Artemis Strapp:
April 19th, 1861

...Secessionists have tried to seal off the city, forcing the first brigade of infantry troops ordered by Lincoln to travel through the city. Violence has erupted and many civilians were killed or injured. As a doctor I was called out to treat them...

Horse-drawn carriages were parked along the muddy, unpaved streets close to the station proper. I picked my way through the angry mob of people shouting. I had a sense that this was just the beginning of a wildfire of violence that would sweep the city, and the nation. Police in their severe uniforms tried to keep the crowd at bay. I stepped over the bodies of the dead soldiers and civilians, holding a handkerchief to my nose against the awful stench of manure, urine, body odor, waste and blood. Even in this profession I have not yet been able to get used to the smells associated with city life.

I consider myself a man of strict personal standards and strong religious and moral convictions against slavery. Those who know me remark of my great depth of compassion for our fellow man and woman and how I am a respected member of Baltimore society held in high regard. To this I cannot speak, but I can attest to my passion for humanity. It is indeed my calling. A calling I hold dear to my heart. One in which, I shall not fail or tire. This is the main reason I am so appalled about the violence happening in Baltimore. I think stronger hearts and minds are needed as we thread the moral needle. More voices are needed to stand against the evil that is the bondage of man. What an evil indeed.

A police officer led me to an injured woman pinned beneath an overturned horse cart.

"Here you go, Doctor. This lady is hurt pretty bad. The cart came right down on top of her. Damn...what a waste. Hey! Come here men! Help me lift this off 'er!"

I waited as more officers lifted the cart off the woman. She screamed in pain. The woman was dressed as a servant or house worker of some kind. She was about twenty-seven years of age and very fair-skinned with high cheekbones. Her hands hardy from working rough patches of land, but it was her eyes that captured me. A wildness seemed to lurk in them.

"Hello, Madam. My name is Dr. Artemis Strapp. I'm here to help you. What's your name?"

"Anna..."

I noticed a pool of blood near one of her legs, and performed a cursory examination revealing a large gash. The leg was deformed, showing evidence of a break.

Journal of Dr. Artemis Strapp:
April 19th, 1861

Her injuries were extensive so with the police officers help, we placed her in a carriage and rushed her to my office in Fell's Point. I could not reach the hospital because of the chaos. During the ride the poor dear talked under her breath. I could not hear most of what she said, but I caught the words "escape" and "forest", and something that sounded like "pack". As the police officer and I moved Anna from the carriage I could see the tall masts of a myriad sea vessels waving in the breeze. I smelled the salt water and heard the creaking of wood against metal as the ships heaved and jostled in the bay.

The port was a non-stop panorama of activity that continued day and night. A great multitude of vessels that entered and exited the Patapsco with no end in sight. The Port near my practice housed a great many warehouses and factories, and these backed into the numerous pubs and several houses of ill repute where sailors spent their hard-earned coin for a few hours of pleasure during shore leave. Immigrants and other residents of this section of Baltimore conversed and interacted in a great throng of humanity that was vibrant and alive. I often would walk the cobblestone streets to feel the energy of the neighborhood. Unlike some, I reveled in the differences this neighborhood presented; the promise for our nation.

But, today my mind was occupied with the saving of a life. I motioned to Judith my faithful assistant and house keeper. She was an older woman with a short mane of sandy brown hair that always seemed to fall into her face no matter how she attempted to pull it back. Judith was widowed with no children. She raised me after my own mother's passing and treated me as the son she had never been blessed with. Judith was an individual of stout heart and steely determination. She was unshakeable and I depended on her.

"Judith, her leg is broken and I expect to find internal bleeding. Please prepare my equipment."

"Right away doctor."

The police officer seemed queasy. He disgusted me.

"If you have other duties I believe we will be fine." I said to him.

"Thank...thank you sir."

I wiped a lock of hair from Anna's face while Judith made preparations for surgery.

"Anna, I am going to do everything I can to save your leg. I promise."

Anna stared into my eyes.

"Your eyes are so...tender...thank you sir..."

Anna fainted.

"Judith! Let's begin."

We started our procedures on Anna.

Journal of Dr. Artemis Strapp:
April 23rd, 1861

I slept by Anna's bed for the next four nights. Judith protested of course, but Anna was on death's door and I felt compelled to ensure she had round the clock care, conventions be damned. At the time I did not understand why I felt compelled to be at Anna's side, but I accepted it as morning accepts the sun.

I have some remembrance of eating when Judith looked in on us, but slumber kept me from speaking to her. Around four in the morning Anna bolted awake, a scream on the edges of her lips. Terror in her beautiful, dark eyes. She glanced around the room, resembling a wild animal more than young lady for several minutes. When her eyes found mine, it seemed to calm her fierce spirit. She lay *back and looked at me. I confess that I had never had another woman look at me the way Anna did since the passing of my wife Cora. No fear, no embarrassment, nothing coy in her glance. Just a strong-willed confidence and appreciation it seemed.*

"Oh...Anna. You are awake. Are you feeling any pain?" I asked her.

"No sir."

I stood up and sat on the bed next to her, careful not to cause her discomfort. I smiled at her. She was so lovely, as if cast from a sculpture of Aphrodite herself. Her skin, luminescent and glowing despite her grave condition. I did not give thought to this at the time.

"I need to look at your leg."

"Of course sir."

I unwrapped the bandage covering her broken leg. I frowned. What I saw confused me on a professional level. It seemed to me...impossible.

"I...well...it appears that you have already started healing. Quite well as a matter of fact. There is almost no bruising. Interesting. I guess I should let you get back to sleep."

"Did you stay this entire time?"

"As your doctor I thought it best if I was by your side if you needed assistance with anything."

"I'm glad you stayed" She said.

"It was my pleasure Anna."

"Sir? Will you stay and read to me? If it is not any trouble?"

I cupped her hand. In my mind it was out professional courtesy, but in my heart, I felt stirrings I had not allowed myself to feel in many years. Emotion that was alien to me, and yet comforting, as if the nearness of Anna was the only place I was supposed to be on this Earth. The emotion and feeling terrified me...and gave me joy.

"Of course, dear lady."

Anna had been displaced because of the impending War and everything she had was lost. Her family had been killed. She was trying to find a way to book passage to France to live with relatives, but her money had been stolen. Even after her convalescence period, I could not put her out. So, I had Judith make up a room that Anna could call her own. It went on this way for months. Anna recuperated, and in that time a curious thing occurred...

We fell in love.

I had been a widower for some time and found that Anna completed my life in a way I had not realized until her arrival. I know she felt the same way for me.

Journal of Dr. Artemis Strapp:
October 4, 1861

Anna and I lay on the floor, next to the fire, warm in each other's love when someone pounded on my door.

As I stood Anna begged me not to answer it. A look of fear and trepidation in her lovely eyes. I assured her I would send whomever it was on their way. She grabbed hold of my wrist (with surprising strength I might add) and again begged me NOT to open it. To my detriment, I did, and was faced with a group of men. Some I recognized, others I did not. The leader was John Noble, a Baltimore City Elder.

"Gentlemen, how can I help you this evening?"

Noble spoke. His face harsh and turned up with hate.

"We have come for your Negro. I mean HER! She is an escaped slave and we are charged with returning her!"

John pointed at Anna.

I laughed of course.

"Wait. You are mistaken Mr. Noble. This is a white woman."

I started to enjoy this joke when I realized the look on their faces did not lend itself to mirth. I glanced back at Anna, waiting for her to confirm what I just told these men. She did not. In fact, Anna drew her knees up against her chest. She would not meet my gaze.

"Passing for white. Look at her! Closely!" Noble spit the words out like venom. I disliked this man to a high degree.

But, the truth was in her eyes. Her secret was out.

"Anna? Is...is this true? Are you...a...Negro?"

"It is true my love."

Noble took my shoulder. I found the gesture repellent and shrugged him off.

"We know you were misled by this slave and don't hold it against you Strapp but move aside and let us do our job."

It went against every social convention I knew, but I was in love with Anna and bound to her no matter what. Till death. Between my shock and disbelief, I felt a new resolve growing. I grit my teeth and faced Noble and his gang of thugs.

"By whose authority are you here?"

"Our authority. As Secessionists it is our duty to maintain the values of this nation!"

"Sir. Baltimore has sided with the Union and I do not, nor shall I ever agree with the aberration of slavery! Never!" I said to them.

Noble stared at me with his devil's eyes. The hate burning so bright it could have lit a flame.

"You are a traitor to every white man who ever lived!"

I was slow in my reaction. I should have anticipated his strike, but I did not. Noble cleft me on the side of the head. The world went black and gray, and I felt myself shift sideways onto the floor. In my haze I heard Anna screaming as the brutes swarmed inside and grabbed her. Noble's voice seemed to issue from everywhere and nowhere as I struggled to stand and stop them. One of Noble's gang kicked me in my ribcage, taking my wind and resolve. I collapsed onto the floor gasping. He kicked again, this time striking me in the face, near my left eye.

"Take this slave to my wagon!"

I heard Anna screaming. "NO! Please don't hurt him! I'll go with you!"

"SHUT UP! I think the doctor was harboring this slave all this time. Too bad he fought us and tried to kill me!" Noble said to his gang of devils.

I could not see out of my left eye. It was useless and blind. I could feel blood soaking my neck and shirt. I turned onto my back trying to use my right eye. I found the muzzle of John Noble's pistol staring back at me. The barrel seemed to gape wide. Inside was blackness and death.

"NO!"

The voice was Anna's...and yet...NOT.

It had a guttural, animalistic quality that seemed more akin to a feral dog or wolf. I looked for my love and saw that she was TURNED! Her features were my Anna's but now tainted by large canine teeth and wolfish eyes that were indeed animal. She grabbed each of the men holding her, one by one, and hurled them with great strength toward the far wall. I heard the tell-tale sound of broken spines as they landed like putty onto the floor.

They lay dead, eyes...sightless.

The ones closest to the door stood in shock until Anna faced them. The men ran into the night screaming for their lives. Then, my Anna faced the only man alive in the room except me. John Noble.

"Get back Demon!"

Noble fired his pistol at her. It seemed to hit Anna, but she did not give evidence of being hurt. Instead she leapt toward him, clearing a space of feet in seconds, and grabbed hold of his windpipe. Anna pulled him close. Noble dropped the pistol from dead fingers.

"What...what....are you...?" Noble whispered.

Anna growled at Noble.

"Your death!"

I shut my eye as Anna killed Noble. I heard the dry crunch of bones as she gnawed his face off his skull. Even in my fear I still did not feel anything but disgust for John Noble, but I felt afraid for my Anna. Now she would have to run...

I heard a horrific roaring sound and feet running.

I opened my eye, cursing myself for a coward. I stood and stumbled to the door and into the street. Anna had vanished into the dark. I could not reconcile with my mind what my eyes had seen. She was...a beast...like a wolf, but only more savage.

And yet, she was still...my Anna.

Journal of Dr. Artemis Strapp:
December 19, 1861

Winter. Heavy snow has fallen on our city. The potential for violence still smothers the air. Strange and savage murders started occurring all over the city. The interesting thing is that the murderer, or animal, only targets Secessionists.

I wandered the city, picking my way around snow drifts and pools of frozen and semi-frozen water. I began following Secessionists. I knew my beloved Anna was still in the city. The monster that was killing people was her.

I knew it.

As the terror coursed through my veins I felt a sense of elation that I would maybe see her one last time. I thought that if I followed the Secessionists, maybe one would be attacked and I could confront her. A morbid thought, but one that compelled and pushed me past any sense of self-preservation or civilized pretense.

The Secessionist I followed that night turned into an alley. Minutes later, a scream throttled the night. I ran in the direction of the sound. Horrified by what I might find, and...yet...

The Beast stood over the body of the Secessionist. Blood dripping from the dark muzzle. The man gurgled his last breath and died. The animal looked my direction. She was a...the only word I could remember from my arcane, supernatural research was...

...WEREWOLF.

The monster began its advance. I had a fearful thought. What if it wasn't her? I had put myself in jeopardy for no good reason if it were not my beloved. Then...the beast stopped. The savage glow in its eyes faded and it just sat there and looked at me. I walked toward it. Took one tentative step after another. Moving closer and closer until I was but a few feet from the monstrous face. I reached out my hand. I had to know if this was her.

I reached my fingers out...and touched the large snout. To my surprise, the werewolf bowed its shaggy head, placing counter-pressure against my palm. I rubbed her head the way I would a large dog. It licked my hand with a rough pink tongue. The once-savage eyes staring at me with compassion and love. I had found my Anna...

TRAGIC LOVE

Wystan shut the manuscript…

He and Alex stared at each other. Alex felt a mix of emotions. Here, on the page, was evidence of what she was. Not just some hazy memory and strange woman talking about destiny, but a waking specter from the past speaking to her as if it was happening now. And, for Alex, it was. She was overwhelmed and excited.

"Did Artemis find out where she went?" Alex asked.

"France. Logs of the first outbound ship report a young woman passenger traveling alone. It stuck out because unlike today, it was still unusual for women to travel unaccompanied. Especially overseas. They, of course, did not figure out she masqueraded as a white woman because her complexion was so fair and her features were more Anglo-Saxon than African. This happened quite a bit around the time of the Civil War and for decades after." Wystan said. "Are you okay? Can I get you some water?"

"I'm fine." Alex said it, but she wasn't fine. She was closer, and yet further from finding out how to end this waking nightmare.

And, that's what it was.

A nightmare.

A horrible secret she had to keep from everyone.

Wystan watched her.

"So, why did you really come to see me? Surely not for a bedtime story. I have never had anyone ask me about my grandfather's journals." Wystan asked.

"Do you believe in werewolves Professor Strapp?"

"Wystan. And, yes. Yes I do. Why? Have you…have you seen one before?"

Alex faced him. She wanted to trust this handsome man who was so odd. She wanted to tell someone…anyone. There was no artifice when he said it. No pretense. He believed his own words as much most people believed the sun would come up in the morning or that they breath air in day after day.

Wystan *believed* in werewolves. Now, Alex had to figure out whether or not he would believe *her.*

Alex wanted to spill her guts. Tell him everything. But, what if he laughed? Or rejected her before she could prove it? And, how would she prove it? Could Alex *wolf-out* on command? How did it even work? The more she thought about it, the more outrageous and impossible it sounded to herself. Even now, the events of the past few days seemed like a distant memory. Fading from the clarity of her mind like a ship disappearing on the horizon.

When Alex stared out at that horizon all she saw was insanity looking back at her.

"Ms. Stone are you hungry? Would you like to eat something? I'm sure airport food hasn't gotten any better. Did you eat already? I have more to share, but it would be better if we did more on a full stomach." Wystan said.

Alex smiled. "No. I was so focused on getting here that I forgot to eat. I think my stomach did a flip when you were talking right now!"

"Perfect! Since you are in *Charm City* as we often call Baltimore, it is apropos that you eat some crab. A Charm City staple I assure you!"

"You talked me into it Wystan. On one condition."

"Yes?"

Alex smiled at Wystan. He smiled back. "Call me Alex. No more Ms. Stone ever again. Deal?"

Wystan smiled again. "Deal Alex."

Wystan and Alex had dinner at a crab restaurant off the pier. They enjoyed each other's company without discussing the real reason for Alex's visit. It was wonderful. For the first time in days she was able to relax and have adult conversation with an intelligent man who seemed as interested in her as she was in him. Wystan talked to Alex about literature, music, poetry, philosophy, and of course history. He was an expert and it showed. Alex was impressed.

She droned on and on about her career in finance, sure that he would be bored to tears. The opposite was true. Wystan leaned in, drinking up everything Alex said. After dinner they walked back to Fell's Point, laughing and joking as if they had known each other years instead of hours. They moved back upstairs to Wystan's sitting room.

Alex felt the mood shift as soon as Wystan picked up the manuscript. Wystan sat on a love seat. Alex moved from her chair and joined him. She laid her head on his shoulder. Wystan was surprised but did not move. He noticed Alex's necklace.

"That's a lovely necklace. Your initials I presume?"

Alex touched it. "A gift from my father."

"Is he still alive?"

Alex frowned. "I don't know. I never met him. I was raised in the foster care system. This necklace was sent along with my birth certificate. The only evidence that I belonged to someone. There was a note too. It said...*Please take care of my Alexandra. Tell her I will always love her.*"

"I am sorry Alex. I really am. Every child should know their parents if possible. It seems a crime to rob them of this. Uh...There is more of the manuscript if you would like to hear it Alex. I don't want to annoy you. Most people find my constant talking more than they can stand." Wystan said.

Alex moved into his body more. "I like the sound of your voice. It's soothing. I don't know why, but I feel so comfortable around you."

"I feel comfortable around you too Alex."

Alex sat up and stared at him. "Why do you believe in werewolves if you've never seen one?"

"I don't know. Faith I guess." Wystan said.

"Faith? Like in GOD?" Alex asked.

"Yes, the same kind. I believe in GOD even though I've never seen him. I believe in science even though I've never been to Saturn or Jupiter. I believe in my great grandfather Artemis' writings even though I wasn't there. I just have faith. In these extraordinary times it seems like we need to rely on something besides our own intellectual greatness. Even the most articulate, complex minds of the past often believed in the spiritual realm. Believed in things seen and unseen. Artemis believed that there was always a reason for events that transpire in the world. He wanted to bridge the chasm of what we think we know and what we have not yet uncovered."

"You really admire him, don't you?"

Wystan smiled at her.

"He was such an ordinary man and yet...If I could accomplish even a fourth of the things he did, my life will be...validated. Silly huh?"

"I don't think so."
"What about you Alex? Do you believe?"
"In GOD? I stopped believing a long time ago…In anything…Can you read some more please?"

Journal of Dr. Artemis Strapp:
September 1, 1862

Because of my reputation as a leading and reputable physician in America, I was able to procure boarding and some work in France as a guest lecturer. I was hired by one of the most elite higher education establishments, the École Normale Supérieure with Louis Pasteur. From there, I followed Anna's trail to the town of Dole, Franche Comté.

One night after my lecture I went to a local establishment. I had learned French well enough to teach and converse, so I asked the Barkeep questions about the area. I still endeavored to find any information about my Anna.

"Monsieur? Are there any wolves in the forest nearby? I am a biologist studying the nocturnal habitats of wolves and want to find out where they might be."

He replied. "I would not recommend you go, but if you must, deep in the eastern edge of the Chaux Forest I have seen them running during the day. At night…I would not care to venture in without armed men. Do you take my meaning Doctor?"

"I do kind sir. Thank you."

Of course, I did not heed his instruction. And, in my foolhardiness, I ventured into the forest without a plan or compass to guide me. I was mad after a fashion. Mad in love. Mad to find my Beloved.

Late afternoon. The sunlight was beginning to fade. I walked through the forest. I was not a woodsman. I just had a feeling that I would find her.
CRASH!

The earth gave way underneath my feet! I dropped into a dark hole and found myself in a cave system. In my mind I perceived that human eyes had not beheld this place in many hundreds of years. I dusted myself off, glanced up at the hole and then into the darkness ahead. My only choices were up, or straight. Anna was not above ground, so I decided to enter the tunnel and see what I might find.

I stumbled along like a blind man a few feet as the light receded. My foot kicked something on the ground. A broken oil lamp. I stooped down to check the contents. After a few minutes I was able to get the wick lit. Now, my vision extended maybe six to eight feet in front of me.

I continued walking and entered a small open area with several other tunnels leading off from it. I attempted to shine the light into each of them.

"Artemis?"

I spun around and found myself staring at a human...ANNA. She was NAKED. I tore my coat off, ran over, covered her, and hugged her tight.

"Are you alright? I...I love you dear Anna!"

"I love you too...but you should not have come here to find me. You must go." Anna said.

"I will not lose you again. Come away with me! We can stay here in France. Far away from America and their horrible ways! We can build a life together! I can teach...you can have our babies."

She kissed me with a fervent passion. I kissed her back and held her. I was determined never to let her go, come what may. I vowed my love to her and knew that the only obstacle that would keep me from her was Death itself.

"I want that and more."

"But...?" I asked.

Sounds emanated from all around us. The clicking of claws on the ground...animal breathing...I stared into the darkness and saw multiple pairs of glowing eyes. I turned to Anna and there was panic in her eyes.

"Go now my love! Please! I beg you!"

"I will NOT leave you!"

Anna moved away from me.

"If you love me...run...NOW!"

I saw the love in her eyes, and not questioning...I RAN as fast as my feet could take me! As I ran I heard the sound of FEROCIOUS

HOWLING and BARKING. I reached the hole to the surface. The night air beckoned to me. I pulled myself up from the hole, crawled out, stumbling into the dense woods. Twilight had crested and it was almost completely dark. Behind me, I heard something tearing itself from the ground. I ran faster. Fell. Stood again. Footsteps were gaining on me but I dared not look back!

The terror I felt as I ran was nothing I had ever experienced before. Stark raving terror...pushing me...propelling me. Branches and twigs scratched and tore at my face and exposed skin, shredding my clothes. I seemed a lunatic, but I was past caring. Survival spurred me onward through the forest.

When I mustered up the courage to glance over my shoulder I glimpsed a NIGHTMARE shape LEAPING for my back...A sharp claw SLASHED me. I felt searing pain course through my body. I tripped and fell to the earth, rolled onto my back and beheld a strange and horrific sight. The werewolf chasing me was ATTACKED by another werewolf...ANNA.

The animals fought each other. A savage, primal battle of superiority that creatures have engaged in for millennia. Both equally matched. But, my Anna was fueled by the extra motivation of protecting the person she loved more than life itself. I was witnessing true love rising above all else to protect and cherish. The battle filled me with disgust, but my heart was won over by Anna's will. She killed her sister werewolf by TEARING into its throat. I was transfixed with horror, standing still. Unable to move. Anna the werewolf stood over the body and HOWLED in victory...

BANG! BANG! BANG! GUNSHOTS cracked in the forest. Anna was blown backward.

"NO!"

I screamed out from the psychic and emotional pain as if I had been hit with the bullets myself. I crawled to where Anna had fallen, forgetting the pain in my back. Knelt beside her. Her canine eyes stared into my human eyes. I could feel her trying to communicate. To express how she felt. I wanted to cross this threshold of the unknown with her.

"Anna? My love? I am here...I am here for you..."

Before my eyes Anna transformed back into the human woman I loved. I cradled her in my arms. I noticed several men with guns walk over in silence. They stared down at us. One of them the Bar

Keep. No one spoke. I did not care. In this moment, Anna and I were the last two people on Earth.
Anna reached out...touched my face with a fingertip.
" ...such tender eyes..."
Anna died in my arms.
I remember screaming at the sky...
Cursing GOD for her death. Perhaps I should have cursed myself for loving?
No...I think not...LOVE is never a curse.
Always a blessing. Always...

Last Journal Entry of Dr. Artemis Strapp:
1862...Physician...Scientist...Lover...Believer.

Wystan closed the manuscript. The tale had shaken him too.

"It has been some time since I read this. I feel the power of his words. And the sadness. Tragic love. Almost Shakespearian yes? Alex?"

Alex was crying. Tears streamed down her face. Wystan moved closer to her. Unsure how to comfort her.

"Why are you crying Alex?"

"I thought...that maybe...he was going to save her... I thought there was a cure."

"Artemis couldn't save her. I suppose the blessing of their love was also the curse that doomed her."

"But, there wasn't a CURE!!"

Wystan was startled at the sound of her voice. Alex was on the verge of panic.

"Why are you so upset about a cure? Did you think there was a cure for being a werewolf? Why would you...?"

The words died on his lips. Wystan *knew*. Alex faced him, face still stained with tears. Wystan was in shock.

"I'm sorry I bothered you Wystan."

Alex ran from the room. Wystan heard the door slam downstairs. He glanced out the windows and saw Alex's figure running down the street. Wystan stumbled back to the loveseat.

"I believe..."

PAULA

Detective Paula Voss walked out of Baltimore Police Headquarters holding a cup of coffee, the life blood of any good Police. Headquarters was a big, smooth-marble and glass-walled building located on Fayette Street. It was where the Department "Brass" and all the other evil geniuses plotted their political machinations. Plotting that Paula had little time or patience for. With an estimated population of over six-hundred and twenty thousand, she and the other Baltimore Police had more pressing things to do than politic.

Her city still boasted one of the highest crime rates in the country for a metropolitan area and was one of the most crowded. This coupled with the recent notorious Police actions against civilians made her job hard. Harder than it should be. But, that was what being a Police in Charm City got you. She'd come to drop off some files and was in a hurry to canvas yet another murder.

An attractive white woman was standing on the curb near where Paula had parked her police sedan. The woman seemed to be waiting for someone. She was looking right at Paula, but Paula was focused on digging her keys out of her pocket.

"Just go to the receptionist desk inside the front door if you have a complaint ma'am," Paula said. She didn't even break stride as she said it. The woman moved aside but kept staring at her. Paula walked around to the driver's side of her sedan.

"Paula."

"That's right. Detective Paula Voss. How can I help you?" Paula said. She was suspicious. The woman might be a reporter set to lure her into providing some spurious or salacious quote that the Brass would dig in her ass about.

"It's Alex."

Paula dropped her keys and looked up. She stared at Alex. In an instant, the memories came flooding back. This was ALEX. Her best friend. The only other person who ever understood her. She had not seen Alex in years. Since she was a girl.

"Alex? Oh my GOD! ALEX!" Paula ran around the car and folded Alex in a hug. She squeezed her tight, afraid that if she let go her old friend would vanish into atoms. Tears rolled down Paula's brown cheeks.

"I missed you girl!"

"I missed you too Paula." Alex was surprised by Paula's reaction. She thought Paula might reject her. She had prepared herself for the worst the minute she left Wystan's house. She was torn and confused, and the only person she could think to run to was Paula.

Paula let go, stood back and appraised Alex.

"Oh! Look at you! So damn beautiful! Wow! And I look like I've been dragged through Western District on my face! Damn! Why didn't you call me? I could have taken the day off. How long are you in town for?"

"It was a last-minute trip. I'm sorry I didn't call...or that I haven't called. You're not mad are you?"

Paula hugged her again. "Mad? No! You just gave me a great excuse to not go to another homicide. Let me call my guys and have them cover. I run the squad, so that won't be hard. Give me ten minutes! And...do NOT leave! Okay? Promise me Alex!"

Alex smiled. Her heart lifted a little bit. "I'll be right here Paula."

"Great! Back in ten!"

Paula jogged off. For the first time in so many days Alex felt like things might be okay.

Alex followed Paula in her rental. They drove to the northern district of Waverly, a quiet area that consisted of row houses and single-family homes. Waverly was a historic community that was safe, had affordable housing, a strong sense of community, and diverse culture. It was a solid working and middle-class neighborhood located near I-83 that provided access to downtown Baltimore, Towson, and the Beltway. Many of her Police colleagues lived outside the city, but not Paula. She wanted to be somewhat close to the community she served.

Paula's house was a beautiful Victorian with brown brick, white trim and matching shudders. There was also a lovely garden just to the left of the stairs leading up to the porch. Alex could tell Paula was proud of it.

"What do you think Alex? Not as nice as my parent's place but it'll do right? I'm joking! Aaron works in finance. I wouldn't be able to afford this place if he didn't."

"Aaron?"

"Yeah. My husband. We've been married for ten years now. I sent you the wedding invite. Don't you remember?"

Alex was ashamed. She did remember now.

What a shitty friend I am.

"And, don't think you're a shitty friend either! I know how busy that job keeps you. Traveling all the time. I'm just glad you're here now!" Paula said.

Alex smiled. It was like Paula was in her head as always. *Well, maybe not so good to be there nowadays.* Alex thought.

Paula led Alex into her house. The inside was more beautiful than the outside. Paula (or Aaron) had exquisite taste. The furnishings and décor resembled a house from the nineteenth century as opposed to one from the twenty-first. There were wooden alcoves, painted murals in the ceilings, and two lovely French doors which opened up to a bright kitchen with an old fashioned-looking wood burning pipe stove.

"Ok...so we do pretty well. Like I said, Aaron's in finance and when it rains it pours. We are blessed I have to say." Paula smiled. She knew she didn't have to apologize for having money, but this is how Paula felt all her life. Like she was the kid who came from money wallowing in the mud with the poor kids. This was not truth, but it gnawed at Paula anyway. She felt like she had less street cred if people knew she had been blessed with a privileged upbringing. Her husband Aaron tried to talk Paula off the ledge about it all the time. He stressed to her that having money was okay, bragging about it was not. Over the course of their marriage Paula had shifted her mindset a bit, but the old feelings bubbled up from time to time anyway.

"I am really happy for you Paula. Looks like things have worked out well. Where's Aaron?"

"Work is his mistress. He sometimes works seventy hours a week."

Alex smiled. "I'm familiar with that. I don't know how people with families do it."

Paula invited Alex to sit at her kitchen table. She poured them some coffee.

"We make it work. We play and travel and laugh and love. It's all good…Wanna hear a secret? Some people in the department think I'm on the take. Can't understand why I still want to be Police when I can afford to quit."

Alex sipped her coffee. "Why do you stay?"

Paula was quiet for a moment. "Someone has to do the job."

The friends drank their coffee in silence. It was nice to just be together. Paula stirred the contents of her cup.

"So, why are you here Alex? Going down memory lane is wonderful, but my cop brain tells me that something else is going on. I can smell it. So…what gives?"

"I just needed to be here…with you. Back in San Antonio, I have no one. Well, I used to. Maddie. Sweet older lady. My neighbor. But, she's gone now and I can't tell anyone what's happening to me." Alex said.

"You can tell me anything Alex. I hope you know that. Wait…you said happening *to you*. Are you in some kind of trouble?"

"Not the kind of trouble you can help with. I don't think anyone can help me."

Paula studied her friend's face. Alex had bags under her eyes. Worry lines creased the corners of her mouth. She had a sense that Alex had experienced some kind of extreme trauma. She wanted to help Alex but didn't know how, which frustrated her because Paula was a helper and healer by nature.

Paula reached across the kitchen table and took Alex's hands in her own.

"Look, Alex. I don't know what's going on with you but listen to me…I am your friend. I always will be. Aaron and I don't have any kids. We have plenty of room here. If you need to come and stay with us It'll be okay. It's an open offer and I hope you take me up on it if you want."

"Thank you…I need to get back to San Antonio, but I'm so glad we got to talk. It was nice to see you again."

Paula smiled. "Yeah, it was. Can you stay a few more hours at least?"

"Sure, Paula."

WENONA

SAN ANTONIO, TEXAS

Wenona moved with the PACK again. They settled under the dark skies looking for easy prey, moving in a tight group along the railroad tracks near Commerce Street. Again, using shadow and darkness for cover. They passed abandoned warehouses and decrepit homes in their search. Attack a human too near other humans and they would be hunted.

So, they preyed on the vulnerable...

The weak...

The homeless...

The kind of population society pretends not to see even when they see them.

For now, this would have to do.

She had called to Alex earlier in the night, but the pup didn't answer. Wenona thought about going into the tall building in her human form, but as of late, each transformation was becoming more and more difficult. After so many years on Mother Earth, changing back and forth taxed her immune system, and could prove fatal over time, weakening her. Even now as she padded along Wenona could feel the brittleness in her ancient joints. The suppleness of her muscles was starting to turn into rigidity. Even her night vision was less acute than it had ever been and her hearing was getting worse day upon day. Perhaps Father Time was catching up with her?

No!

Giving in to her aging body might lead to vulnerability to their enemies. And, Wenona would never capitulate or give quarter. Wenona was leading the charge of a new era for her sisters. One where *mankind* was placed back down the food chain where they belonged. If she had to live another hundred years she would make it so.

Wenona glanced up toward Sister Moon.

It was hidden by clouds. Even though the PACK did not gain actual power from Sister Moon, they still felt her pull just as the tides did. A wave of emotion came over the PACK members whenever

Sister Moon was at her zenith. They felt a freedom and energy that stimulated and excited their senses. The ideal time to hunt was when she was exposed in her full glory. As Wenona thought about Sister Moon she looked back in time. Back to when Mother Earth was lush, green, and fertile. Back to a time when everything seemed so simple.

CHAUX FOREST - DOLE, FRANCHE COMTÉ: 1573

Night crawled over the land as Wenona, just twelve years old, carried a water bucket back to her village. The walk back from the river was long and winding, traveling through a great wooded area. She tried not to be afraid, but stories about bear and other predators eating children had been told to her so often by Father that each waving branch or blowing leaf held hideous terrors for her young mind. Several yards ahead Wenona could see the clearing. To her, the clearing represented safety and home, since her small dwelling was a stone's throw away from it.

Wenona entered the clearing. She was safe.

A monstrous shape appeared to the left of her. Another stepped from the shadows to her right. A scream welled up in her throat, dying there as one more ominous shape cut off her path.

It stood in front of her. At least seven feet tall. Dark. Hairy. Hot, fetid breath billowing from the wrinkled snout, mixing with the cold air.

She turned in a small circle.

Several more beasts entered the clearing, cutting off all avenue of escape. Tears flowed down her small cheeks as she realized she was going to be eaten by these creatures. But, alas, this was not to be.

Their behavior was NOT menacing. They just watched her. Wenona stared back at them...too terrified to move but wanting to run screaming for her family.

Sudden, sharp, stinging pain enveloped her. Pain that radiated from her toes to the crown of her head. She fell to the grassy ground and coughed up blood. Then, spasms and convulsions took hold. Her entire body shaking. The animals moved closer, forming a protective ring around her.

Wenona SCREAMED...her screams turning into HOWLS...a sound that seemed to go on forever...

Wenona woke up to more screams. This time, the screams did NOT come from her. They came from people she recognized. Her family. Wenona stood, but the world felt different to her. She felt more connected to the ground. In fact, she felt more connected to everything around her. The forest. The wind. The animals. She could hear the trees speaking. Not in a language she understood, but in some ancient way, communicating, no, communing with each other.

More screams. She tried to run to them. She swayed, falling to the hard earth as if she had never used her legs before. Wenona looked down and realized she had not ever used THESE legs.

She had FOUR legs instead of two. Hairy animal legs that resembled those of a large dog or wolf. Wenona stared at her hands. They were still hands in the functional sense, but where nails should have been she had five long, dangerous-looking claws. She screamed in horror and was surprised at the sound issuing from her throat. It was not a human scream, but instead, an animal sound.

A howl...Just like a WOLF.

Somehow, Wenona stood. She was alone in the clearing. She ran toward her home, testing her new legs. As she gained confidence, she ran faster. Driven by the knowledge that her family needed her.

She pushed faster, cresting a hill overlooking her home. Terror overtook her. Her home. The only home she could remember, was on FIRE. Even worse was the sound emanating from inside. A horrid shrieking that chilled her blood. Whoever was inside was being roasted alive. Wenona raced down the hill, stopping short of the fiery inferno. The black smoke choking her. She backed up looking for a way in. Her Brother, Sister, Grandfather, Father, and Mother were inside. She wanted to help them escape.

Another scream...her Mother. Cut short by something else.

A dark shape burst from the side window where Wenona would sit and watch her Mother sew. The shape cleared the burning structure holding something in its giant jaws. It was a beast just like the ones from the clearing. Only this animal had searing red eyes. It dropped the object onto the ground and Wenona saw it was her Mother...

The giant wolf-like being looked over at Wenona as if wanting her to watch. It bent its muzzle down toward her mother. It growled and with one giant bite, crushed her Mother's skull.

Wenona ROARED.

She leaped at the animal but was brought to the ground like a pup. One hand-like paw pinned Wenona to the grass. Wenona struggled to no avail.

Wenona never forgot the slaughter of that night. It was forever seared into her nightmares.

Days later she turned back to her human form, along with several other PACK members. She was shocked to realize that all of them were female. The oldest woman was named TELBA. This was the one who killed her family. She seemed to be in charge of the rest. She told Wenona they would travel on a long journey to Paris. Wenona was still just a girl, and having no choice, she went along without complaint.

As they rode by wagon across the French countryside Wenona became excited, the horrors of the days receding from her memory as they crossed mile after mile. As she watched pasture after pasture roll by she wondered about her family. She believed they were her parents, but she looked much different than all of them. Telba told her that the PACK had been watching for many years and that in Paris Wenona would meet her real Mother.

Telba described Paris to her. In Paris, the assassination of King Henry threw the country into petty squabbles over power. Louis XIII was still too young to rule, so the Queen-Mother, Marie de Medici, ruled as regent in his place until the King came of age. Marie de Medici announced to the public that she would take in one orphan girl every year, provide an education for them, and give them a court position so her son the King could demonstrate his love for the French people. The Queen-Mother requested that Wenona be brought to her private audience chambers.

The Queen-Mother, MARIE DE MEDICI, rested on a divan reading a book of French poetry. She had the look of someone who was once attractive. Her harsh, lined features hinting at the beauty she once was. Every few seconds, she stared out at the royal courtyard. Her son, LOUIS XIII, fifteen, paraded in front of her. The boy trying on different outfits. He was small for his age and pale. Several Royal Courtiers fretted and fussed over him. She dismissed all of the courtiers with a wave of her hand. They scurried from the room. Louis watched his mother as Telba entered with Wenona.

The Queen-Mother held up a finger, silencing Louis before he spoke. She smiled and placed a hand on Wenona's head.

"You are safe here. Do not mourn little one. The carcass in Dole was not your true Mother. It was only keeping you safe until it was time for you to undergo the CHANGE. Now, you are one of the PACK for all time. Here, in this place, you will be given every advantage, every chance to learn and be educated about the World and how the humans operate in it. Know that I am your TRUE Mother Wenona! I waited until the time was right and now we can be together as was intended by Mother Earth and Sister Moon!"

Wenona was stunned.

The Queen-Mother herself was one of the PACK. Wenona stared at the boy-King standing near the dais. His head was lowered, eyes staring at the floor. Then Wenona understood. The Queen-Mother was the real power behind the throne. The boy Louis but a pawn in some larger scheme Wenona did not then understand.

For the next several years the Queen-Mother sheltered, cared for, and taught Wenona all she could until Louis came of age and into his own as King. His jealousy of Wenona infected him. Louis wished to rid the country of these demons in human clothing. His close advisor, Armand Jean Du Plessis, who would later be named Cardinal Richelieu by the King, conspired with Louis and the Queen-Mother was exiled to Compiegne in 1630. Richelieu realized that killing the Queen-Mother was too risky but exiling her sent a stronger message to others who would think to conspire against the young King and his powerful advisor.

Wenona accompanied the Queen-Mother during this exile which included a stay in Brussels in 1631 and Amsterdam in 1638. Their travels continued until the Queen-Mother was shot dead by a silver bullet in Cologne by an agent of Richelieu's. Assassinations continued in Dole and the surrounding areas as the King purged the country of the PACK and all enemies of the monarchy. The history texts did not recognize these events, but for Wenona they were real.

When the King and Bishop's forces began to exterminate the PACK, the sisters were driven underground or spread to different parts of Europe. Some, including Wenona, sailed to the New World where they were free to roam and be true to their savage nature. When the Queen-Mother was killed Wenona swore a blood-oath on humans.

An oath that lasted over four hundred years.

Wenona refocused on the hunt. They stopped under the dark bridge structure of the highway. The homeless population was thin tonight. Word of the mysterious and brutal deaths had spread. The ones who did brave the elements instead of the shelters huddled together in large groups, making them less desirable as there was strength in numbers. The PACK moved on from this area, slinking further inward toward downtown. Drawn by the city lights, but nervous about so many cars and traffic.

Wenona led the PACK through street after street, each time finding them empty of prey. She could feel them getting restless. They moved back to the park, defeated and angry. Upon entering the park, they observed two human females on the perimeter. One of them seemed familiar. Wenona moved closer to catch their scent.

PREDATOR

Dana and Robin wandered the edges of the woods. Both were dressed in jeans, jackets and boots instead of their normal on-duty slacks and jacket ensembles. Robin thought it was strange when Dana wanted to meet at Gevaudan Park, but hey, when the Boss calls, you go.

"Not to be a killjoy or anything Boss, but can you please remind me why we're out in the woods at night again? I didn't take you for the hunting kind."

Dana allowed herself a small grin.

"We're Murder Detail remember? All we do is hunt."

"Yeah…good point. But, that really doesn't answer my question. WHAT are we hunting?"

Dana was focused on a small section at the edge of the woods. It was the same spot where she found Elijah shooting off his gun that night, and where she had felt like someone, no, *something* was watching her.

"Ah-ha! This is what I wanted to show you!" Dana said.

She motioned Robin over. Dana was holding a piece of shiny, iron-gray fur in her gloved hand. Fur that looked the same as the fur at every crime scene they had been to in the last week.

Robin frowned. She was irritated.

"You gotta be fucking kidding. Same fur. This doesn't make sense. How does an animal…an *animal*…go from here to downtown, kill some homeless folks…then a taxi cab driver…then uptown INSIDE a condominium and attack an old lady…then back across town again to murder that Brian douche-bag dude? Even what you told me about what that Left-Foot dude said. A dog that stands up? What the fuck? I think he was high. I don't get it. AND, even IF I did believe this crock-of-dog-pucky horseshit…We would have to assume that it's…"

"…Intelligent. Yeah. I had trouble wrapping my head around that too Robin. By the way, you forgot about Abraham Moore's church. That is on the east side. This thing…or things…cover a LOT of ground. Miles. From what I remember about Gevaudan Park it is centrally located with lots of bike trails and feeders in and out that branch and connect to other hiking trails."

Robin was nodding her head. "That was part of that city-wide health initiative several years ago right? Trying to get people to do more outside activities. There was talk about building more hiking trails and parks."

Dana nodded. "Correct. So, follow my logic. If I were a predator and wanted to move around in my hunting ground without detection I would need an avenue that was mostly invisible to the casual observer..." Dana pointed at the highway overpass near them. Robin followed Dana's finger. She studied the overpass and then looked back at the woods.

"The highways are too high profile, so I would need multiple ways in and out like the connected hiking trails and easy prey like our homeless vics."

Robin followed this. "But, what's not tracking for me are the Moore attack and the condo attack. Like how the hell did some animal open doors, wait for their victims, and then attack? No dog in the world can do that! Not without human help that's for sure!"

"You're right. I don't think it's a dog Robin."

"Not a dog? Then what? A giant kitty? This is Hinkey and Fubar all rolled together in a big shit sandwich! None of this makes sense Dana! None of it!"

"I think we're dealing with something else. Something dangerous that understands how to hide and think like us. I watched a documentary once about wolves. They travel several hundred miles within a given territory tracking their prey. In the space of a day. That is a lot of moving around. The pattern of this predator seems similar." Dana said.

"Wolves? That can open doors? Hey Boss...I'm all for alternative theories and whatever, but nothing we have supports anything. We don't have any probable cause, no witnesses, and the only evidence besides body parts we have is this stupid-ass fur! Also, I know a little something about wolves and they avoid humans at all costs. They do not attack them and certainly don't attack them by opening doors and crap!"

CRACK!

The sound emanated from the woods as if a branch or tree limb had broken. The women paused. Their sense of danger on high alert.

"You heard that right?" Robin asked.

"Yeah. I did."

Dana had the same feeling as before when she was picking up Elijah's shell casings. The feeling of being watched. It was stronger than ever now. "You feel that?"

Robin nodded without looking at Dana. Her fingers caressing the handle of her service weapon.

"Yep. Fucking Fubar."

A growling noise in front of them...

"Step back...slow." Dana said.

She and Robin moved backward, one tentative step at a time. They could feel the energy of something dangerous near them. They continued to move back until they were about fifty yards away from the perimeter.

"I think I just peed myself!" Robin hissed through clenched teeth.

Dana was peering into the darkness of the woods. At first, she thought her over-taxed brain was playing tricks on her, then, she saw it.

A big, shaggy head staring back at her.

Blood-red eyes.

Savage eyes.

Intelligent eyes.

It was their *Predator*...

Robin saw it too now.

"What...the fuck...is that?" Robin asked.

It picked its big head up and HOWLED into the night sky! The sound shook them to their core. Robin closed her eyes. Dana kept staring. Two hunters locked in on each other.

Dana gripped the handle of her service weapon. With one thumb she undid the retention strap on her holster.

I see you.

A barking noise and the eyes were gone in a flash. The sense of danger evaporated as well.

Robin seemed to be in mild shock. "What...what just happened? I don't know what just happened. I think I'm shaking and I definitely peed myself. Yeah."

This was different than being confronted with criminal activity or human violence. Dana and Robin were trained for that. They understood that. What they encountered tonight was something else.

Something unexplainable to the logic centers of their human brains. But, in that primitive part, they felt and understood the FEAR.

"We just met our predator."

"Why did it growl at us?"

Dana looked over at Robin.

"It was a warning."

THE ORION COMPLICATION

Eli and Chapa drove to Cappy's Tactical Range on the far southside, past the San Antonio Police Academy off Highway Loop 410. It was their go-to shooting range and had been for years. The range sat on thirty private acres nestled behind rows of trees so it was invisible from the highway. Eli, Chapa, and other Operators and former Operators liked to hone their skills there, away from the prying eyes of civilians. Arnold "Cappy" Rogers was a former Vietnam-Era Green Beret who was well-respected in the Spec-Ops community. Everybody knew Cappy. And Cappy had one rule: *No Cowboy shit on his range!*

Cappy's Tactical was an outdoor range where you could shoot almost anything you wanted except explosives. AK-47s, Shotguns, Uzi submachine guns, etc. anything that an Operator would use they used here at Cappy's. He had designed several tactical courses for different weapons and scenarios. Cappy's even had a sniper's nest set up with targets marked out to seven-hundred yards. Chapa suggested that they brush up on their skills considering the mission they were about to undertake. Eli agreed. Firearm shooting is a perishable skill. If you don't use it, you lose it.

The brothers stood on the ready line holding MP-5 submachine guns. Each man wore double ear protection. Inner custom foam inserts and outer rubber and plastic full cover head gear similar to the kind airport workers wear on the tarmac to keep out the chaotic and deafening sounds.

Cappy's disembodied voice reached their ears over a speaker.

"Shooters! On the ready line! The line is hot!"

Eli looked over at his brother...they shared a quick smile. Then they began strafing the targets downrange with multiple rounds. Each man placing precise bullet holes in the target. Over and over until they had emptied all their magazines.

"Cease fire! Cease fire! Shooters, make your weapons safe!"

Eli and Chapa held their weapons at the ready position, waited a beat, then relaxed, put their weapons on safe. Eli pulled his hearing protection down.

"Let's reload and go to the shoot house." Eli said.

"Roger that bro'!"

Cappy joined them on the short walk over to the Shoot House. This plain, wood sided building housed life-size human targets made out of cardboard. Some were bad guys. Some civilians.

BAM!

Chap and Eli exploded through the door and began a live ammo exercise where they crisscrossed in different directions. Clearing rooms and covering each other. They moved in and out of fake bedrooms, kitchens, living rooms, and bathrooms like one hive-mind. Leap-frogging one another. Moving from a place of deep instinctual training woven into them from their years as active duty SEALS. The brothers cleared one room and moved to the next. Two dangerous forces of nature. When they were done in the Shoot House the score was: Bad guys ZERO, no civilian casualties...

Eli smiled at Chapa.

"Didn't lose a step." Eli said.

"Damn skippy! Let's test those sniper skills bro'! Loser buys first round." Chapa said.

Eli grinned. "You're on."

Chapa lay on his stomach on Sniper Hill with a .300 Win Mag, a semiautomatic rifle similar to the one used in Iraq by the late-Navy sniper Chris Kyle. Chapa used his come-ups (adjustments) to sight in on a target five-hundred yards away. Cappy and Eli sat on a pair of metal stools in the Range Instructor's tower which overlooked the course. Eli had a radio with him and looked through a pair of binoculars. Another radio tuned to the same frequency lay on the ground next to Chapa.

POW!

Eli's voice squawked from the radio next to Chapa. "Good hit! Dead center! Coming up!"

The men high-fived and changed positions. Chapa raced up the back side of the hill, joining Cappy in the tower. Eli aimed on a target. Checked his come-ups. Same distance away...

POW!

Chapa's voice squeaked through the radio. "Good hit…just left of center…clean kill…Not as good as mine though. I want Guiness, just thought I'd tell you!"

Eli smiled as Chapa's laughter sounded over the radio.

Eli and Chapa cleaned their weapons at the weapons bench. Cappy joined them. Even in his seventies Cappy was in fantastic shape. He was tall and lean, with hard muscles that spoke to a disciplined and regimented lifestyle. He rubbed his gray buzz cut, then took a sip of coffee.

"Damn good shooting gentlemen. Still have your skills."

"Thanks Cappy." Eli said.

"Yes sir! We appreciate you letting us come out today!" Chapa added.

"Good to have some real operators out here again! You know you're welcome anytime. By the way, think there's someone here to see you boys. Real stick-up-his-ass type. Out in the parking lot. Just wanted you to know! Take care!" Cappy said.

"See ya Cappy!" Chapa said.

Eli and Chapa walked to the parking lot. A man stood next to a rental car. He was parked near Eli's Jeep which told Eli that he might have known the license plate number. The man was in his late forties. White. Lean, very fit. Eyes intense and edged with…cruelty? He was dressed as a civilian, but it was obvious he was Military through and through. This was a man who was used to things being done…HIS way.

"Smells like Government to me." Chapa said.

"Think you're right." Eli replied.

"Captain Moore? Chief Petty Officer Chapa?" The man said as they approached.

They eyed him.

"That's correct. How can we help you?" Eli said.

"My name is Major Carl Orion. Used to be with Delta."

"Heard the name before sir." Chapa said.

"I work at the Pentagon now and I have been tasked with finding very highly qualified operators for an assignment. Because of the SEALS you were our first choice."

"Using independents who are retired means something major." Eli said.

"Yes it does Captain. You need to come to Washington with me asap so you can be properly briefed." Major Orion said.

This pissed Eli off. "Excuse me Major. We're civilians now. No one orders me. I gave my twenty years in service. Chapa too."

A slight twitch at the corner of Orion's mouth. He wasn't used to people NOT obeying him. He tried to change tactics.

"I am asking you to accompany me to Washington to see if you will be on our team."

Eli still wasn't convinced. It was going to take a lot more than some stiff like Orion to make him march back into taking-order-land again.

"What team would that be Major?" Eli asked.

"That's classified." Orion said.

Eli started putting his weapons and gear in the back of the Jeep. "Pass. Thanks though." Eli said as he closed the rear hatch.

Now it was Orion who was irritated. "Captain Moore I think you need to consider…"

Chapa interrupted. "Let's go check it out, Eli. No harm. We don't like it...we walk."

Part of Eli was annoyed with his brother that he would take this stranger's side. But, the Pentagon didn't send high-level Intel folks out to recruit former Operators every day. As much as he hated to admit it Orion might be right. It could be important. This thought and Eli's sense of duty tugged at him.

"How soon? Chapa and I are in the middle of something right now. Not sure when it'll be done." Eli asked.

The twitch in Orion's face again. "I can give you a week, but I assure you that this is pressing. A matter of National Security. Boarding passes have already been arranged. I'll be in touch. Good day."

Orion didn't wait for an answer.

What a dick. Eli thought.

Orion climbed back in the rental. He drove up next to Chapa and Eli and buzzed the window down. "I expect your full cooperation in this matter Captain. As you probably realize you and the Chief can still be recalled to active duty if necessary because of your Inactive Duty status. Just a reminder."

Orion attempted a smile. It was more like a parting of the lips and exposing of his teeth.

Eli did not smile back. "Sir." The implication: *Fuck you.*

Orion drove off.

"So?" Chapa asked.

"Smells Hinkey to me." Eli said.

Chapa patted his brother on the shoulder. "It must be something pretty darn important if they sent HIS ass all the way from D.C. I didn't think guys like that got out of their coffins until dusk, much less traveled. What do you think? Worth stopping the mission for now?"

Eli's face was grim. "Nope. We're still a go. We can deal with Orion after you and I handle what we need to handle."

"Roger that bro'." Chapa answered.

OPERATIONAL PLAN

That night Eli, Brick, and Chapa huddled around the small desk in the surplus store. A city map spread out in front of them.

"So, what's the plan?" Brick asked.

"We need to figure out how they move around." Eli answered.

Chapa grinned. "A little recon huh?"

Eli nodded. He pointed to red Xs on the map. Brick pawed at the top of the filing cabinet in the corner. He took down a small case, pulled out a pair of eyeglasses and put them on.

"Peepers ain't as good as they used to be Yella'."

Chapa smiled. Eli continued.

"I've plotted several trails in the park near major roadways. Each one of the

trails correspond to a system of drainage tunnels that lead right into the city. I think it's how they move back and forth. I want to check them all."

"Roger that." Chapa understood what was needed. This felt like being back in

their world and he loved it.

Brick pointed at one X in particular.

"What about this one? Looks like a main feed."

"That's my assessment as well. Chapa and I will concentrate our focus there.

How's your contact?"

The big gap-toothed smile gleamed at them.

"He'll be there. Man owes me a favor from way back. He knows I'm gonna

collect or take it out of his ass. Excuse me…I mean…The man owes me." Brick said.

This time Eli and Chapa burst out laughing. As strange as it might have been to civilians, for Operators, similar to police officers and other emergency service personnel who risked their lives, humor was part and parcel of dealing with violence. It served to release the tension, pre-mission, so that later, when the shit went down, it would be all business.

The men agreed to meet Brick at the store in six hours. This would give them time to plot the trails, check sight lines and vectors for the best shooting positions. Chapa and Eli walked each drainage section from their map. They shined their tactical flashlights around, looking for evidence of their prey. In the main connector Brick had pointed out Eli located canine footprints.

Their first victory.

It confirmed how the werewolves moved around. Now, it was a matter of picking the perfect ambush point. Chapa found some high ground near an intersection of walking trails not far from the main drainage sector. They figured that once the werewolves were clear of the drainage they might travel into the woods using the walking trails.

Brick met his weapons contact at a warehouse on the deep South side. The big man waited on the loading dock as a large delivery-style truck backed up. Brick's contact and the driver opened the rolling door on the truck, hauled out a long wooden crate, and pried it open. Inside, numerous military-issue weapons. Brick approved of the shipment, handed over a large envelop stuffed with money, and shook hands with his contact. The two men drove away. Brick used his hand-dolly to load the crate into his truck.

Hours later, the former soldiers met back in front of Brick's place.

"We're all good Yella." Brick said.

"Thanks Uncle Dan."

"What's up for tomorrow Eli?" Chapa asked.

"Rally back here and gear up." Eli said. He glanced at his Uncle. "You good for this Uncle Dan? We're going to need as much firepower as possible. Two of us might not be enough. Every hand on deck."

Brick grinned at him. "I got this Yella. I'm gon' be right next to you boys in the shit…Just like me and Abe in Nam!"

"Good. I knew I could count on you." Eli said.

"Sounds like a plan!" Chapa said.

"Uncle Dan, do you mind dropping Chapa off? I'm going to hang for a minute." Eli asked.

Chapa eyed his brother.

"You alright Bro'?"

"Yeah. Just need some alone time."

Brick swooped Chapa in a head-lock with one massive arm.

"I got him...Come on knuckle head! Night Yella."

"Goodnight Uncle Dan. See you later Chap."

Brick and Chapa climbed in Brick's truck. Eli watched the truck ease out of the parking lot and head toward the interstate. Eli jumped in his Jeep and headed back to Gevaudan Park. This time, Eli parked near the service road where passing cars wouldn't see his Jeep. He hiked from the Jeep into the woods near the spot where he encountered the werewolves. Eli opened the end of his tac light, switched the clear lens out for a red one, and melted into the woods SEAL-style. The moment Eli crossed the threshold his training took over.

Eli was back in SEAL-mode.

He was alert to every sound and movement. With each step he tested the ground without making any noise. To human ears Eli would be undetectable. But, a human was not the only one walking in the woods this night.

A sound on Eli's right made him spin, gun up and ready. A woman stood in front of him. Wenona. Eli lowered his weapon. She was dressed for the cold weather: jeans, boots, jacket. Eli noticed the streak of white in her dark mane.

"Lost in the woods are you?" Wenona asked.

"Uh...not really. Just looking for something."

Wenona smiled, exposing her white teeth. Eli had the vague sensation that she was a meat eater. Her teeth looked sharp.

"With a gun? Deer perhaps? Don't hunters use rifles to prey on that species?"

Something about her tone and accent made him uncomfortable.

"What are you doing out here?"

Wenona laughed.

"Me? Surviving. It is a curious thing about survival. All creatures have it in them to want to continue to exist. To live the way they have always lived. Would you not agree?" She said.

"Sure."

Eli maintained a discreet distance between them. While the woman didn't appear to be a threat, his senses told him she was. And, listening to his senses and instincts had kept him alive during many life and death encounters.

Wenona moved closer, trying to close the gap.

"In the end, I believe survival is relative. The deer wants to live but is killed by the wolf. The wolf wants to live but is killed by man. And man wants to live but is killed by other men."

"I agree." Eli said.

Eli took a shooter's stance now. Weapon held at the low ready.

"I have a question for you Hunter…"

"What?"

"…Which one of us will survive?"

"It's relative I suppose."

Wenona's eyes changed color right in front of him. They became red. Like the werewolf he shot the other night.

It's her!

Eli brought the Glock up and FIRED…

Wenona roared and leapt sideways, the bullet just missing her.

Eli tried to track her movement, but Wenona had already vanished into the darkness. Her voice rang out. It's rage and blood lust evident. "Your time is at an end Hunter. Soon I will come for you…as I did your Father."

"You BITCH!"

Eli fired off round after round into the woods in all directions, hoping just one would find its mark. Wenona's mocking laughter floated back to him.

NEXT STEPS

Once Brick dropped Chapa off, Brick drove back to the surplus store. He lumbered inside and sat at the tiny desk.

The SCOTCH…It called to him.

He opened the drawer and pulled it out, set it on the desk, label-side facing him. Brick stared into the amber fluid, fascinated by the tiny bubbles floating around.

One more drink won't hurt right? I'm smart enough to have one drink and that's it. Of course. It will steady my nerves for the fight ahead.

Brick stared at his hands. They were shaking. Brick was ready to fight, but also afraid. The fighting man he used to be was not the same man staring at the bottle in front of him. He was terrified of not being able to do what he used to do. Back in Vietnam Brick was one of the most feared and respected soldiers on both sides of the conflict.

On one dangerous night patrol he took on an entire squad of VC soldiers who had wandered into the perimeter of a camp he and his fellow soldiers had just left. Not wanting the VC to move toward his troops Brick rushed them. He charged the entire squad with only his sidearm and a knife, killing many of them and scaring off the rest. From that moment on his legend grew and Brick was known to the VC as the *Black Ghost.*

Could he be the Black Ghost again? Could he be fearless and run headlong into battle against this deadly enemy? Brick wanted to say yes to the questions he asked himself, but he wasn't sure. He was weak and stupid. He didn't even know if the Black Ghost still existed.

Brick unscrewed the cap, brought the bottle to his lips. A moment's hesitation, then Brick swallowed the rest of the Scotch all at once. Never pausing to take a breath. He drained the bottle as if it had never been full. He sat back. His stomach lurched. Brick could feel the liquor coming back up. He grabbed the small trash can next to the desk and vomited into it. When he started dry heaving, Brick noticed it…BLOOD.

Brick wiped his lips and stared at his fingers. They were stained with blood. He pushed back from the desk, bumping into the filing cabinet. A photograph fell down. Brick bent over to pick it up. He smiled at it. The boozy haze settling over him like a shroud. It was the exact same photograph that Abraham had in his office.

The brothers in Vietnam. Both young, wearing camouflage uniforms and holding M-16s. Writing at the bottom of the photo:

ABE & BRICK, Cambodia, '68.

Brick plopped back into the chair, his mind drifting back two or three years ago...

The morning was misty. The air cool. The brothers could hear small animals scurrying in the underbrush and birds taking flight overhead. The men walked through an extension of Gevaudan Park that was owned and operated by the State. In certain sections hunters were allowed to do their thing on a semi-annual basis. An impromptu hunting trip, and one of the last times they had been close to each other.

"When does the boy come home?" Brick asked.

"He didn't say. Or least he didn't tell me. Probably told his mother though."

Brick placed a hand on Abraham's shoulder. "Go easy on yourself Abe. That boy has a head like a rock sometimes. Kinda like us huh?"

Abraham laughed.

"Just like us. Ahhhh! Remember those summers when we would go with Daddy hunting in the woods? It was great! No one to worry about. Just us and the deer."

"I hear you big brother! I'm glad you called me. We haven't hung out in awhile and I..." Brick said.

Abraham stopped walking.

"Abe? Hey. What's the matter?"

Brick stopped next to his brother. He stared down at the ground. In front of them...a large, dead, WEREWOLF.

"Oh, Lordy...not here too."

Abraham stared at Brick with a look that seemed to say "I knew this would happen".

Brick pulled himself from the memory. The booze had kicked in with a vengeance now. He was supposed to do something with the boys. But, he couldn't remember what that was. It felt like something important...maybe...

I'll just rest my eyes a bit. Yeah. Just rest 'em up till I figure it out.

Brick tilted his head back and minutes later began snoring.

THE HARD WAY

Dana sat in her car watching as Alex pulled her Jag out of the condo parking garage. Dana settled in behind it, shifting into surveillance mode. She had no problems keeping the Jag in sight as it weaved in and out of rush hour traffic. After a twenty-minute drive Alex pulled into a large military-friendly bank off the frontage road of IH-10. Dana eased into the parking lot, near the back, and waited.

Alex was in and out in twenty minutes. Dana trailed the Jag by two car lengths as Alex drove to the Rim Shopping Center at the junction of I-10 and 1604. Dana dialed Robin as she waited for Alex.

"Yep." Robin sounded business-like this morning. No jokes. No laughter. Dana guessed that the encounter in the woods spooked her. Hell, it had spooked Dana too.

"Robin, I want you to go to Stone's bank and find out what she was doing there. I'll text you the address."

"Something fishy?"

"Not sure. She's at the Rim, shopping right now or wandering. Can't tell which."

"Okay, Boss."

Alex got back in the Jag. She drove downtown, ending up a few blocks away from her office. She parked at a meter on the curb and started walking. Dana parked her car near a "No Parking" sign. She placed an official police decal on the dashboard, locked up, and followed Alex on foot. Her phone rang.

"Talk to me, Robin."

"Seems like Ms. Stone closed all her accounts. Pulled everything. Strange huh?"

"Not for someone taking a trip…Keep digging. I'll let you know when she stops again"

"On it," Robin said.

Dana tailed Alex for the better part of four blocks. Alex wandered without a distinct sense of destination. She stopped to stare into a clothing store. Dana was a full block away, hidden by passing pedestrians, and shop signs. From Alex's view there was no way she could know that Dana was tailing her.

And, that's when Alex turned and stared right at her…

What the hell? There's NO way she can see me.

Alex picked up her pace and disappeared into an alley between buildings.

Dana sprinted to the alley, turned the corner…NOTHING. The alley was empty. Dana couldn't figure it out.

Where is she?

Dana started to leave the alley when she heard a rushing of air…Something dropping to the ground…a light IMPACT…

"Why are you following me, Detective?"

Dana spun around. Her eyes wide.

Alex stood there. Calm. But, a dangerous energy seemed to radiate off her. Dana kept distance between them.

"You seem to have a lot of secrets. What're you hiding?"

Alex's expression shifted. She faced away from Dana.

"Nothing you want to find out."

Dana reached in her coat pocket. Held up the evidence baggie with Alex's necklace inside.

"What about this? The initials, if I had to guess, would be Alexandra Stone. Correct?"

"It was a gift…from my Father. It's the only thing I have left of him. Can I have it back please?" Alex asked.

"Nope. Evidence. Found at a crime scene. Actually, a murder scene…Here, take a look at the victim."

Dana pulled up a photo of dead Brian on her phone.

"Brian Delaware, forty-five. Married with two kids. Whoever killed him was pissed! Tore his throat out. Whew!"

Alex averted her eyes from the photo.

"I need answers from you that don't include *I don't remember*". Dana said.

"So do I."

"Yeah, well that's not going to do it for me. We need to talk for real. At the station. I won't even put the cuffs on if you behave."

Alex was nervous.

"Look. I'm sorry I can't help you Detective Adams, but I HAVE to leave."

Alex took another step. Dana pulled her weapon and pointed it at Alex.

"STOP right there! We've just passed the easy way. Turn around."

Alex stared at Dana. A weird, tortured expression on her face.

"I'm sorry Detective."

Alex jumped at Dana before she could react, with animalistic grace. Alex landed on Dana's chest, smashing her back-first onto the ground. The impact taking all the wind out of her. Dana's Glock skittered several feet away from her. Alex picked Dana up by the neck, pinning her against the building wall. Dana struggled, trying to break Alex's grip.

Alex reached into Dana's coat pocket. She pulled out the evidence bag with her necklace inside. Her eyes were FERAL.

"Do NOT come looking for me."

Dana started to blackout when Alex let go. Dana slid to the ground, delirious from lack of oxygen. Alex stared down at her.

"I'm sorry."

Alex jogged from the alley…

Dana coughed a few times. She crawled over to her Glock, aimed in Alex's direction. But, Alex was already gone. Dana collapsed onto the dirty ground.

B.O.L.O.

Dana walked inside the house, dropped her gun and badge on the kitchen table, and shuffled to the sink. Pain radiated throughout her body from her meeting with the alley floor.

"You're late...*MOM.*"

Dana glanced over and realized Troy was sitting at the kitchen table, feet up on it, book in hand.

Well, at least she reads.

Dana didn't answer. She was just too tired to argue. She opened a cabinet and fished out a couple of pain meds from a prescription bottle that had expired. She tossed them back dry, then stuck her head under the faucet to chase them down with water.

"Why aren't you at school?" Dana said between gulps of water.

Troy smirked at her mother.

"Young lady, I asked you a question. Why the hell aren't you at school!"

"Please Dana. NOW you want to play supermom? Like you care."

"Don't you DARE talk to me like that!"

"Give it a rest...*MOM.*"

Before Dana could think about her reaction, she had crossed the kitchen and grabbed Troy on the arm...HARD. She shook her.

"Don't EVER talk to me like that! EVER!"

Dana felt her mind exploding. All the anger and loneliness boiling up. All she had ever done was for Troy. Damn near killing herself working crazy hours so Troy could have a good life. Everything she did was for Troy. EVERYTHING. *Why didn't this little shit appreciate it?*

"MOM!"

Dana realized she was still shaking Troy. She let go when she saw fear in Troy's eyes.

Oh my GOD....

"Troy...baby...I'm..."

Troy stood there, shaking. Dana couldn't tell if it was from fear or anger. Tears rolled down Troy's face.

"Baby..."

Troy ran from the room, leaving Dana standing in the middle of the kitchen. Dana heard a low rumbling noise. A car with a big engine block. It stopped outside the house.

"TROY!"

Dana ran outside just as Troy climbed into a dark colored, older model Trans Am. The car sped away too fast for Dana to see the license plate number. Dana was numb. Her mind a blank. She went back inside and dialed on her phone.

"This...is...uh...Detective Adams, badge number four, seven, nine, four. Place a B.O.L.O. on a dark blue or black Trans-Am. Nineteen-eighty-three or four model. Four passengers, teenagers...Thank you." B.O.L.O. stood for *Be on the Lookout For* in police terms.

She hung up.

The dam broke...Dana leaned against the kitchen sink and cried until her face hurt.

Troy sat in the Trans Am with three other teenagers. Nancy, Troy's best friend, was the kind of girl who thought she knew more about the world than she did. Nancy's boyfriend Lucky, the owner of the car, and at seventeen, the oldest one. Lucky was the class clown. Always on the edge of trouble. The last teenager was Jack. A quiet boy with smoldering looks, wild hair, and a hollow soul. Jack and Lucky sat in front. Troy and Nancy in the back seat.

"Did you guys get into it again?" Nancy asked.

Troy lit a cigarette and puffed on it. She coughed.

"Lucky, can you buy us something to drink? Maybe have your cousin hook it up?" Troy asked.

Nancy watched her friend's face. She knew Troy was hurting, but not how to help her.

"My parents suck too," Nancy whispered to her.

Troy rolled down the window. Tossed the cigarette out.

"At least you know who your Dad is." Troy said.

Nancy reached out, stopped. She didn't want to embarrass Troy. She fingered the charm bracelet she wore on her left wrist. It had been a gift from Troy for her fourteenth birthday. Troy wore one too on her right wrist. They considered themselves sisters-from-anybody else's-mother.

"Forget it." Troy said.

"Hey! I already got it hooked up." Lucky said with a smile.

He pulled a bottle of rum from underneath the seat. He took a swig, passed it to Jack who also drank from it. Jack sent it back to Troy. She guzzled it down. Rum splashed down her neck.

"Hey! Not too much!" Nancy said.

"Who cares?" Troy said. She leaned back in the seat and closed her eyes, letting the false warmth wash over her. Nancy wrestled the bottle from her and gave it back to Lucky.

Lucky glanced into the rear-view mirror at them.

"How 'bout we go to G-Park tonight?" Lucky said.

"Yeah! It'll be all dark and creepy and shit! We can stay till the sun comes up." Nancy said.

"Sure," Troy said.

"Works for me. Right Jack?" Lucky said.

"Screw it. Whatever." Jack said.

Nancy smiled. She leaned against Troy and whispered again.

"I think Jack likes you."

Troy didn't answer. She was already buzzing. In the front seat Lucky showed Jack two condoms he pulled from his pocket. Lucky smiled. Jack's eyes were empty. Lucky turned the music UP.

Troy let the music wash over her.

Music.

One of the only things that gave her comfort. In music Troy could escape the real world. She could escape Dana…her friends…school and the incessant pratter of people her age babbling on and on about mindless crap that didn't matter to her. She could escape the therapist Dana made her visit twice a month. She could escape ALL that crap. Just release and sink into a place where she never felt fear, or hurt, or anger, or sadness.

Troy wished she could listen to music all day, every day for the rest of her life. In music, Troy felt life. She felt whole. Once Troy left for college she would make it a standing rule that music would come first in her life, to the exclusion of all else. This is why she was going to travel far away from San Antonio. To Georgetown maybe, or Julliard. Somewhere, anywhere to start fresh.

Dana stared out the windows of the Murder Detail. The morning brought rain and clouds with it. The afternoon sky was now an ugly grey color that didn't help her mood. Robin walked in.

"Sup' Boss?"

She stood next to Dana and saw the red-rimmed eyes and bruise on the side of her face.

"What happened to you? You look like shit!"

"Slipped in the tub."

Robin didn't buy that.

"Ok...well, tell me about Stone then. Did you find anything else out? I was waiting for your call."

"Dead end. She window shopped for a bit, then headed into work. Stay on the financial angle though. Something may turn up. Oh...and I want to sit on Abraham's brother tonight. Meet me here and we'll take my car."

"No problem. Sure you don't want to talk?"

Dana faced Robin.

"Thanks anyway," Dana said.

Dana walked to her desk. She dialed Troy's number...No answer.

CALM BEFORE THE STORM

Eli and Chapa pulled into the surplus store parking lot that evening. Eli used a spare key Brick gave him to open up. Across the street, Dana and Robin sat in her sedan watching them. Robin leaned forward to get a better view.

"What's your boyfriend doing here?" Robin asked.

"Don't know. Maybe he just came to visit his uncle. By the way, he's not my boyfriend."

"Whatever you say," Robin said. She grinned.

"And, is it against the law for single Moms to date?" Dana asked.

"No. I'm glad you're dating, or whatever. If I'm lucky, maybe you'll get laid and stop giving me grief. You're always nicer after you've had sex." Robin said.

"Guess I haven't been nice in lately."

Rain poured down, obscuring the view from the windshield.

Raining on my life. How fitting...Oh no...here comes the pity party. Poor old Dana...Waa, Waa, Waa!

Her Dad's voice boomed at her...*Soldier on Dana. Get your mind right baby girl.*

"I don't think it would work anyway," Dana said.

"Why not?"

"You know me."

"Anything you want to talk about Boss?"

Robin didn't make a joke this time. She knew it must be serious if Dana was willing to share her feelings. This was not a normal occurrence.

"I just wish I had another chance. Not too many guys are up for the old instant family. Know what I mean?"

"Where's Troy tonight?"

"I don't know. She took off earlier. I've been trying to reach her all day. Maybe she's with Nancy."

"Isn't Nancy that wild girl? Thought you didn't like her? Bad influence and all."

"Troy's the wild one. Actually, I hope she's with Nancy."

Dana got quiet again. Robin changed the subject.

"The other night at the park. How did you know where to look?" Robin asked.

"I found more of that same fur there." Dana said.

"Wait? When? You were at G-Park? By yourself?"

"Uh...Elijah was there. Shooting his gun."

Robin stared at Dana like she had taken a long walk off a short pier.

"Let me get this straight Boss. Your boyfriend-not boyfriend was shooting his gun...in the Park...which is illegal by the way...and you don't think that's strange?

"He's grieving. The man just lost his father."

"Yeah...and I need to get laid! But, let's be real here. Didn't you think that was suspicious? Plus, you found some of that fur as well? I think your boy is tied up in this. I'm not sure how, but he is neck deep." Robin said.

Dana mulled this over.

She'd been so caught up with telling Elijah about Troy that any kind of connection didn't even occur to her. Abraham was killed by these animals. Elijah was in the parking shooting at something. Then running into their Predator. The connection was there. She just had to find the pieces and make them fit.

"So, why'd you want to sit on the big man here?" Robin asked.

"Brick Moore's had lots of brushes with law enforcement. He's ex-military and knows every low life pushing dope or guns. He might have caught wind of something, especially if it involves some kind of military." Dana said.

Robin smiled.

"And...you figure you can use his brother's death to guilt him into cooperating."

"That's the plan," Dana said.

"Teach me Obi-Wan...I am your Padawan!"

Dana side-eyed Robin.

"You are a mess, Robin."

"And you fucking love it," Robin said.

"You know what?"

"What?"

"The Moore attack, the taxi cab, and the married man at the Pearl, those attacks seemed personal somehow. As if our predator wanted to kill them as opposed to just eat them like the homeless victims. And, before you say it doesn't make any sense I want to point out what happened the other night." Dana said.

"Hey, I'm not complaining! But, my argument still stands. How do we build a PC case against an intelligent wolf-dog or whatever? No judge in the world is going to sign off on that, much less the Captain. Basically…we're screwed." Robin said.

Dana stared at her partner.

"We build as much of a case as we can with the evidence we DO have. But, as far as the Predator, we might be on our own because someone needs to stop it. I'm not going to let any more people die if I can help it. I'm telling you this because if things go sideways I don't want you getting shafted. Understand me Robin?"

"Yeah, I understand. But, understand this…I'm your partner, do or die. If you go, I go. Period."

"Thanks, Robin."

"You got it, Boss."

Dana smiled.

Alex stood in the middle of her living room staring at the boxes.

Why do I need boxes if I'm giving up my life?

Howling drifted to her ears from outside.

Alex walked out on the balcony. Another long howl in the distance rode the night. She stared down into the blackness of the park beyond the city lights.

She's calling to me.

I am being called to HUNT.

I don't want to go, but what choice do I have? Do I have any choice?

The life I used to know is gone…over. The only thing I have now is the PACK. They're my family now and I need to be one with them. They need me…and I need them.

A low growl filled her chest…

GEAR UP

Chap followed Eli into the tiny back office. They stopped when they spotted Brick. He was leaning back in his chair. Passed out. Eli walked over and picked up the bottle of Scotch on the desk. He tossed into the trash can. Chapa held his nose. The room reeked of vomit.

"Damn! Dude...Brick's seriously out of it."

Eli could see blood mixed with vomit in the trash can. He frowned.

Brick twitched in his sleep. He mouthed words Eli couldn't understand. Eli leaned over his uncle.

"Toss me that roll of paper towels Chap."

Chapa grabbed a roll of paper towels standing on a smaller table in the room. He threw it to Eli who tore one off and wiped Brick's mouth with it. Brick opened his eyes. He stared at Eli in a moment of clarity.

"The silver! Elijah, it's the SILVER!"

Brick leaned forward. His head about to hit the desk. Eli caught it and guided Brick's head onto the desk.

"Never knew he was an alcoholic," Chapa said.

"Me neither."

Chapa wandered over to the stairs and looked down. A large wooden crate sat at the foot of the stairs. Chapa went down and opened it. Inside were military-issue weapons. MP-4s, which were a better, more compact version of the old M-16. Uzi machine guns, AK-47s, and several kinds of pistols. Both semi-automatic and standard revolvers. Several ammunition cans were stacked next to the box.

"Eli! Check it out!"

Eli came down the stairs. He inspected the weapons along with Chapa. He noticed an object in the corner.

A RIFLE Case.

Eli placed it on the ground and unzipped it. Inside, a Haskins .50 caliber model Sniper Rifle. An older model designed to kill a man with one shot at a range of over half a mile. Chapa glanced over Eli's shoulder.

"Man, that is nice! Was it Pop's?"

Eli nodded. Chapa picked up one of the MP-4s. Pressed the bolt release. It made a sharp, satisfying clacking noise. Chapa smiled.

"How'd Brick get his hands on this stuff anyway?"

"Black market arms dealer Uncle Dan hooked up with during the War. They kept in contact over the years. Brick sells what he can, takes a percentage of the profits."

"Damn! How'd you find out?"

"Came by one time when I was on leave. You were on the pirate ops along the Ivory Coast remember?"

"Yeah."

"I walked in to surprise him. Boy, I surprised him all right. Caught them making a deal. Uncle Dan nearly crapped himself. I stuck my gun in the guy's mouth and told him if I ever saw him around my uncle again I'd kill him. Brick was so worried about upsetting me. He started begging me to forgive him and promised me that he would quit."

"Why didn't you tell me bro'?"

"I know how much you love him. Guess I didn't want to tarnish his image to you. Stupid right?"

Chapa patted his brother on the back.

"Trying to protect your little brother huh? I feel you. Well! I'm just glad he still knew the guy. This is exactly what we need!"

"Let's put this stuff in the Jeep. I'm ready to go hunting."

"Roger that Eli."

Eli walked back up to Brick's office. He stared at his Uncle. "Damnit, we needed you."

Chapa came over. "Brick is human. We make mistakes…we screw up. That's what we do. And you know what Eli? It's okay. Cut him some slack. His heart's in the right place."

Eli's thoughts turned to Dana. She had lied to him for a long time about Troy. Never once giving him the choice to be involved in her life the way he would have liked. It sucked. Part of him wasn't sure he could ever forgive her for it. But, Chapa was right. People screw up. The last words he had with Abraham weren't filled with love or kindness and he would have to live with that. Knowing he made a choice to argue with his Father instead of show love, regardless of how Abraham's words cut him. Sometimes we just have to cut the people in our life some slack or we can't move on he thought.

These thoughts weighed on him, but he and Chapa had a mission to complete. The men left Brick snoring away on his desk. They turned off the lights and left the surplus store.

Dana and Robin watched as Eli and Chapa exited the store. They carried several large military duffel bags. They climbed in Eli's Jeep and drove off.

"Want to follow them?"

"They're not suspects," Dana said.

"It just seems kind of strange to me. Loading his Jeep in the middle of the night. I could'a swore I saw a rifle case. And why are they dressed in black fatigues? Tell me that."

"Maybe they're going hunting."

"This late at night? Hey Boss…you uh…hitting the sauce? You know, tipping a few back before work? I mean, I won't tell if you won't but you just seem off…AND, I still think this whole thing is a goat rope."

"Come on. Let's go talk to the big man." Dana said.

They climbed from the sedan and walked across the street to the surplus store.

"Tell me something Boss…how come you don't know anything about this guy Brick if he's Navy-guy's uncle?"

"Eli never talked about his family much. Just his Mom and Chapa. They're the only ones…I don't know."

"Hinkey."

"What?" Dana asked.

"It's Hinkey I'm telling you." Robin said.

Dana was about to knock on the door.

"What does that even mean?"

"I don't know…weird…strange…spooky…Basically whatever the hell you want it to mean."

"Don't use words around me I don't know Law School."

"Old lady." Robin grinned at Dana.

Dana pounded the door.

"Police! Open up, Mr. Moore!"

Robin eased to the other side of the doorway, while keeping an eye on the windows. Dana rapped on the door again.

"Police!"

She scanned the parking lot. Brick's truck was the only vehicle around.

"That Moore's?" Dana asked.

Robin pulled out her notebook. Checked a page.

"Yep. That's it."

"Well, he must be inside. Either sleeping or hiding out."

"Think he knows we're looking at him for something?" Robin asked.

"Doubt it. Come on. I don't want to waste time here. He lives and works here. He's not going anywhere."

"You're the Boss, Boss!"

Robin followed Dana back to the sedan.

While Eli drove, Chapa reached back and pulled out a smaller box from the back seat. It was wood grain with a high gloss finish. He opened it. The box was filled…with SILVER BULLETS for their Glocks. He climbed in the back seat and checked the ammo cans. They also contained various silver calibers for all the weapons they had.

"Oh, man! Now I really do feel like I'm in a werewolf movie! It's SILVER Eli! How did Brick get hold of this? And, why silver?"

"Your guess is as good as mine. I get the feeling that he's been preparing for something like this for quite some time. Hey…remember Panama?"

"How could I forget?"

"We hit that animal with everything we had, short of explosives. It was hurt but didn't die. Nothing happened until I stabbed it with my knife…The blade was made of silver. I didn't make the connection until just now. Silver must affect their nervous system somehow. Break it down. It's lethal to them for whatever reason."

"Which gives us the edge," Chapa said.

"Exactly."

Chapa put the box back, stared out the window. He could see G-Park coming up on their right.

"How do you know they'll still be in the park?"

"They're animals, Chapa. They need the cover of the forest, or the closest thing they can get to it"

"Roger that bro…roger that."

Eli parked the Jeep at an abandoned service station a brief walk to G-Park, in the rear of the building. They got out and stood next to it putting their gear on. Semiautomatics secured in tactical holsters strapped to their thighs. PAS-7 infrared viewing devices that worked off body heat. MP-4 submachine guns. Chapa had a riot shotgun slung over his back. Eli carried Abraham's .50 caliber sniper rifle, and a CAR-15 machine gun with laser sighting. The men loaded the weapons with the silver bullets.

The men wiped black and green grease paint on their faces, giving them a bizarre, ghost-like appearance. Eli tied a black bandana around his head. Chapa wore a black NAVY baseball cap turned backwards. The weapons they carried were black, blending with their black fatigues.

Eli and Chapa stared at each other.

A moment passed between them that only they as *OPERATORS* understood. On every mission they knew DEATH waited just around the corner. Every time they slipped in the water, dropped into a hot zone, or crawled on their bellies toward a hostile target. Death walked right next to them.

DEATH and FEAR.

But, both men knew they would face it together. Each was willing to lay down their life for the other without thinking. It was the SEAL way. It was THEIR way. This mission was personal now.

The brothers had faced danger the summer of the photograph from Ellen's house too. Chapa had bucked up to a high school boy named Drake known for terrorizing middle school kids. Drake robbed them, roughed them up, and humiliated them whenever he got a chance. That summer Drake cornered Chapa alone while Chapa was waiting on Eli to show up at the pond. When Drake arrived with his entourage of snaky-ass friends Chapa went on high alert.

Drake tried to intimidate Chapa but miscalculated with the former foster care warrior. Chapa punched Drake in the mouth and squared off with the other three goons. That was when it got dangerous...Drake pulled a switchblade on Chapa.

"What's up Bitch? Gonna cut your ass now!" Drake said.

"Shut up pendejo'! Don't talk about it just do it!" Chapa said.

He was a cocky little shit, smaller than most kids his age at the time, but with the heart of a lion. Drake stalked over. Chapa backed up just out of slicing range. He'd seen enough knife fights as a kid to understand the dangers. Drake edged closer. Just as the older boy lunged a shape came flying out of the shadows...ELI.

Eli tackled Drake, sending the two of them plowing into the muddy shore of the pond. Drake's buddies ran over to mess with Eli, but Chapa punched one of them. They scattered like roaches, running for the street while Eli proceeded to beat the ever-lovin' shit out of the middle school bully. Chapa threw the finger at the fleeing boys and went over to help his brother.

It was a BAD day for Drake...

Soon after, attacks on middle school boys stopped. Act of GOD everyone in middle school thought. When the Moore Boys heard this they just smiled at each other and bumped forearms together.

Eli and Chapa bumped forearms together like they had since they were boys. Eli pulled Abraham's dog tags out from under his shirt. Kissed them. Stuffed them back inside. It was time. "Let's get some payback." Eli said. Chapa nodded. "Fuckin' A. I got your Six bro."

PART III

FULL MOON

VIOLENCE OF ACTION

Eli and Chapa established a secure perimeter on the small slope they scouted a day earlier. They laid down in a thicket of shrubs and spread camouflage netting over the top. They checked their ammo once more. Chapa took out the PAS-7 infrared viewing device from his pants pocket. It was about the size of a pair of binoculars. He peered through the PAS-7 at a small trail about six hundred yards away.

"Uh, Eli..."

Eli checked the sights on the sniper rifle. He answered without looking at Chapa.

"Yeah."

Chapa tapped him on the shoulder, causing Eli to stop what he is doing. Chapa continued to look.

"Oh my GOD..." Chapa whispered.

Eli snatched the PAS-7 from Chapa and looked through it. He held his breath as he watched SIX werewolves creep from the shadows and sit in a circle.

Judgment time.

Alex was a werewolf again. She and Wenona were with four other PACK members:

A big SILVER and BLACK animal. The fur on its hide was spikey.

A DARK BROWN one with ONE EAR.

THREE-TOES, a smaller werewolf, reddish-brown in color, with three toes instead of five, on its right paw, and

Another one with a smooth LIGHT BLACK coat.

Alex trotted up to Wenona. dipping her head just enough to acknowledge the huge werewolf's presence. Wenona crouched down into the grass and waited. The other PACK members did the same. Alex crouched next to Wenona. She stared in the direction of several humans.

188

Troy, Nancy, Jack, and Lucky walked together in a group on the trail. They laughed and smoked cigarettes, oblivious to the danger a few hundred feet away. Wenona raised herself up off her belly and growled at the PACK members. She nodded her shaggy head at Alex.

The werewolves waited for their prey...

Chapa set up the tripod while Eli dialed the settings for the telescope sight. Chapa edged closer to Eli so he could effectively spot the targets for him. Eli stared through the scope, aiming the cross-hairs at the animals in the circle. They appeared fuzzy because he didn't have the proper range yet. A few more clicks and the animals' images jumped into view with a frightening clarity. He moved the sights of the weapon over each animal, stopping on the big, black one.

"There she is." Eli whispered.

Chapa grabbed another PAS-7 from his backpack. Turned it on. He stared at the werewolves.

"She? Why she?"

Eli kept his focus on the werewolves. Chapa held a range finder in his hand. He squinted at the small device to see how many meters to the target.

"They're all female."

"How do you know that?" Chapa asked.

"Just a feeling. Also, remember what Brick said the other night? When he talked about the big werewolf with red eyes and a slash of white on its head he said he saw *HER* last night. Not *IT*."

Chapa pondered this as he stared through the PAS-7.

"Hey, you see this?"

Eli didn't respond. He saw them. Civilians. Teenagers walking into a shit storm. From their position though, he and Chapa couldn't see Troy. She was hidden behind the others as they walked.

"Spot me Chapa."

Chapa concentrated on the range finder and checked the come ups.

"Range to target, five-seven-eight meters, wind coming from the northeast, two knots. Good to go."

Eli slowed his breathing to compensate for the upcoming trigger pull. His index finger caressing the trigger...

Nancy and Lucky lagged almost a hundred yards or so behind Troy and Jack. Troy turned to check on her friend. Nancy smiled.

"Go on, we'll catch up." Nancy said.

"Don't find us! We'll find you!" Lucky said.

Nancy hit Lucky on the arm with a playful tap. He leaned in and sucked on her neck like there was no tomorrow. Jack and Troy continued to walk up the trail.

Wenona turned to the other werewolves. She leapt from the bushes. Raced toward the teenagers...

Eli squeezed the shot off a second after Wenona broke cover. The shot passed the group of animals and hit a tree. Alex was still rooted to the ground watching Wenona run at the humans. She heard something whiz by her head. Her animal instincts took over. She hurtled after Wenona. Now, the other werewolves ran from the bushes toward the young people.

Missed! Eli thought.

Chapa was staring at the werewolves loping away. Eli glanced downrange. He SAW Troy walk deeper into the park.

Oh no...NO!

Chapa seemed to be in a state of shock after seeing the werewolves in the flesh.

Chapa dropped the range finder. "Did you see how fast they are?" Chapa asked.

"CHAPA! RANGE ME! NOW!"

Chapa scrambled to find the range finder on the ground. Eli took matters into his own hands and tracked ahead with the sniper rifle. He fired two shots, one after another. The shots struck the silver and black werewolf in the chest and neck. It howled once. Fell to the ground. It lay there bleeding. Two more bullets ripped into the werewolf's hide, showering Alex in blood and muscle tissue. It gasped and died.

Wenona pounced on the first teenager before she was aware of anything. Nancy tried to scream. She began to choke on her own blood as the werewolf sank her canines into Nancy's jugular vein. Wenona dragged the girl's body into the underbrush. Lucky was terrified. He screamed and started running the other way. The dark brown werewolf and Three-Toes chased Lucky down the walking trail.

Eli fired three more shots, missing as the beasts ran out of sight. He moved the rifle back toward the kill site. He spotted the grey werewolf leaning over the carcass of the one he killed. Wenona was nowhere to be found. Eli sprang up., ripping the netting off their hiding spot.

"I'm going after those two! You get the grey one!"

"I'm on it!" Chapa said.

Eli tore down the slope in the direction of the teenagers. Chapa picked up his MP-4 and sprinted in Alex's direction. Alex heard Chapa running at her before she could see him. She watched the body of her dead comrade as it transformed into a woman's body. An old woman.

"Don't you fuckin' move!"

Alex snapped her head up at the sound of his voice. Chapa's MP-4 was fitted with a muzzle suppressor. He fired three rounds at Alex. One striking the carcass, and two missing her head by inches as Alex dashed into the bushes. Chapa ejected the empty clip. Rammed another home on his weapon.

An ear-splitting roar sounded behind him.

Chapa whirled around just in time to avoid having his head separated from his shoulders. The light black werewolf, bounded at him from the shadows. Chapa ducked a second before she had time to strike at him with her sharp claws. The werewolf sailed over him, ending up on the other side of the trail. She landed on her feet like a cat.

The werewolf snarled at Chapa. Chapa pointed his automatic, aiming at her head.

"You don't even know what time it is do you?"

She bared her fangs, preparing to leap...

Chap felt the surge of adrenaline he always experienced in the thick of battle. Part fear, part excitement. Hard to quantify, but present. He smelled the crisp night air and noted the crystalline breath leaving his mouth and nose. The battle thrilled Chapa and it was where he was most himself. Chapa understood that and accepted it.

Other men might shy away from enjoying the chaos and violence of war, but not him. He thrived in this kind of environment. Lived for it.

In some sense…he *loved* it.

Chapa pulled the trigger. BAM! The werewolf's head snapped back. She yelped, falling on her back. One kick at the air and she was gone. Chapa looked down at the two werewolves laying on the ground. Chapa covered his nose as a terrible smell assaulted his senses. His eyes watered. The toe of his boot touched something in the dirt. He picked it up. Nancy's charm bracelet. Chapa shook his head. Put the bracelet in a pocket. He spit on both corpses, and then dashed up the trail to find Eli.

Troy and Jack made-out near an old tree stump. Jack tried feeling Troy up, but she kept him at bay. The faint sounds of screaming reached her ears.

"Stop. Wait, did you hear anything?" She asked.

Jack was only thinking about one thing.

"Nope."

She pushed him off. Jack did not like this. His bearing more aggressive.

"I know I heard something. Stop it." Troy said.

"What did you think was gonna' happen when we came out here? Now quit messin' around and give me some!" Jack said.

Troy saw the expression on his face and realized she was in trouble.

"No! Leave me alone!"

She kneed Jack in the groin, causing him to double over. Then she slammed a hard elbow into the side of his nose just like Dana had taught her. Blood sprayed onto the grass. Jack fell to one knee. His face was a mask of rage, and his words were slurred from the booze and blood in his nose.

"Stupid bitch…I'm dunna' gonna kick your a…"

Troy held her hands up in fighter mode, preparing to launch a kick into Jack's stupid face when his threat was cut short by the werewolf that crashed through the trees, grabbed his neck, and dragged him to the ground. The boy didn't even have time to blink.

Troy screamed. Her survival instincts kicked in and she raced over to the tree stump and ducked down behind it. On the other side, the werewolf savored the still-pulsing meal.

Eli stopped on the trail when he found the bloody remains of a teenage boy on the ground in front of him. He grimaced.

Lucky wasn't so lucky anymore...

Eli dropped to a squatting position when he heard a noise. Panting sounds, like animal breathing, came from a twist in the trail ahead. He switched the laser sighting on for his CAR-15 machine gun. It was a shorter more compact version of the MP-4.

Eli HATED the feeling welling up inside of him.

Fear.

But, not fear of being killed or maimed, but fear of who he had to become to deal out violence. Even after a career of dispensing out violence Eli had never really gotten used to it. Was he good at it? Yes? Did he thrive on it? No. Leaving the SEALS had been the worst/best decision of his life. Leaving his team and the bonds he had forged with those men was the worst. Not having the camaraderie anymore. The best was leaving all the violence and aggression behind. Allowing himself to have another life. Maybe an academic life. A family life.

And yet...here he was...using the tools of violence once again.

It made him sad.

Click.

Eli turned off his feelings. No time for that.

The former SEAL melted into the woods...

Through a small gap in the bushes, Eli stared at the two werewolves. One devouring Jack's body in large gulps. The other werewolf sniffing the grass near the entrance of the park, as if searching for something.

She's looking for TROY.

Eli stepped from the shadows like an angel of vengeance.

He stood twenty feet away. Three-Toes looked up at him. She growled, baring her fangs. Eli stared back without a trace of fear.

The three-toed werewolf stood up. Walked over to him. Eli aimed the laser sight at its chest. Pulled the trigger in a quick three round burst.

The bullets punched into the werewolf's midsection and exploded out its back. It was blown five feet away, landing on its side. Three-Toes convulsed once and died. The reddish-brown werewolf watched its companion die. It raced at Eli, howling in rage. Eli dropped the sniper rifle on the ground in front of him. He pulled his silver-bladed knife, slashing the animal while rolling out of harm's way. She dropped to the ground, weak from blood loss, shuddered, and died.

Eli heard a sound coming from behind the tree stump. He picked up the sniper rifle and swiveled it in the direction of the noise. He sliced the pie as he approached. Moving one step at a time sideways, in order for him to see what was there before he exposed too much of his position.

Eli lowered the rifle. He knelt down next to the tree stump.

"Hey, Troy…it's me. Come on. You're safe."

Eli stared at Troy's terror-stricken face inside the tree stump. A few seconds later Chapa ran up just as Eli was helping Troy out of the tree stump. The girl was shaking and crying. Eli put his arm around her shoulders. Troy slumped against him.

"Is it really you Elijah?" She asked.

Her eyes were unfocused. She was in shock.

"Yeah, it's me kiddo. Are you hurt?"

Troy shook her head "No". Eli checked Troy for visible injuries as he talked. Her eyes rolled back in her head. Troy slipped into unconsciousness.

"Who's this?" Chapa asked.

"My daughter." Eli said.

Chapa's eyes widened. Eli gave him the "not-right-now" look.

"Anyone else make it?"

Chapa didn't answer, telling Eli what he needed to know.

"I confirm four kills on the targets, two escaped."

Chapa showed Eli the bracelet.

"I found this. Must have been one of the kids."

"Don't worry, we'll get the rest." Chapa said.

"Yeah. We will."

"Hey bro'…I'm sorry…Back there with the range finder…you know that's not like me. It's not normal." Chapa said. Eli could tell

194

Chapa was embarrassed. Eli stared at his brother. Nodded his understanding.

"Nothing about this is normal Chap. Help me get her to the Jeep."

Eli kissed Troy on the forehead.

"C'mon baby, Daddy's got you."

Eli and Chapa rode in silence. Neither man wanted to speak about what happened in the park. They had seen death before, but the manner in which the kids had been killed was just awful. The more Eli thought about it, the angrier he got. These animals...these monsters needed to be swept from the face of the Earth. Exterminated. He knew that some science geek somewhere would want to study them instead of wipe them out. But, he was a SEAL, or used to be, and when you engaged the enemy you put them down. Not to be studied and prodded or used for research.

NO!

Put down, never to get back up again. If the brothers had anything to say about it, they would ensure that happened. Down. End of story. Eli would never let that happen. No one was going to study the monsters who killed his men.

Not on my watch.

Troy stirred in the back. Eli glanced back and saw her staring at him. Her eyes red-rimmed.

"Hey. How you feeling?" Eli asked.

"Is she dead?" Troy asked.

Chapa stared over at Eli. The pause told Troy what she needed to know. She began crying.

"I'm sorry baby. We tried to save them." Eli said.

Chapa took Nancy's bracelet from his pocket. He tapped Troy on the knee and handed it to her. "I'm really sorry Mija'." Chapa said.

"What are they? Those things. Wolves?" Troy asked.

Eli met her eyes through the rear-view mirror. "Not exactly. They are...something else. But I promise you, I will never let them hurt you. NEVER. Do you understand me Troy?"

Troy shook her head YES. Chapa turned around again. She stared at Chapa. He seemed familiar, but she couldn't place from where. "Who are you?" She asked.

"Chapa...Eli's brother." Chapa said.

"The crazy one?" Troy asked.

"Yeah, I guess so."

Troy was silent. Eli and Chapa didn't want to traumatize her any further by asking a million questions. They understood that when civilians were subjected to violence they processed it in different ways.

All in all, Troy seemed more together than the situation dictated.

Damn...she's a tough young lady. My daughter. Maybe like Father/Daughter.

"How come you guys were in the park?" Troy asked them.

Chapa spoke up. "Eli and I were tracking them. We plotted an ambush. Got four of them."

"Wow. Four? That's crazy." She said.

"Troy, I'm going to share confidential, top-secret information with you because I think you can handle it, and I know I can trust you." Eli said.

Troy sat up straight in her seat to listen.

"One of these things attacked Chapa and I last year on a mission. We killed it, but not before it killed some of my men. It was fast, and deadly, but we killed it. So, I'm telling you that these things CAN be killed. And, if anybody can do it we can. Do you believe that?"

Troy considered this. She liked that Eli had trusted her enough to tell her this information. It made her feel *Special. Important.*

"I believe you." Troy said.

"Good." Eli said.

"Where are we going?"

"To my Uncle Dan's place. He knows too and can help us."

"Okay Elijah." Troy settled back into the seat. She pulled her headphones out, found her phone was still working, and selected her favorite song from her playlist.

Chapa nudged Eli in the front seat.

"She's a tough kid."

"I know." Eli smiled.

ASSAULT

Before the hunt, when both women were still human, they sat in the Sanctuary, dressed in shirts, winter coats, jeans, and boots. If someone happened upon them they would have seemed just like two modern women almost anywhere in the world. Except, these two women were not ordinary in any way.

Wenona had lit a small fire in the middle of a pile of cinder blocks. A three-foot opening in the top of the Sanctuary roof vented the smoke to the outside. The amount of smoke so small that vehicles miles away on the highway overpass would not notice it. Wenona stared at Alex, who in turn, stared at her feet as if she wanted them to carry her far away from the Sanctuary.

"Alexandra listen to me. Tonight, when we encounter the prey. Do NOT hesitate. This could get the PACK killed. Do you understand?

"I understand." Alex said it more to herself.

"Repeat this…No hesitation…no mercy…no quarter." Wenona said.

"No hesitation…no mercy…no quarter." Alex repeated back to Wenona.

No hesitation…No mercy…No quarter.
No hesitation.
No mercy.
No quarter.

"Wenona, why do you want these humans dead?" Alex asked.

Wenona did not speak for several moments. When she began Alex could read the weary lines of hundreds of years of suffering and being hunted on the older woman's face. Wenona had been through more than Alex would ever know and lost more than Alex would ever lose. At this moment Alex felt a great wave of compassion for Wenona. She reached over and grabbed Wenona's hand. Wenona smiled at Alex and placed her hand on top of Alex's.

"After the extermination of most of my kind in France, years later a man named *Strapp* led human hunters into the underground lair of the PACK."

The mention of Wystan's great-grandfather caused Alex to shake. She managed to control her muscles enough so Wenona would not see that her words disturbed Alex. It wouldn't have mattered anyway. Wenona was lost in her thoughts as she stared into the depths of the burning fire in front of them.

"The men burned it, destroying my remaining sisters. So, I and some others fled to the New World on a boat, where we lived as scavengers. Fighting for scraps with other large predators like the bear, wolf, and mountain lion. Living a loathsome existence. In the Old World we were Queens! Now, in the New one, we were nothing but shadows of our former selves. A mockery of a once-proud and superior race. As the villages and settlements evolved into towns and cities we attempted to continue our ways…hunting as of old…But, alas…it was not to be. The old days were long gone. Replaced by this modern era.

"The years passed and I received word from abroad that another Queen Mother was killed in an ancient land known as Vietnam. It was US soldiers, two brothers, who performed the deed. Decades later my beloved Telba was destroyed down in Panama by another group of soldiers. My sister Caynin witnessed the attack by the American soldiers and recounted it for me:

Minutes after SEAL Team Two egressed the clearing, Security personnel from General Mendez's compound arrived. Once on scene they tried to make sense of the apparent fire fight.

"Hefe!"

One of the junior men called the commander over. He pointed at the body on the grassy jungle floor. The men stared. Transfixed by the sight. Some crossed themselves. Others stared wide-eyed. Others glanced at the jungle itself as it something was waiting to pounce on them.

On the grass lay the body of a naked woman. Her body ravaged by multiple bullet holes.

Deep in the jungle, past the vision of the men, Caynin crouched down watching. Upon seeing the body of Queen Mother Telba Caynin let out a plaintive wail. A cry of mourning and anguish that whispered into the night and trailed away like a phantom. She continued to watch as the security personnel fled the area. When they were gone she devoured the great Queen Mother Telba's remains as required according to custom.

"I fell into a frenzy upon hearing this dreadful news about my Telba. It served to reaffirm the blood oath I swore when the Queen Mother in France was killed. And, on that day Alexandra, I vowed to wipe the soldiers spawn from the face of Mother Earth." Wenona said.

These revelations were shocking for Alex as she experienced history doubling onto itself, leaving them at this particular moment in time.

"Wenona, may I ask you a question?"

"Anything young one," Wenona answered.

"Do you know where I come from? I mean…who my parents are? I know it's a silly question, but since I'm part of the PACK now, and you seem to know so much about this all. I just thought you might know." Alex said.

Wenona stared at Alex. When she did Alex had the feeling of warmth. Of belonging. Wenona reached over and held Alex's hand.

"Parents…such a crude term for how legacy is passed down in the PACK. We are a society of Mothers and Daughters. It has always been such and will always be so."

"Then how do we…reproduce?" Alex asked.

"When a PACK member has come to full womanhood she mates with a human male and procreates. This male is selected with care and watched to ensure the bloodline is pure and untainted. Then, the PACK member mates in the human manner. She is guided by the PACK to the Place of Waiting for the allotted time until the glorious Birthing commences. She is protected and soothed by the Dula Mothers. They guide the pup into this World."

Alex didn't want to ask, but she had too.

"What about the man? What happens to him?"

Wenona gave her a look that spoke of distaste.

"The selected one is killed by one of the Hunters. Once this is done the PACK communes with Mother Earth and Sister Moon, celebrating the arrival of the new member. It is a joyous and wonderful event! The only sadness that occurs is that the PACK is only gifted with one pup every twenty seasons."

Alex started weeping. Wenona squeezed her hand. "Why do you cry little one? This is a beautiful event!"

"My Father…this means my Father is…dead."

Now, it was Wenona who seemed just the slightest bit sad.

"The selected male who conceived you…he…" She stopped. Wenona stood and pulled Alex up by the shoulders. "No! We will not dwell on the past! Our time is NOW! Gaze upon me…"

Alex wiped her eyes. She stared at Wenona.

"…Gaze upon your TRUE Mother Alexandra…I have watched and waited for you. Waited until the Change took hold. That is why it took so long to come to you! I am sorry if I caused you pain over the years…if you thought you were alone in this world! But…you are NOT alone any longer! Now that you are among us I will teach you the wisdom of our kind! I will share everything I know so that one day YOU will take the mantle of Queen Mother for our PACK! This…will be my gift to you Alexandra. Sweet daughter."

Alex couldn't believe it…and yet…she knew with a certainty. She FELT it in her bones…in her soul…She had found her MOTHER at last.

The question of what Elijah and Chapa were up to nagged at Dana.

Why were they moving all that equipment into the Jeep at night? Why were they dressed like that?

Dana slowed the car, checking oncoming traffic, then pulled a U-turn in the street. She accelerated back in the direction of Brick's surplus store.

"Whoa! What gives?"

"We're going back to Brick's. I DO want to know what the heck they were up to." Dana said.

Robin grinned. "Now that is what I'm talking about! Let's go balls-deep on this Brick guy. See what he coughs up!"

Dana side-eyed Robin. "That mouth. Geez!"

Robin grinned. "And again…you fucking love it."

The two detectives crept up to the door. Dana peered through the windows, but massive amounts of dirt and grime obstructed her view. She tried the knob.

"We can't do that Boss. No PC."

"Sssh. I'm not looking for evidence. I just want to talk. Besides, he's on probation." Dana said.

"Forgot about that," Robin said.

Dana pushed the door open and flashed Robin a smile. They entered the surplus. As Dana and Robin made their way through the store, a shadow watched them from behind a shelf. Dana looked into the back room. The desk was empty.

"Nobody home," Robin whispered. She turned around and stared into the barrel of a shotgun. Brick glared at them. Dana whipped her gun from the holster, drawing on the big man.

"I sho' hope you guys ain't sellin' nothin'."

"Drop it! Police!"

Brick regarded her like a tick on a dog's back. His eyes bloodshot.

Damn it! He's one big boy! Dana thought.

"I don't believe I'll do that just yet. Mind tellin' me what you folks are doin' in MY home?"

Dana lowered and holstered her weapon. Brick continued to hold the shotgun on Robin.

"Look Mr. Moore, we just want to talk." Dana said.

Brick tilted the barrel of the shotgun up at the ceiling. He smiled.

"Ma'am -- If I was gonna shoot -You'd already be dead. Can't be too careful. Bad folks in this neighborhood."

Robin wiped beads of sweat from her brow.

"We've heard."

"Mr. Moore, we have some information about your brother's death. We think it was a canine-involved attack." Dana said.

Brick didn't even twitch. "So, you think some kind of animal killed my brother huh?"

"The evidence is mostly inconclusive right now, but yeah. Maybe a trained attack dog or something."

Robin checked out some of the junk in Brick's store while he and Dana talked. Dana took a pad from her coat.

"Did Abraham have any enemies?"

"Everybody loved that man." Brick said.

"What about you? Any enemies? People you can think of who would want to harm your brother? Any weird situations or events that transpired that he was involved in?"

"My brother was a righteous man of GOD. He was a gift. An absolute gift. And as for enemies? Nah Ma'am. I pretty much keep to myself and don't bother nobody."

Robin wandered back over.

"Is that so? What about the guns?" Robin asked.

Brick rubbed his bald head. Smiled.

"Well, I been in a spot of trouble once or twice, but I served my country. Two tours in Nam."

"And we appreciate your service. But, right now, we really need your help." Dana said.

Brick smiled at the compliment even as he kept a wary eye on the two detectives.

"I really wish I could help you folks out Ma'am, but I don't know anything."

"You're sure? Nothing out of the ordinary that comes to mind?" Dana asked.

Brick showed her the gap-toothed smile again.

"No ma'am."

The phone in Brick's back room rang. He glanced over at it. After a few minutes, an old-school answering machine picked up.

It was Chapa. "Hey Tio', we're comin' in with a package!"

Robin's cell phone rang.

"Detective Malcheck. Yeah, yeah Gevaudan Park. Multiple bodies…wait a minute…"

Robin pulled a pen from her pocket. Dana and Brick stopped talking.

"Right, right, dark blue Trans-Am. Nineteen-eighty-three or four model."

The words froze Dana. *Troy*.

"Tell me." Dana said. Robin held a finger up, cutting Dana off while she listened and scribbled on the note pad.

"Got it. Thanks. Yeah, I'll tell her." Robin hung up.

"Robin, tell me what you just found out!"

"Something about a B.O.L.O. you put out on a Trans Am. Patrol spotted the car near G-Park. Some dumb-ass kids got killed in the park by wild animals." Robin said it without thinking.

Dana's face went ashen. She slumped to the ground.

"Oh no. No, no, no..."

"Dana! What did I say? Wait...no way Troy was there!"

Brick watched them. He shook his head.

"Troy...was in that car." Dana whispered.

"You're kidding right? Tell me you are!" Then Robin realized what had happened. Her mind raced back to the other night. The park. The dangerous predator lurking in the woods. The various murder scenes she and Dana had investigated. Now this was personal. This predator, or predators...no these *monsters*...had attacked and possibly killed Dana's daughter. The thought filled Robin with rage.

Alex waited outside the surplus store. She had transformed into her werewolf form again and joined with the PACK not far from her condo. She followed them through the drainage tunnels, along the hiking trails, until they arrived here. At first Alex didn't understand what Wenona wanted, but the minute she saw the humans inside framed in the open doorway she knew. So, she stayed outside as a sentry, a guard in case more humans arrived. Wenona understood Alex was still new to the PACK, and as such allowed this.

No. This can't be happening! No. No. NO!

Dana started to sob. She bent over heaving, trying to catch her breath.

"Lord, Lord, Lord. They done it now. Killing babies." Brick whispered to himself.

Dana pulled her gun from the holster. Walked over to Brick, shoved the barrel under his chin and cocked the hammer.

"You tell me right now what is going on, or I'll put your brains on the ceiling!"

Robin stared at Dana. She'd never seen her partner lose it like this before. "Dana?"

"Hold up! Take it easy! Chapa and Eli are on their way in!" Brick said.

"Talk! What did that to my daughter? I know you know what I'm talking about!"

"You ain't gonna' believe nary a word of it." Brick said.

Robin took a step toward Dana. Not sure what she was going to do but determined not to let Dana make a mistake that would end her career, or worse, land her in jail.

"Don't do this Boss."

Dana pushed the barrel deeper into his corded neck. "TELL ME!"

Brick grimaced from the pain. Brick's eyes stretched wide as he realized she *WAS* going to kill him.

"Wait Ma'am! I'll tell you everything! I know what killed your daughter. Were..."

BAM! Eli, Chapa, and TROY burst through the door. Troy's face tear-stained.

"Troy? -- TROY!!!" Dana screamed. She ran over and scooped Troy in her arms. Her little girl...her BABY was still alive.

"MOM!" Troy sobbed into Dana's chest and neck. Eli and Chapa stood off to one side as this reunion took place. Dana opened her eyes and locked with Eli's.

"You saved her?"

Eli nodded. Dana whispered the words *Thank You* to Eli.

Brick walked over to his nephew, head hung.

"Yella...I'm sorry I let you down...the bottle got hold of me again 'cause I was weak just like yo' Daddy said I was."

Eli stared at his uncle. "You need to get it together Uncle Dan. We've got a fight coming and we need you sober. Understand?"

"I can do it Yella. I can! Just don't give up on me."

Robin was watching this like a tennis match.

"Elijah...that your name?" Robin asked.

"Yes." Eli said.

"I think it's time we get some answers from you all about what the hell is going on here!" Robin said.

"I was trying to tell you earlier." Brick said.

Eli was annoyed. "Look Detective..."

"Malcheck." Robin said. She was annoyed too. These guys were hiding some serious shit and Robin wanted to know what it was.

"I don't have time to go into it all right now. We need to regroup and plan our next move." Eli said.

Robin kept pressing. "Regroup for what? What are we up against? I think we have a right to know. I don't really give a shit if you're some kind of badass Navy SEAL or whatever. WE are the police, and YOU need to come clean right now!"

Chapa walked back to the door to close it and noticed something. Movement in the parking lot. A trick of the light perhaps? Chapa continued to stare, his night vision shot from standing inside the store under the florescent lights. What seemed to be one shadow moving across the parking lot became multiple shadows. Chapa squinted at them.

"Oh shit...Eli..."

Eli was still squaring off with Robin, his back away from the front door.

Dana came over. "So, what IS going on Elijah? Maybe this is the time for us both to be honest with each other."

"Look..." Eli started. He wasn't sure where to start. With Panama? The stuffed werewolf down in the Vault? His encounter with the werewolf lady in Gevaudan Park? Which was the most plausible scenario to tell that wouldn't lead to he and Chapa being arrested?

"Eli!" Chapa yelled.

"What is it Chap?"

Everyone turned in the same direction. Through the open doorway they saw the shapes of several large animals slinking toward the store front.

"Lordy! They comin' to get us!" Brick said. He stepped back away from the door.

Chapa did a quick mental count. "Uh...there's a lot more than two Eli."

Eli turned at the sound of Chapa's voice. Chapa was scared.

Eli joined him at the door. Dana and Robin came over as well. They all stared out into the darkness. Wenona lead the PACK, her eyes seeming to glow in the darkness. She roared when she spotted Eli and sprinted toward the front door.

"SHUT THE DOOR!" Eli screamed.

Chapa slammed the door shut. BAM! BAM! BAM! BAM! BAM! BAM! The door was pounded and hammered by the animals outside. Howls shook the windows. The door was solid but started to buckle nevertheless. Eli pointed at the back of the store. Brick already knew what he had in mind.

"I'll lead 'em inside Yella!"

"Those are the animals that killed your father aren't they?" Dana asked.

"Yes. Werewolves." Eli said.

Dana whispered the word. "*Werewolves.*" As if speaking it would give life to it. However, these things were indeed real. THIS was their predator from the woods. Brick stared at Dana. "Ma'am, I got a secure room in the back. Let's get your daughter there. They won't get in."

It only took a moment for Dana to decide. "Troy! Go with Mr. Moore!"

Brick smiled at Troy. Even though Brick was a huge man children trusted him. They seemed to sense his gentle nature.

The door started to buckle inward. More HOWLING.

"Call me Brick sweetie."

"Go! NOW!" Dana yelled. Troy, still shell-shocked, nodded and followed Brick toward the back.

"Wait a minute! You're saying those animals are werewolves? No way!" Robin said.

"I don't give a damn if you believe me or not!" Eli said.

Dana pulled her weapon. Robin keyed off her and did the same.

"Eli! The rest of our gear's in the jeep!" Chapa said.

BAM! One last barrage on the door and then nothing... Absolute silence.

"They're not going to give up easy, are they?" Dana asked. Eli shook his head to indicate *NO*.

CREAK! They looked UP...and heard the sound of claws climbing up the side of the building and onto the roof.

"The fucking things can climb?" Robin asked. "Uh Dana...I believe your intelligent wolf theory now!"

Dana didn't answer. All of them were tense and waiting for what might happen next.

CRASH!

The windows upstairs shattered. Hairy paws reached inside and tore at the metal grating over the windows. The sounds from outside were getting louder. The pounding on the front door resumed. Upstairs the tearing became more frenzied as the werewolves realized they were almost inside. Wenona and a few other werewolves began to squeeze through the ragged openings.

"Up there!" Eli said.

Dana and Robin started shooting at the animals upstairs. The animals reacted to the hits but kept coming through.

"This isn't working!" Robin shouted.

Chapa noticed Robin was too close to the front door. "Careful!"

The front door burst inward. Robin spun just in time to have a werewolf jump at her. It slashed Robin on her arm, dragging open a huge gash. Dana rolled to the side into a bunch of shelves as the beast leapt over her.

"AHHHHHH!" Robin cradled her arm.

"ROBIN!!!"

Dana crawled over to her friend. She checked the wound. The flesh was peeled back like orange rind, exposing white derma below. Blood pumped from the wound, spraying the floor and Dana's jeans. She pulled her belt off to make a field tourniquet. "Come on partner! Hold on! I got you!"

Robin stared at her. "Don't get so fucking dramatic on me Boss…It's just a flesh wou…" Robin passed out.

"NO! wake up damnit! You wake up Robin!" Dana screamed at her.

Dana willed Robin to live. This was NOT the way she was supposed to go out. Robin was too young. She loved Robin like a sister in some ways.

Eli and Chapa opened fire on the beast with the weapons they were holding. The animal flew back into some shelves, bleeding from a dozen mortal bullet holes. Chapa ran over and finished it off with a head shot.

"She's alive! Help me!" Dana said.

Eli and Dana lifted the unconscious Robin and supported her together. Chapa covered their retreat. Upstairs, Wenona pulled herself through a window. She stood on the platform, on the edge of the loft area looking down at Eli and Dana. Wenona roared at them, launching herself into the air…Dana saw the monstrous shadow heading right for Elijah.

"ELI!"

Eli moved out of the way just as Wenona landed on the floor in the exact spot they were in. Chapa fired to cover his brother, backing the werewolf leader up. She ran behind the shelves to escape the lethal silver bullets. Dana and Eli raced to the stairs as fast as they could, dragging Robin with them.

Alex paced back and forth outside. Her animal and human mind racing and contradicting itself. Her animal urge was to join her sisters in the HUNT. To go inside and rend and tear at the prey. It was a compulsion that was almost overwhelming. The wind brought the scent of the prey to her nostrils. Alex growled and bared her canines. Licked her lips. She started to bolt toward the front door, but something stopped her.

For some reason though, the human side of her was still aware. She remembered the journals of *Artemis* and his love *Anna*. Somehow, those two people attempted to look beyond their differences and try to live in peace. She felt revulsion at her own thoughts and killing impulses. She backed into the woods, hiding in the shadows, her tail between her legs in a submissive position.

Alex whined. A pitiful sound. She was afraid. Afraid of what she was becoming, and of what she still was…

THE VAULT

Brick led Troy down the World War I bunker-looking stairs to the vault with the iron bar. He undid the locks, lifted the bar off and flipped the lights on.

"Go inside. It's alright."

Troy stared at Brick, then at the room. She took a deep breath and walked inside. She screamed. Brick had forgotten to tell her about the stuffed werewolf inside. He rushed in after her.

"It's okay! It's dead! See?" Brick said. He touched the stuffed werewolf to show Troy.

Troy was almost paralyzed with fear. She huddled underneath a large desk. Brick groaned in pain from both his reconstructed knees as he knelt down near her. Brick and Troy heard gunshots coming from upstairs.

"Hey…I need to go help your Mom out okay? I'll be right back. Wait here."

Troy nodded. She still couldn't speak. The trauma of the night was almost too much for her to process. Her best friend Nancy was dead. Lucky and that dickhead probably dead too. Monsters wanted to kill and eat her along with her Mom and Elijah. The whole world was crazy and she just figured this out. She wanted out of it all, but this was the first time she couldn't run from her problems or drown them in music. She had to face it somehow.

Yes. She needed to be brave.

Like Elijah.

What would a Navy SEAL do right now? He wouldn't sit around and whine like a little baby. No. He would grab a weapon and fight back.

Right! I need to help them fight back somehow! But how? I'm just a fifteen-year-old kid. And there are monsters upstairs. REAL monsters who want to kill us.

"Come on Yella! Hurry!"

Eli saw Brick holding the vault door open for them. He and Dana moved faster, hustling Robin through the door. Chapa brought up the rear. The lights in the building went out! As a couple of werewolves ran into the stairway Chapa fired multiple rounds at them. The muzzle flare from his weapon lighting up the area.

"Eat this!"

Chapa fired another short burst at the animals, striking one and making the other scramble backward. He dove into the vault doorway. Brick slammed the huge metal door home. The werewolves pounded on the door. The sound, thunderous.

"Don't ya'll worry! This door was built to withstand Nazi bombs. Ain't nothin' getting through that!" Brick said.

"That shit was hairy!" Chapa said. No one laughed. "No pun intended."

Eli and Dana laid Robin on the floor. Eli helped her adjust the make-shift tourniquet on Robin's arm. Robin was still unconscious and it worried Dana. Brick came over.

"She's lost a lot of blood Ma'am. She'll be okay for now, but she's gonna need to go to the hospital sooner than later."

"I know. Thank you." Dana walked over to Troy and hugged her.

"I was so scared. Thought I lost you baby! I'm so sorry for earlier. SO sorry! I didn't mean to hurt you."

"I know Mom. I'm sorry too." They cried together. Tears of sadness mixed with joy for having found each other again.

The group huddled together a few feet from Robin. Eli stared at Dana. Both of them wanted to talk about Troy, but this was not the time. That could come later, IF they survived this night. For now, Eli was in operational mode. Potential options raced through his mind. None of them good.

"What's the plan bro'? Personally, I want to take the fight to those fuckers!" Chapa said, deferring to Eli as he had on numerous SEAL missions.

"We're outnumbered and stuck for now. No. We need another option. We need our gear from the Jeep." Eli said.

"Damn straight." Chapa said.

Dana stared up at the stuffed werewolf on the dais. She didn't comment on it but gave it a wide berth just the same.

"What's in the Jeep Elijah?" Dana asked.

"Concussion grenades." Eli said.

"Enough to blow those sumbitches to Kingdom Come!" Brick said. "Pardon my language Ma'am. But, I maybe have a solution. See that lid in the floor there?"

Brick pointed down. They stared at a metal grate, maybe a foot and a half feet in width.

"Where's it go?" Eli asked.

"Down to a partial cellar from years back. Runs under the building...Connects to the sewers. I used to store the weapons and ammo there. I would bring 'em in from street-side, haul 'em down there and leave 'em till it was time to ship 'em out."

Chapa stared at his uncle as if he had discovered a new life form. "You are some kinda legend Tio'! Damn!"

Dana wasn't impressed but saw merit in the plan.

"If this works I'll think about not reporting you to the ATF," Dana said.

Brick smiled at her. "I like her Yella! She's got some sass on her!"

Eli was frowning. He bent down and examined the opening.

"It's too small for any of us to fit Uncle Dan." The adults sized it up. The opening WAS too small.

"Shit!" Chapa said. "There's got to be another way!"

Brick shook his head. "Sorry knuckle-head. That's it."

Troy walked up behind them. She stared at the opening.

Be brave.

She tapped Eli on the shoulder.

"I can do it," Troy whispered.

"What's that Troy?" Eli asked.

"I can fit. I'm the only one who can fit."

"NO! It's too dangerous! You are not going!" Dana said.

Eli knelt next to her. He stared into her eyes. Troy loved that Eli always treated her the same as everyone else. He never spoke to her like a child. Eli valued Troy's opinions.

"Do you really think you can?" Eli asked.

"Eli! She'll be killed!" Dana said. But, even as she said it Dana knew it might be their only way out of this.

"What do you want me to do if I make it?" Troy asked.

"In the back of my Jeep are several grenades. Concussion grenades. Like police SWAT Teams use. You pull the pin and throw them like a baseball. After ten seconds the grenades will explode and stun anything within the radius. If we can stun the animals then we might be able to kill them and get out. Understand?"

Troy smiled. "I understand." She looked at Dana. "I can do it, Mom. I can."

Dana hugged Troy again.

"Guess I'll have to trust you," Dana said.

"Yes, you will," Troy said with a smile.

The werewolves started to storm the door. Eli and Chapa stomped on the metal grating. It loosened. They kept at it until the metal broke free with a wrenching noise. Troy stripped out of her jacket and knelt down.

"Here you go Baby Girl." Brick handed Troy a small flashlight. Eli handed her the Jeep keys.

"Go straight down. When you reach the cellar there's another opening like this -- a lot larger though. It should take you into the drainage ditch. From there you can walk until you reach the street." Brick said.

"Where does it come out?" Troy asked.

"The parking lot will be about twenty feet away," Brick said.

"Time to go," Eli said.

"Troy!" Dana came over.

"Yeah, Mom?" Dana held her daughter. Squeezing like they'd never have another chance to hug. "You know I love you right?"

Troy looked into her mother's eyes.

"I love you too Mom."

"When you get back...I have to tell you something important. About Eli -- about all of us..."

Troy was puzzled. "Tell me when I get back." She said.

Eli touched Dana on the shoulder.

"We're running out of time."

Dana backed off. The strain too much for her. She turned her back and walked to a corner of the room.

"I love you kiddo," Eli said.

Troy smiled. "I love you too Elijah."

Troy crawled into the opening, wriggling through until they could only see the soles of her boots. Eli looked up from the grating at his Uncle.

Brick whispered to Eli. "What if she doesn't make it Yella?"

"She will," Eli said with the power of conviction in his daughter.

"What IF?" Brick asked.

Eli stared at the hole his daughter just crawled into.

"We have to face them. Go for the crates outside. Try to fight them off. Kill as many as we can." Eli said.

"Damn straight! I'm sick of this hiding crap!" Chapa said.

Dana walked back over. She made sure NOT to look down at the cellar opening. Eli took Dana's hand.

"Hey…she's going to make it. Okay?" Eli said.

"Okay." Dana said. "Eli…"

"No…after tonight. We'll deal with it. But, regardless of what happens between us, let's promise to put Troy first." Eli said.

Dana managed a smile. "I'd like that."

Chapa wandered over, trying not to intrude. "Uh guys…hate to break up all this lovey-dovey talk, but we got shit to do."

"Roger that Chap. Alright! Let's give Troy whatever cover she needs! If we can keep them busy in the building that won't even know she's outside." Eli said.

"Right out of the manual Yella! Flanking maneuver!" Brick said.

Eli noticed a few spare boxes of silver ammunition on a shelf. He walked over, grabbed them and handed them out so they could reload. He passed a box to Dana.

"You need these for your weapon. Silver. It's the only thing that will kill them. Everything else just seems to piss them off."

Dana didn't question or hesitate. She began loading her mags with the bullets.

"Hey…What...about me?"

They looked over at Robin. She was in a sitting position and looking very pale.

"Dana. Where's my rig? Do I get some of those bullets too?" Robin asked.

Dana came over, picked up Robin's weapon from the desk where she placed it when they entered the vault, and loaded it with silver bullets. She handed the gun to Robin.

"You good partner?"

Robin racked the slide on her service weapon, chambering a round. "Fuckin' A."

Eli pulled his silver knife. He admired the shiny blade on it and the weight of it in his hand. "This saved my life in Panama."

Brick looked at the knife. "Yo Daddy's knife from 'Nam. I remember it saved him a time or two also. Probably why he gifted it to you."

Brick took Eli by the shoulders.

"This ain't no accident Yella. You know that right? This here is Fate and Destiny all rolled together. What we do here tonight is going to determine how that destiny is going to play out. Understand me?"

"Yes sir I do Uncle Dan." Eli said.

Brick took hold of Chapa's hand too. He bowed his head.

"Lord...I know I'm a sinner and all, and not worth a split nickel...But...IF you are up there listening and would be obliged to give this old soldier one last shot I would hope that you bless these boys, these Police, and the girl. Give us righteous power and victory over our enemies...If you see fit to do so. Amen."

"Amen." Eli said.

"Amen." Chapa said.

"First time I prayed in...Well...it's been a while."

Eli smiled at his Uncle.

"It was a good thing. Thanks Uncle Dan."

Brick put his soldier-face on. "Moment of truth Yella."

Eli stared at their faces. Dana...Brick...Chapa...They were his family. And he would do anything to protect them. He nodded at Chapa.

"When Uncle Dan opens the door we head to the crate outside. There are more weapons. We load them with silver and then engage the targets. Conserve your ammunition. Shoot only what you can see. Short controlled bursts. And keep moving! We push the fight to them no matter what." Eli said. Eli glanced at them. They seemed ready.

"Ready Chap?" Eli asked.

"Always bro."

Brick placed his hand on the door handle. Eli did a silent countdown with his fingers.

FIVE...

Dana braced herself.

FOUR...

Chapa aimed low. Dana high.

THREE...

Robin readied herself from her sitting position.

TWO...

Brick began to pull the handle. Eli reached *ONE.* Brick yanked the door open...

THE YOUNGEST WARRIOR

Troy sat in the concrete drainage ditch, covered with algae and muck from the filthy sewer water she just crawled through. She waited a few minutes to get her bearings, listening for sounds of the predators she knew were inside the surplus store.

The parking lot sounded quiet. Feeling safe enough, Troy climbed up the shallow embankment toward the street. She did a quick peek, craning her neck and head around until she could see the entire parking lot. Eli's Jeep was close to her. She scanned the building perimeter for more werewolves. The coast was clear.

Be brave.

She climbed all the way out of the drainage ditch, every nerve on edge, senses hyper-vigilant to all the noises outside. She crossed the street and hid behind the Jeep. Still no werewolves...

She unlocked the door and climbed inside. Something watched Troy enter the vehicle. A low growl. The shape moved across the street in the direction of the Jeep. Inside, Troy scrambled over the back seat. She found the pouch with the concussion grenades.

The Jeep rocked from side-to-side, pounded from the outside by some great force. Troy covered her mouth to stop the scream in her throat. She glanced out the window. The rear windshield of the Jeep exploded, showering glass all over the back seat.

Alex shoved her head through.

Troy screamed.

She kicked Alex in the muzzle, causing the werewolf to howl in pain. Alex pulled her face from the broken windshield.

Alex shook her stinging muzzle. She smashed into the Jeep once more. The human inside was cagey and smart so she would have to try another tactic. Alex lowered herself within a few inches of the pavement and circled around toward the hood. She couldn't tell if the

215

human had some kind of weapon or not. Better to be cautious than foolish. As she passed the rear tire she heard movement from inside the vehicle. She could smell the fear emanating from the human.

It smelled delicious.

Soon, Alex would tear the savory flesh off the bone, drink the still-pumping blood, then join her sisters inside as they purged the remaining humans from existence.

The emergency lights Brick had installed several years ago kicked in during the first assault, so now the hallway and stairs were bathed in a fiery red glow. As their eyes adjusted to the darkness in the hallway outside the Vault door a werewolf leapt from the darkness...

Dana reacted. Firing point blank into the animal's head. It fell at her feet, thrashing and crying out with a strange, almost human sound. The animal gurgled and began to change. Dana watched the hideous transformation.

"Oh...my...GOD..." Dana said. She felt a surge of vomit threatening to come up. She had never seen anything like this and would never forget it either.

Brick stared down at the now dead woman on the floor.

"Don't look at it Ma'am. It ain't nothin' pretty."

"Seal Team Two back in the shit huh?" Chapa asked.

"Yeah. Back in it." Eli said.

Eli opened the crate. Hauled out several M-4s. He tossed one to Brick. Handed the other to Dana. "These are already loaded. Just pull the charging handle. One clip finishes, switch it here. Jam the other home. Got it?" Eli said.

Dana pulled the charging handle on the machine gun. She tested the weight of it in her hands. Dana breathed deep to calm herself. "I got it." Dana said.

Eli took the retention strap of the M-4 and placed it over her head so the weapon hung underneath her arm. "Keep it slung like this. In case you fall down or stumble. When you go dry in your mags switch to your sidearm but do not drop this."

"Okay."

Howling sounds from the other room galvanized them into action. The werewolves were waiting...

"The deck's a little more even now." Eli said.

"Right. It's only seventeen to four." Dana said with a grim smile. Eli and Dana stared into each other's eyes.

"Come on. Our daughter's waiting." Dana said.

Come on Troy. I know you can do it baby. Dana thought.

Troy was bounced around inside, but unhurt. She scrambled over the back seat to the driver's seat. She fumbled around as she tried to stick the keys in the ignition. Alex jumped onto the hood of the Jeep. She began smashing her bony head into the windshield, using it like a battering ram. The animal had taken hold of Alex once again. Inside her mind Wenona's voice raged like a splinter.

No hesitation.

No mercy.

No quarter.

Alex continued to bash the safety glass. Her human mind and instincts suppressed. Troy screamed, but kept her wits enough to start the ignition. The Jeep roared to life. Spider-web cracks spread across the length of the windshield as it started to cave inward. Alex smashed harder. Troy slammed the Jeep into gear, driving straight toward the front door of the building. Alex dug her claws into the hood, riding it out instead of jumping off.

Troy jammed her foot onto the accelerator. The Jeep sped up.

Be brave.

Alex turned her head as she realized what was about to happen just as the Jeep exploded through the front of the store…

FIRE IN THE HOLE

Eli, Dana, Chapa, and Brick heard the tremendous crash of the Jeep plowing into the building.

"Oh my GOD...TROY!" Dana started to run up the stairs. Eli held her back.

"Wait! We don't know what that was! There's no smoke from the concussion grenades!"

"Let go! My baby's up there!" Dana pulled herself from Eli's grasp. He frowned but ran up the stairs first, followed by Dana then Chapa and Brick. Eli stopped at the top, holding his fist out to signal for them all to stop.

The landing was empty.

Eli peeked into the short corridor, looking for any sign of werewolves hiding and ready to strike. The corridor was empty. He whispered to them.

"It's clear. Quiet."

Eli padded toward the main surplus floor.

The Jeep lodged itself through the front counter. Alex was propelled thirty feet into the air and against a wall. She lay in a pile of clothing and shelves. The crash disrupted the actions of at least five werewolves who were waiting for the humans to round the corner. The animals were still disoriented from the crash. Some of the animals trapped under the wreckage of the building wall that had fallen on top of them. Others trapped under the Jeep's tires. Troy was dazed, but she managed to free herself from under the deflated air bag, reach into the grenade pouch, pull one out. The Jeep's hood had broken off and lay several feet away.

Be brave...

Pull then throw.

Troy pulled the pin, opened the door and threw the concussion grenade into the middle of a group of werewolves. They heard the noise, saw an object fall near them, and were blown backward by the force and stunned. Troy launched another one in a different direction. Same effect.

YES!

Eli heard and felt the concussive pressure wave from the grenades. He saw yellowish smoke billow from the main floor.

"NOW!" Eli shouted.

Eli entered the room, strafing targets as fast as he could acquire them. He put down two werewolves in short order. Dana came up behind him. She scanned the wreckage and spotted Troy standing by the front door of the Jeep. Troy saw her too. "TROY!" Mother and daughter found each other. They hugged. Troy was beaming with pride.

"I did it!"

"I knew you would baby! Now let's move!" Dana said.

Dana and Troy moved toward the large front counter. Dana backed up with Troy behind her. No sign of any werewolves near them. Just as they were about to step behind it for some kind of cover a large werewolf jumped from between two shelves and landed right in front of them. Dana pulled the trigger on the M-4. Nothing. The animal advanced. It savored their fear, anticipating a meal. Dana pulled the trigger again. Still nothing. The animal started to lunge at them.

"Damnit! COME ON!" Dana realized it was on *Safe* mode. She flicked the selection lever up to *Semi* and unloaded the entire clip into the werewolf's torso just as it moved their direction. She screamed as she did, her finger pulling the trigger over and over and over until the magazine ran dry. Tears streamed down her face.

"You ok?" She asked Troy.

Troy was shaking. "Yeah…I'm okay Mom."

Wenona tried to gather her senses. She was stunned from the blasts and her ears were ringing. She knew the prey was close but her vision was blurry. She heard shooting all around her and the dying cries of her sisters cutting through the air. She growled and shook her large head, trying to clear it. But, Wenona had lived a long life. She was a cautious hunter. She stayed hidden among the shelving. The advantage had been lost to the humans. Stealth was her greatest weapon now.

Eli, Chapa, and Brick opened fire on the animals. The men were right back in their world. Maybe for the last time.

The werewolves scrambled over one another trying to escape the deadly silver bullets. Even a grazing wound caused severe and immediate reactions. Brick and Eli continued to shoot every target they saw. Chapa was shooting like a madman in every direction. "Here you go!! Get some of this! What? You too? Take it! Take it!"

Wenona hadn't joined the battle yet. She watched as her fellow warriors were cut down. Then she spotted her opportunity. Eli ran out of ammo.

"Brick! Reload!" Eli shouted.

Before Brick could throw Eli a magazine Wenona sprinted out from her hiding spot between shelves. She hit him dead center in the chest with her head. Eli flew backward into several shelves.

"Yella!" Brick shouted.

Robin was the only one left in the Vault. She struggled to stand but didn't have enough strength. She could hear the chaos and gunfire above. She wanted to get into the fight but had to wait it out down here like some civilian.

A growl from just outside the door reached her ears.

In the darkness Robin could see a dark shape claw its way into the room. The glow from its eyes made the werewolf look demonic. The werewolf snarled and advanced toward her.

Robin kept her eyes on the approaching monster while raising her gun. The werewolf, sensing her prey was too weak to move, padded forward in an unhurried manner and displayed her canines. Robin had the gun almost all the way to a shooting position. The werewolf gathered her legs under her belly.

Robin brought her weapon to eye level and shot the werewolf through the forehead. It fell back and flopped once, then died. Robin smiled. Now *this* was what she had been waiting for.

Brick ran out of ammunition. He scowled as four werewolves crept forward. He realized that except for one other animal Chapa was dealing with, these were the last ones. The PACK surrounded Brick. He stared back at them. Defiant.

"You sho' don't scare me. It's you who oughta' be scared!"

Brick reached behind his back, pulled a grenade from his pocket. He started to pull the pin. The werewolves came closer.

"Come on...that's right. Ole' Brick's got something fo' ya! Yeah, just keep coming."

Brick pulled the pin.

"FIRE IN THE HOLE!!!!" Brick screamed.

Dana understood. She grabbed Troy, jerked her to the ground, shielding Troy with her own body. The shattered hood from the Jeep was near them. Dana grabbed it to cover them. Chapa on hearing this dived behind an old metal desk in the corner. Wenona realized the mistake they made. She leaped away before the other werewolves understood the danger they were in.

BOOM!

It was NOT a concussion grenade! The entire building shook from the blast. Dust and concrete filled the air. Debris fell from the ceiling. Silver or no silver --- those werewolves were DEAD.

But...

...so was BRICK...his crucifix fused into the remaining floor.

There was so much devastation in this part of the store that almost nothing remained. Spot fires burned every few feet. Dana pulled the hood off them. She and Troy stood amidst the rubble. Dana glanced around.

"ELIJAH! ELIJAH! Where are you?"

No answer.

GRROWL!! ALEX stood in front of them. Dana looked down. Her machine gun was buried under rubble. Dana looked back at the werewolf in front of them. They were in trouble.

"Mom!"

Dana held her daughter. Trying to shield her from the certain death she knew was coming for them. "I know baby, I know! Shut your eyes!"

Mother and daughter closed their eyes as Alex stalked closer to them. She growled, ready to leap on them and rip the flesh from their pulsing bodies. Several feet away from them Chapa was pinned by a piece of ceiling. He could see what was about to happen. His weapon was just out of reach.

Chapa clawed at it with his fingers...

"No! No!!" Chapa screamed. It couldn't end this way. Not on his watch. It couldn't.

Alex opened her mouth. Saliva dripped from the long canines. She prepared to leap...

Dana waited for it.

Why couldn't I protect you Troy? Why? I failed you baby. I'm so sorry.

Dana dared to open her eyes when nothing happened. She looked into the ice-blue eyes of the grey werewolf in front of her.

Awareness came to Dana, and RECOGNITION.

...The werewolf was ALEX...

Alex recognized DANA too.

Her human consciousness came rushing back, pushing away her animal instincts in a flash. Alex knew she was NOT going to kill them. She was different for some reason. Apart from the other PACK members. But, this would be the only way she could embrace who she was. The only way she could live life on HER terms.

Alex sat on her haunches like a large dog. She stared into Dana's eyes.

Dana pushed Troy behind her.

"Wait here."

"No Mom! Don't go near it!" Troy said.

"Look. She's different now. See how she's just sitting there?" Dana said.

"What if it's a trick?"

Dana stared at Alex again. All traces of the savage ferocity...gone. Dana felt like she was staring into the same sad eyes like on the day she interviewed Alex in her apartment.

"It's not. Trust me baby. It's going to be alright."

Dana took a step toward Alex. The werewolf did not move a muscle. Dana took another step. And another. Until she was inches away. Dana held her hand up, palm out. Alex sniffed Dana's hand and lowered her head. Dana placed a hand on Alex's bony forehead.

"I know Alex...I know."

Chapa was watching this exchange. He couldn't believe it.

ROARRRRR!

Alex spun and saw Wenona towering over her. Wenona nodded in the direction of the women. Alex swiveled her mangy head between Wenona, Dana and Troy. Alex roared back at Wenona. DEFIANCE in the sound.

Alex stepped in BETWEEN Wenona and Dana and Troy.

"What's going on?" Troy asked.

"I think she's protecting us." Dana said.

Alex and Wenona faced off. Wenona growled again. She wanted Alex to move but the pup stood firm. This infuriated her.

A PACK member, protecting HUMANS. *Sacrilege!*

"Hey! We're not finished yet!"

Eli stood behind Wenona. He was covered with dirt and grime, but okay. He held his Father's silver bladed knife in his hand. Wenona faced him, a snarl on her face.

"C'mon girl." Eli said.

Wenona walked over to him. They circled each other like prize fighters. She held back, understanding that Eli was a formidable adversary. She snapped at him. Slashed with her claws. Eli danced just out of reach. This happened several times, frustrating Red Eyes.

"C'mon!" Eli said just as he slipped on a piece of broken tile. He stumbled and fell backward. Wenona jumped on Eli's chest, her claws sinking into his shoulder, making him scream out in pain.

"ELIJAH!" Troy screamed.

Wenona issued a victory howl up at the rafters. The spawn under her claws at last. Now, she could wipe him from the face of Mother Earth.

Eli gripped Abraham's knife with his other hand. As the werewolf lowered her head toward his face he stabbed upward...plunging the silver knife deep into her neck. Wenona's howl was cut off...

She made a gurgling noise in her throat. Eli pushed the blade further into her flesh and watched the glow of life start to fade from the savage eyes. Wenona sagged, falling over with a thump onto the floor.

"This is for my father."

Eli used the knife to leverage her to the side. Eli rolled onto his back. All his strength gone.

Dana and Troy ran over to prop him up.

"Okay, that was too close for comfort!" Dana said.

Eli managed a weak smile.

"You're not kidding." He said.

Troy wrapped her arms around his neck. "Elijah!"

"Troy, I think it's time we had that chat now." Dana said.

Troy stared at them.

"Okay...?"

"I'd like you to meet your father." Dana said.

Troy continued to stare at them. She didn't quite comprehend what Dana just said.

"Yes…your Father…I'll explain it all later baby." Dana said.

Troy looked from Eli to Dana and back to Eli. "My father..." She whispered it like breathing for the first time. Eli stroked his daughter's hair.

They heard a noise behind them. Chapa was trapped underneath the pile of rubble waving his arms like a madman.

"Uh...guys? I hate to break up this little family reunion but...Can you get me the hell out of here?"

Dana, Troy and Eli came over and pulled Chapa free. Eli and Chapa hugged when he stood up.

"Damn brother…that was way too close." Chapa gasped.

"Yeah. Glad you made it Chap." Eli said.

Robin staggered into the room. She gasped when she saw the destruction around her. Dana smiled at her partner.

"Damn! I missed all this going down!" Robin said.

A loud howl erupted from behind them. A howl of mourning. They had forgotten about Alex. Eli glanced around on the floor for a weapon. He spotted an MP-5 under some shelving, grabbed it, aimed the weapon in Alex's direction.

"NO!" Dana shouted. She jumped in front of Eli's weapon, blocking his view of Alex. "Don't kill her."

Eli scowled. "Why not? She's the last one! They all need to be put down. Move Dana."

Dana pushed the barrel of Eli's weapon down.

"Alex is different. She saved our lives. I don't know why…but she did. We can't kill her Elijah. It has to end here."

Dana locked eyes with Eli. He could see the determination in hers. Eli lowered the weapon. All of them looked over at Alex. She was laying on the floor next to Wenona. She placed her snout against her mother's dead body.

She's in mourning, Dana realized.

Alex stood and faced the group. Eli, Chapa, and Robin were still wary, but Dana walked closer and nodded at Alex.

"Thank you."

Alex raced away. Through the ruined building. Out into the street. Alex loped into the woods, stopping just long enough to glance back at the surplus store. She let out a plaintive bark, then surged deeper into the forest. Dana watched her shadow disappear.

Chapa held onto Eli while Dana came back over to help Robin. Troy stood near them.

"We need to get you and Robin here checked out." Chapa said.

"Yeah…" Eli spoke but he was staring at the spot where Brick died. Chapa looked over also. "Tio` was a great man." He said.

"Yes he was Chap…yes he was."

The two former SEALS knew that Brick was in a better place now…standing tall next to their father Abraham.

THE BLACK SITE

After the battle for Brick's surplus store Robin and Dana put their heads together to figure out what kind of call to make on the radio. The whine of approaching fire engines sounded in the distance making the situation that much more critical. When the Station Chief from Fire Station 28 showed up Dana badged him explaining there were multiple bodies inside. Dana decided to call it in as shots fired, but the situation was contained. Before she could make the call, three black, armor-plated SUVs squealed into the parking lot. A Homeland Security Federal Agent walked over to Dana.

"Detective Adams?" The Federal Agent asked.

"Yes?" Dana answered.

"By order of the Department of Homeland Security this crime scene is now a federal government priority. You are relieved of command."

"What kind of bullshit is this?" Robin asked.

"I don't understand Agent…" Dana said.

The Federal Agent produced an official document with the Homeland Security Seal and held it up for Dana and Robin to inspect.

Before Dana could protest more Agents escorted Eli, Chapa, Troy and Robin over. They were told to relinquish their firearms, walked over to the waiting vehicles, and confined there by several serious-looking men and women in dark suits while the Federal Agent spoke to the Station Chief. He told the Station Chief that this was now a matter of *National Security* and that a suspected terrorist cell had blown themselves up right when the detectives arrived to question a suspect. The Federal-Agent-in-Charge ordered the fire fighters to stand down as there was a Federal Incident Response Team on the way.

The city fire fighters withdrew and a large, oversized white van pulled in. The parking lot was cordoned off and personnel in HazMat suits debarked, unloaded black zippered body bags, along with nefarious equipment that Eli had never seen before. The HazMat team entered Brick's store, set up large work lights.

Eli wondered what the hell the HazMat team was doing inside.

The Federal Agent walked over to the SUV carrying Elijah and Chapa. He gave them a grim stare.

"I'm going to ask you and your people to wear these. Procedure." The Federal Agent held out two blindfolds.

"Why?" Eli asked.

The Federal Agent kept staring at Eli and Chapa but didn't offer up an explanation. Eli watched from behind the Federal Agent as several HazMat team members walked from the ruins of Brick's surplus store carrying several long black plastic bags that he knew contained the remains of the werewolves. *This is surreal*, Eli thought.

"Whatever." Chapa said as Eli passed him the blindfold. The brothers placed them over their eyes. The Federal Agent checked to make sure the men couldn't see. He closed the door and climbed into the passenger seat. He nodded at the driver and they sped away.

Minutes later he, Chapa, Dana, Troy and Robin were driven down Interstate Highway 90 exiting 36th Street, to the old Kelly Air Force Base compound. The SUVs parked at a non-descript building in the middle of what used to be a vast military installation that started as Kelly Field in the late 1920s then morphed into Kelly Air Force Base until the early 2000s when the base was shuttered.

The grim and silent Federal Agents ushered them inside, down long, narrow hallways with empty offices, and into separate rooms that resembled interrogation rooms. Dana had to be restrained when they took Troy to another room. Chap and Eli both knew they were really in some kind of Black Site, so they waited it out without saying a word. Robin cursed everyone who made eye contact with her. They all waited three hours until Major Orion entered Eli's room. He sat opposite Eli, studying the former SEAL from his side of the dented metal table.

"Captain." Orion said.

"Major." Eli answered.

Neither man spoke again for a full two minutes. This was a game of chicken and the one who spoke first lost. Eli was used to waiting though.

In the rain.

In the snow.

In the desert.

In the mountains.

Underwater.

In some bombed out building on the other side of the world while men you had never met tried to kill you.

Waiting was a big part of SEAL life. Waiting was easy.

Another hour or two wouldn't hurt him. The only thing that irritated him was knowing his daughter was also waiting in a room just like this. Probably scared and hungry.

And THAT pissed Eli off.

Orion lost.

"This is why you need to come to Washington Captain Moore." Orion said.

"Why?" Eli said.

"Captain…Don't insult my intelligence and I won't insult yours. This problem you experienced tonight is NOT localized."

This got Eli's attention. He sat forward. "How so?"

Orion stood. "Follow me. Our transport is fueled and waiting. We'll swing by your place so you and the Chief can pack."

Eli stayed seated. "Let my family go and then we can talk. Keep them in here and you won't be able to call for help from this room fast enough. Understand me Major?"

Orion's mouth twitched. He shrugged. "Very well."

Orion opened the door and Eli followed him from the room.

Dana, Robin and Troy stood in a small lobby area waiting. Two armed men stood near them.

"What the fu…err…What the hell Boss? This is some conspiracy type crap here!"

Dana nodded at her partner. She stood with an arm draped around Troy's shoulders. "You okay baby?"

"Yeah, Mom. The men were nice. What are we doing here anyway?" Troy asked.

"I'm not sure," Dana said.

Eli walked in the room. Orion behind him. Dana and Troy rushed over. They group-hugged. Orion stood by the doorway, giving them space.

"How's your side?" Dana asked.

"They bandaged me up pretty good," Eli said.

"Where's your brother?" Robin asked.

"In another room. I'm going to see him in a few. You guys okay?"

"Yes. What do you think they want Elijah? They wouldn't tell us anything." Dana said.

"They know about the werewolves...somehow they know. Chapa and I need to go to Washington with Major Orion and figure out what the deal is." Eli said.

"They know? How could they know?" Dana asked.

"Beats me," Eli answered.

Troy held on to Eli's hand.

"You're leaving?" Troy asked.

Eli cupped her chin in his hand. He stared into her eyes. "Just for now. But, I WILL be back. Promise."

Troy smiled at her Dad. "Okay. Don't break it or I'll come find you, Elijah!"

Eli smiled. "Roger that."

Orion raised his hand at Eli signaling that the family reunion was over. Eli nodded at him. "Gotta go. I'll call you as soon as I can Dana."

Dana hugged his neck. She looked into his eyes. "Come back okay?"

Eli kissed Dana. "I will." He leaned down and kissed Troy too. "Troy...help your mom out okay? Try to get along."

"I will Elijah," Troy said. Orion walked over.

"Everything's been arranged with your department Detectives. They've been informed of the confidential nature of the situation and there is no further need for police intervention. You are free to go."

"That's it? No apology? What a crock of shit!" Robin said.

Orion stared at her like she was some kind of vermin. "Take it as a gift Detective Malcheck." Orion ended the conversation by walking away before Robin could get another word in. Robin shot the finger at Orion's back.

Eli smiled at them. "See you." He turned around and left the room with Orion. Robin stared at Dana.

"Not my boyfriend huh?" She grinned.

"Shut up," Dana said. "Let's get out of here." One of the guards motioned for them to follow him. As they left the room Dana glanced over her shoulder but Eli and Orion had already disappeared down the long hallway.

229

Eli opened the door to the room Chapa was in. Chapa smiled when he saw Eli. He jumped up from the metal chair.

"Damn! Glad you're here! Hey Major I have to take a piss!" Chapa said. Eli laughed. Orion did not.

They walked down the hallway and left the building, AFTER Chapa peed. Outside, everyone climbed into one of the black SUVs and drove off.

"Where we headed bro?" Chapa asked.

"D.C.," Eli said.

"This about what I think it's about?" Chapa asked.

Eli faced his brother in the seat. Orion rode up front with the driver. Eli lowered his voice.

"Yeah. I think what we faced is the tip of the iceberg Chap." Eli said.

GOING HOME

BALTIMORE, MARYLAND

Alex stood outside Paula's house. She was nervous…and scared. The last few days had worn her out. She was at the end of her rope. Paula opened the door and smiled at her.
"Quit standing around girl! Welcome home!"
Alex smiled.

Wystan poured over his grandfather's manuscript, along with ancient texts and tomes about mythology and shapeshifters. He had contacted many academics who specialized in these kinds of mysteries. When Alex flew back to San Antonio Wystan began searching for anything about some kind of cure. Any shred of evidence, no matter how small. He knew he had to find it. Wystan felt certain that it was not merely chance that lead Alex to his door, but FATE. Wystan knew, like his grandfather before him, it was his destiny to not only uncover some kind of cure or peace of mind for Alex, but also that he was on the cusp of discovering a new species.
On the cusp of discovering…greatness.
Wystan called up an old colleague, Val Rubin from Siodmak University in Minnesota. She was the closest to an expert in Lycanthropy he knew. She was headed to a small town called Cold Water. He wasn't sure about her current research, but she sounded excited and promised to share her findings with him. Val also mentioned that she had received a call from a woman named Alexandra Stone about the same subject. Wystan smiled when he heard this. Maybe they could publish the paper together Val proposed. He said yes and thanked her. His mind (and his heart) were spinning.
On one hand, it seemed impossible that Alex was actually a werewolf. On the other, it all made sense.
Impossible, crazy, irrational sense…kind of like Love when Wystan thought about it. Love could not be measured, quantified,

counted, consumed, experimented on, tallied, or analyzed. But, yet love was real. People experienced it and shared it. It felt as real to some as breathing air. So, by this anecdotal notion, Alex could indeed be a werewolf. Of this he was certain. Wystan was certain of something else. Something that had been lurking in the corners of his mind since the day he met her. Wystan was infatuated with Alex and knew he would help her even if his life depended on it. He would follow Alex to the ends of the Earth as Artemis had followed Anna or go into the pit of hell with her. Perhaps, he was in love with her?

Someone rang the doorbell downstairs...

The sound was a chime doorbell he had installed several years ago. He glanced out his study window but couldn't tell if anyone was standing at the front door. He climbed down the stairs, irritated that he was being bothered while in the middle of his research. Whoever was standing outside was going to have to come back another time. Wystan had important work to continue and interruptions were not part of his plan.

Yes, Wystan was going to explore the world his great grandfather Artemis Strapp had explored back in the 1800s. A world not bound by imagination, but by the concrete structure of shapes we have only seen on the periphery of our limited vision. A world where the real and mythic collided into something else. Wystan was terrified too. More terrified than he had ever been. When he thought about the horrors associated with these discoveries it gave him pause. And yet...noble, heroic efforts always came with risk. Yes, they did.

Now, the person knocked. Wystan hurried to the front door. He unlocked it and yanked it open, ready to give this annoying person who could not read the *Do Not Disturb* sign a thorough talking too.

"WHAT? Can't you see that this establishment is closed?" Wystan glanced at the person. He stopped talking...

It was ALEX. She smiled at him. "Hi, Wystan. I need you to help me find my Father."

Wystan overcame his shock. He reached out his hand. Alex took it, still smiling. He stared into those sad, beautiful, ice-blue eyes. Eyes that lifted him up and took him to another place. Eyes he could drown in. "Whatever you need dear lady." Wystan led Alex inside and closed the door.

THE END

Thank you SO much for reading my book! As an independent author it is often difficult to let people know your book is out there. One small way you can help is by leaving a short review.

Reviews are SUPER important to indie authors for two reasons:

- One: It legitimizes the book when others see that people have read it and reviewed it.
- Two: It really does help sell books!

I want to give you the best reading experience possible, and I also want to share this book with as many people as I can!

So, PLEASE leave a short review for my book. It means a lot.

Author's Note:

HUNTED has been a long time coming. I first came up with the concept in 2000 after the Y2K scare (What a waste of time that was!). I believe I had just watched or re-watched one of my favorite werewolf movies, either *An American Werewolf in London* (Still the best transformation scene ever bar none!!), *The Howling*, or *Wolfen* (I know, not officially a werewolf movie!). I knew I wanted to write a werewolf story, but was unsure where to begin. The version you just read has existed in different variations over time. It started as a bad novel at first, then became a screenplay. HUNTED stayed in this format until December 2017. I rewrote it over and over again. Tried to get it financed. Had a series of on again-off again near-misses as I tried to realize my vision.

When I first began to daydream about writing my werewolf story I wondered: What kind of person could fight back against these powerful animals? Then I thought about soldiers. To be more specific, Navy SEALS. The best Special Operators in the world in my opinion.

I had an idea that a Navy SEAL (ex-SEAL) would fight against some werewolves. But why? And what about the werewolves themselves? What I decided early on was that the werewolves would NOT be the result of some supernatural or demonic curse. I wanted something that felt more natural. I wanted my werewolves to seem as if they existed in the real world, or could exist in the world. I also wanted them to be female. I love the idea of a matriarchal society, similar to many Native American tribes. One where the women influence and direct the inner workings of the tribe or clan, and where their word is of studied importance. As I researched legends and the general mythology surrounding werewolves and shape shifters I realized that most societies have some kind of version of them. In keeping with this, I decided to mold my werewolf society to reflect this global nature.

So, now I had my werewolves to a degree, and my protagonist, the Navy SEAL. Elijah Moore. Elijah, the name of my youngest son at the time, and Moore my Mother's maiden name. Elijah would be the driving force hunting the werewolves because they killed the one person in life he needed closure from, his father. Elijah and his adopted brother Chapa, also a Navy SEAL (Yes, far-fetched that

BOTH brothers would make it through BUD/S!), would take the fight to the werewolves using their warrior skills. And, that part gave me the action lift it needed.

But I still didn't have a story. How would these two entities clash? Where could I bring them together? Who else would populate this world I wanted to write? Why and to what end?

I love movies from the seventies. I do. There was a grittiness and realness to them that is often lacking from current films. Many of these films were spawned out of the turbulent decade adjacent to the sixties and featured nihilistic endings, grimy surroundings, and the people who lived in these films seemed like real people instead of glossy Hollywood stars.

So, I decided to bring my werewolves to the city. In my mind I was channeling the 1981 film *Wolfen*, based on the book of the same name by the eminent Whitley Strieber, and *Nighthawks* (also made in 1981!!!), the gritty terrorist film starring Sylvester Stallone, Rutger Hauer, and Billy Dee Williams (Yes! Lando!! And he was badass in this film!). I love both of these films so much and the rundown, decaying New York City of the seventies they portrayed (even though both were made in the eighties).

In my secret place I can see characters from both films existing at the same time. Image if Stallone's *Deke DeSilva* met up with Albert Finney's *Dewey Wilson* and they chased down the wolves in the city only to discover that Rutger Hauer's *Wolfgar* was the werewolf leader! Aaaah yes! Now THAT is the film I want to see!

I did not read the actual novel *Wolfen* until many years after I wrote my story, but I had seen the movie many times, so I am not surprised by the influences. However, my versions were actual werewolves who transformed from human to werewolf, and back again in some instances. More the classic version than the intelligent species of wolf in Strieber's novel. And, I struck on something else. I wanted to have a homicide detective investigating the murders (ala *Wolfen*), who was connected to the Navy SEAL by way of a child.

Detective Dana Adams was introduced and became the main protagonist. Dana was the character who would keep the story grounded in reality. She was a single mother (I was dating my wife who was a single mother at the time!), and significantly, she was African American. I felt it was important to have a Black Woman front and center in the action. Moving the story forward, finding the pieces that fit together. The clues to the puzzle. And I also made a conscious decision to have her just *be*...to not fall back on the tropes of her and Robin (who was originally a guy named Ken who I hated!) bantering back and forth, throwing racial slurs at each other. That is not the book I wanted to write or read! Kind of like the *Rush Hour* movies which I love. I am all in, except the racial schtick got repetitive.

So, I placed two strong women detectives together and let them dictate the pace of the investigation and what happened. Best thing I ever did! I love these two women and enjoyed spending time with them!

But, I also wanted an avatar for the werewolves and wanted to tell the story from their point of view.

And thus, Alex Stone was born. She would be the guide for the reader of a human discovering she was something different than she thought. To me, Alex is the heart of the story. She never asked for this tortured werewolf life. In some sense, Alex undergoes the classic Hero's Journey:

• At the beginning Alex is in one place in her life.

• Then she is thrust into this New World of killing, hunting and becoming a werewolf.

• Alex resists the Call to Action (in this case kind of bad...killing and eating humans!) at first. An event spurs her on and she moves forward.

• Alex enters the Cave, and for a time decides to embrace her nature.

• She meets a Mentor in Wenona, who attempts to guide Alex on the path of what it means to be a werewolf.

• Alex ends up embracing a new destiny as she decides not to kill the humans and to forge her own path! She is changed forever and cannot go back to the life she had at the beginning of the story.

Not perfect, but if I were to place an overlay of Alex's journey on top of the Hero's Journey map it would be very similar. I know all this may be a lot to digest, and some you may not care. But, I write this in the hope that some of you who took a chance on this novel and enjoyed it will want to know more about how this story, and these people came to be.

So, now you have an understanding about why I wrote **HUNTED**. I have loved these characters for almost twenty years. Eli, Dana, Robin, Chapa, Brick, Abraham, Ellen, Troy, Wystan, Paula, and of course Alex. They have spoken to me. Told me what they wanted.

Their hopes and dreams.

Their nightmares.

I have listened to them whisper to me in the middle of the night, and shout at me during the day. I have longed to introduce them to readers…and now I have. And this is not the end. I have more stories to share with you about this family I have created, and with your permission and blessing, I will write them for you until their stories are done.

Oh, for you researchers out there, I have taken many fictional liberties with this story. Several locations in San Antonio I made up. There is NOT a Gevaudan Park in San Antonio! This was a figment of my imagination. I created an amalgamate of several city parks so I could have one large, central park where the PACK could be free to roam throughout various parts of the city. My version of Central Park in NYC, but wilder! I mention this because one of you shrewd readers will point this out to me at some point, and I will have been found out! So, I figured I would beat you all to the punch! □

Thank you for your support and trust. I will try not to let you down as I continue to pull these characters from my imagination!

Keep dreaming. Keep reading. Keep hunting…

Kevin L. Williams

Made in the USA
Columbia, SC
09 October 2024

43390786R00130